FRIENDS AND NEIGHBOURS

Minna is passionate and demanding. Beth is more reserved, less flamboyant, a hardworking helpmate to her doctor husband and happy with the quieter pace of her small village, Chantry Green. To Beth's surprise, Minna declares she and her husband Jimmy are ready to settle down to peace and stability. Although Minna is her best friend, Beth sometimes secretly envies her, but with Minna's move to Chantry Green the two friends are brought into closer proximity and Beth learns that, amazingly, she herself possesses the one thing her glamorous, have-it-all friend has always yearned for...

FRIENDS AND NEIGHBOURS

by
Rose Boucheron

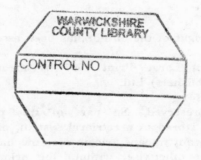

Magna Large Print Books
Long Preston, North Yorkshire,
England.

British Library Cataloguing in Publication Data.

Boucheron, Rose
    Friends and neighbours.

    A catalogue record for this book is
    available from the British Library

    ISBN 0-7505-1190-7

First published in Great Britain by Judy Piatkus (Publishers)
Ltd., 1997

Copyright © 1997 by Flora Gorman

Cover illustration © D Hughes by arrangement with
Allied Artists

The moral right of the author has been asserted

Published in Large Print 1997 by arrangement with Judy
Piatkus (Publishers) Ltd.

Magna Large Print is an imprint of
Library Magna Books Ltd.
Printed and bound in Great Britain by
T.J. International Ltd., Cornwall, PL28 8RW.

Chapter One

On this lovely July morning the sun shone down on the village of Chantry Green with its little pond and two eider ducks, while roses, pink climbing 'Compassion', ran riot over old Mrs Prior's wall and tubs full of rampant petunias and geraniums stood outside the prettiest house in the village. Indeed all the residents had gone to town this year, having to work overtime with watering on account of the dry summer, but it was worth it, for visitors came from far and wide to see the show.

Driving out of the village towards Chantry Park, that splendid and tasteful development started in the thirties, the gardens became even more spectacular, although many were hidden behind high hedges and walls, secured by wide wrought-iron gates, locked and electronically operated. Just a touch on the switch and they would slowly open as in grand houses in old Hollywood movies. Not for everyone, though. If you neared the gates of some properties, dogs could be heard barking, sometimes appearing from nowhere and enough to scare anyone but the bravest away.

If, however, you took the road out of the village towards London, you drove down a tree-lined avenue and came across a large Victorian house standing like a sentinel. This was not considered the best part of Chantry Green—after all, location is everything—but the residents there thought themselves quite superior to the inhabitants of Chantry Park, for they were not part of an estate, prestigious though it was. Not that the houses in Chantry Park were alike, indeed they were all different, but the place had no history, no background. The houses had been built in the grounds of Chantry House, which had burned down after the First World War. Whereas at this end they were all different—Edwardian, Victorian, a row of Georgian cottages—individual. Still, in this part of the world, where Berkshire meets Surrey, everyone was aware that they lived in a most desirable part of England, whatever their individual status.

The Victorian house, Chantry Gate, was bathed in sunshine on this lovely morning, and it was worth a climb just to see the view it commanded. Elizabeth Meldrum slowly ascended the stairs to the second floor. There was a time when she had run up and down these stairs to make beds, tidy the children's rooms and playroom, and inspect the au pair's room—the only

6

one they had had—but that was thirty years ago...

The view was magnificent, or at least she had always thought so. Chantry Gate had been built in 1887. There was a stone plaque outside to prove it, set into the front wall of the house, with the name of the architect on it too. From the front bedroom you could see for miles, to Windsor Castle on a fine day, and sometimes, fleetingly, when the sun was shining, the thin thread of silver that was the Thames. Sometimes, too, if the wind was in the right direction, you could smell chocolate from the factory in Slough, and once, when Windsor Castle was on fire, the stench of burning wood carried miles and hung over the area for days.

The house was a landmark to visitors to Chantry Green. It was the first house to come directly into view as you drove down from London. When Beth had first seen it late in 1965 it had been nothing, an empty old house that no one had wanted. The developer who had bought it with ambitious plans in mind had obviously thought her mad even to consider it, and put it down to a young woman's curiosity. She learned later that he had wanted to demolish the house and build four new homes but had been prevented from doing so, finally gaining permission for just one new house so long as he retained the old one. The tennis court, stables and garage were to be levelled and the site of the new house was already marked out. In the sixties no one had been drawn to these wonderful old houses—their full potential was yet to be realised.

The glazed front door led to the wide hall, paved with black and white tiles, its lofty ceiling ornately plastered. There was a drawing room with an immense fireplace, a study with a window overlooking what was now the defunct tennis court where loosestrife and pink vetch and willow herb grew in magenta abandon, the sorrel and grass as high as the surrounding fence.

The front-facing dining room had a window seat and long windows, and built-in shelves to either side of the fireplace. It was all just waiting for a loving family to take over. The kitchen was huge and at one end stood an Aga. Beth's eyes gleamed. She had read about Aga cooking.

The builder grinned. 'There's a thing,' he said. 'We could take that out for you. I expect you'd want a gas cooker?'

'Oh, no!' she cried. 'No.'

'What would you do with it?' he asked, genuinely puzzled.

'Use it!' Beth cried. 'Cook with it!'

'It partly heats the water,' he said, 'but of course it's not enough. No heating in these old houses.'

She bit her lip. She had forgotten that—more expense and another barrier to Geoff's approval.

'Could we see upstairs?' she asked. Off the half-landing was a Victorian bathroom, with white tiles and a large white bath on legs, then up a few more stairs to four large square bedrooms and another family bathroom. Up yet again to two more bedrooms and a playroom, and that view. The house had a lovely feeling to it, as though it had been lived in and loved.

'Oh,' she breathed, opening the window to let in fresh air. 'It's beautiful.'

And there was the lane leading to the village of Chantry Green, a lane that in spring and summer was fringed with blossom trees, the houses set well back from the road. She wanted this house more than anything she had ever wanted in her life.

In the garden, now cut in two with thick stakes marking the boundary—thank goodness the new house would be fairly well concealed and not on the side nearest the village—she stood stock still.

'What happened to the people who lived here?' she asked, but knew he wouldn't tell even if he knew.

He shook his head. 'I dunno.'

It would be too big for us with all this

garden, Beth consoled herself. Half would be enough... If she could only persuade Geoff to look at it, surely he would love it as much as she did?

'Course, you'd have to get in touch with the agent,' the builder said.

'Yes, of course. It was nice of you to show me round.'

'I'm not supposed to. You're lucky I was here.'

There was a window broken here and there, and the garage doors were off their hinges. The house must have been empty for some time, but until today she had never seen a FOR SALE board there.

'If you've got a car, you'd have to build a garage,' he said. 'The new building plot is the other side of those markers.' As though he wanted her to be sure just how much land was on offer.

Beth nodded. 'Yes, I realise that.'

Excitement at the prospect of living here was almost too much for her. They had been looking around for some time, ever since Geoff had taken up a new appointment as one of three partners in the general practice in Ledsham. Moving to this area meant that the boys could cycle to school, and there was a girls' school nearby for Belinda.

'Well,' she said, a little breathlessly, 'thank you again. I'll go and see the agent straightaway.'

The boys were doing their homework upstairs before she dared broach the subject, although Geoff was well aware that she had something to say. She had sat through the meal with an air of suppressed excitement. Only after she came down from bathing Belinda did she tell him.

'Come on, let's have it.' He grinned. 'You're busting to tell me something.' He looked down into her shining blue eyes, fair hair tied back carelessly, her neat, trim little figure beneath the flowered apron she always wore to do the washing up.

She took down a tea towel and handed it to him.

'I've seen a house!' she said, eyes shining.

'Oh, so that's it?' And she told him, trying not to let her enthusiasm bubble over, and watched the indulgent smile slowly fade from his face.

'Oh, Beth!' A frown took over. 'And just what are they asking for that?'

'Seven thousand, five hundred,' she blurred, as if the quicker she said it, the less it would seem.

'What!' he repeated, staring at her. 'You must be joking!'

'We could offer less, not everyone wants a Victorian house.'

'Exactly,' he said. 'Darling, no one with

any sense wants an old house with all its problems.'

'It's a beautiful house, Geoff, a family house,' she said firmly. 'And a good investment. It would last us forever.'

'It'd have to,' he said grimly. 'I'd have to take out a mortgage.'

'We could, couldn't we?'

'Look, Beth, I was looking to spend only a thousand more than this will fetch, give or take.'

'Well, what's this worth? The agent said four thousand—that's what those people offered last time and they were prepared to wait.'

'Well, then,' he said triumphantly. 'A three-thousand mortgage. Sorry, Beth, it's just not on.'

'Please, Geoff, just come with me to view it, and you'll see what I mean.'

'What's the point?' he asked. He was the logical one, but he hated to disappoint her.

He went with her, though, as she had known he would. Having made the appointment to meet the agent, they drove there on Saturday, with the three children in the back of the car. Geoff's eyes widened as they drew near.

'Not this one?' he said, seeing the board as they approached the high yew hedge. His shoulders sagged.

'Yes, this is it,' she said with a casual air, heart beating fast as he drove between a pair of high white gates and onto the gravel drive, coming to a stop beneath the gabled porch. He looked at her in sheer disbelief and saw that her eyes were alight with excitement.

'Elizabeth—'

But she was out of the car, taking Belinda's hand, while the boys were making their way round the back where an old, open conservatory stood. He followed them, seeing the building plot marked off and the half garden.

They all met up at the front of the house where the agent, shiny red face, trim little moustache and splendid teeth, was waiting for them.

'My husband, Dr Meldrum,' said Beth.

'Well, now.' And he held out his hand to Geoff. He was a little in awe of doctors. 'Robinson, Read and Son.' He looked around him. 'Fantastic place, isn't it? The finest house in the neighbourhood—your wife has good taste, Dr Meldrum.'

It wasn't until he went into the cool hall, and saw the size of the rooms, and felt the atmosphere enveloping him, that Geoff began to feel the same surge of excitement that had swept through his wife. As he went into each room, and finally on the top floor looked out at

13

the view in front of him, he knew that, however difficult it would be for him to purchase, that was what he wanted to do. He saw their bedroom, his and Beth's, Ian's room, and Jon's, and the one with the old-fashioned flowered wallpaper was just waiting for Belinda to move into. And there was the perfect study for himself.

Going down the stairs, he thought, I'm mad. Absolutely mad. I can't afford this—quite apart from the money that would have to be spent on it. Central heating, plumbing, and God knows what else... No, it's ridiculous.

Beth came in with Belinda from the garden, looking at him, searching his face.

He sighed deeply. He hated telling her, and his own disappointment showed. 'Look, darling, it's lovely—I know what you mean—but it's beyond us, I'm afraid.'

Her face dropped. She looked utterly wretched. 'Even with that lovely study? It's just what you need.'

'I can't see a way round it,' said Geoff. 'We would be committing ourselves so heavily, and there are the school fees, to say nothing of—'

He tried to find a way out, a loophole.

'Anyway, you're seeing it as it is now. How do you like the idea of only half a garden? It won't look the same, you know, once it's cut off and they start building.'

The agent, who had been silent, could see the mental tussles going on inside their heads. He had the wife in the palm of his hand, and the husband was on the brink—they usually gave in, though, in nine cases out of ten. The women were even easier.

'May I make a suggestion, sir? You could put in an offer,' said, quietly and sympathetically. 'It would be quite in order to offer a lower figure.'

Geoff had been toying with just that idea, and even then knew it would be too much.

'There's a hell of a lot to do to the house inside,' he said.

'Yes, sir, that's what I was getting at. In view of that...'

Geoff looked at Beth, the disappointment showing in her face, the two boys standing beside her expectantly.

'It's super, Dad, couldn't we buy it?'

'I know, but it's a bit beyond us, I fear.'

They trooped home and it was as if the sun had gone in and storm clouds hovered overhead.

'Have a think,' the agent had said. 'I'll be pleased to put in any offer—within reason, of course.' Nice young family. He thought he had it in the bag.

And so he had.

Six, seven-fifty the developer had settled for, glad to get the money to enable him to continue work on the new house. It wasn't everyone's choice. Rather them than me, he thought.

Geoff had lifted Beth off her feet and swung her round. 'How about that then?' he had cried in sheer exuberance. Only later did he become worried as the estimates for the work came in. They had always come to more in the long run, but somehow they had managed. It was the best thing they had ever done. The house was made for them. They had worked hard for it.

Thirty years... Beth closed the window slowly, tears falling unheeded. There was a great lump in her throat. Downstairs past the packing cases filled with china awaiting the morrow and moving day. She could hardly bear it. Crates of books—so many—but Belinda would be over tomorrow to help her move. Chairs stacked, crates of china...how efficient removal men were today. They would be here again early in the morning.

Geoff—she still couldn't believe that she would never see him again. Her husband, lover, friend, the children's father, senior partner in the local practice that had grown to seven partners. What had they said? An aneurysm, just like that, suddenly—all over in a few minutes... Don't think about it, don't even think about it.

She reached the wide hall with its black and white tiles and sat on the bottom stair. The great Victorian mirror still hung there, sold to the new purchasers. No one else wanted it, and she certainly wouldn't have room. Besides it belonged to the house now. In the drawing room hung the long heavy curtains she had bought ten years ago in one of Phillips' sales because they were twelve feet long, and lined and interlined, and there were swags and tails to match. She had been so excited when she bought them, and they were still here—even after so many cleanings. Pelmets and swags had gone out of fashion when poles came in but they were back now.

The children had grown up, reached maturity and married from this house. Thirty years...she couldn't remember living anywhere else. Small grandchildren played in the garden of the 'new house' next door, as they still called it, quite mellow now and hidden from view by tall trees that had grown over the years, a rose arbour, two of the old originals still there, and the wall clad in wistaria that Geoff cut back every August.

Don't think about it...

On the sideboard in the dining room were the photograph albums she had kept out to look at, and going into the kitchen she poured herself a glass of red wine and picked up the first one, sitting on the window seat as the setting sun shone gold on the far wall. This was the nicest room in the house, where the family had gathered at Christmas, birthdays and weddings.

She opened the album, smiling despite herself. This was how it had looked when they moved in. The boys, so young, and little Belinda, laughing into the camera in their new garden. Oh, joyous days! And then the house when it was painted, and the white gates mended, the three children in the porch, the trees and hedges as they grew...looking outside the window she saw the strawberry tree, *Arbutus unedo*. Imagine, it had been eighteen inches high when they'd bought it. Now look at it. She hoped the cutting she had in its little pot would grow in its new home.

Oh, and here was Minna, darling Minna, and Jimmy, and this one taken in the South of France, and Sheila and the girls—how pretty they were, and what beauties they had grown into. And here was Belinda in the dress Beth had made for her. What a scream, little fat round Belinda—who would think she would grow up so slim and elegant? And here was Bernadette with young Annelise, looking into the camera, her lovely blue eyes so clear and candid.

But that was before Laurie—oh, and Gina, how photogenic she was. Beloved Gina. How could Beth have coped without Gina—and whatever happened to Laurie Featherstone? She put the album down and opened the next one, but was it such a good idea to delve into the past?

Perhaps not, but she was going to just the same. Memories, that's what life was made up of, memories good and bad, and how lucky she had been until now. Geoff's sister had died at forty-four, had never known the joys of seeing her children grow up.

Here was Jon on his wedding day, how happy he looked. A wonderful day, and Laura looking so lovely. And here was Ian. He'd always sworn he would never get married but along came Sophie, and that was that, while Belinda, who'd always said she would marry a farmer and have ten children and bake scones in a farmhouse kitchen, had done almost that. She hadn't married a farmer, she had married a barrister, but she had achieved her lifelong ambition of being a cook.

Beth wondered what the new people would be like, if they would change the old house in any way? She knew they were a musical family, and Chantry Gate would soon reverberate to the sounds of piano and violin, but she would never come back. She would never want to see what someone else had done to her beloved house.

She finished the rest of her wine, closed the album and went into the kitchen. It had stayed as it was, Aga as well, with massive Victorian cupboards that took all their china and had never been filled to capacity. They hadn't wanted to change it except for the flooring.

Through the kitchen window she saw the clumps of paeonies—they had been there since the beginning, filling the air with their scent. Well, she would buy new ones. Paeonies hated to be disturbed and had a long life.

She had stood at this window all those years ago, looking out at a row of markers, watched as the bulldozers moved in and the builders followed. Workmen digging the foundations, bricks slowly growing higher, day by day. It had been awful, but she wasn't going to give in. It was Chantry Gate that mattered. They would put up a wall and trellis and trees to block out the other house. Central heating had been installed, and the house rewired, and hadn't that been a bill! Then the plumbing. There seemed to be no end to it, but by now they loved it so much they couldn't imagine living anywhere else. And she had vowed she would keep it Victorian—she had never liked modern furniture anyway. It was the greatest excitement of her life, to choose the wallpapers, and after the children had gone to school, to bring out the ladder and tackle those high ceilings. She must have been awfully strong or determined, she thought now. Had thought nothing of climbing high on the ladder, dealing with reams of folded, pasted wallpaper, had been quite alone in the house yet never felt the slightest bit nervy. Not like now, when you heard such stories about people living alone being mugged; it didn't bear thinking about. How the quality of life had changed! She had been lucky living when she did.

'If you had had proper training,' Minna had once said, 'you could have been an interior decorator.'

But the general consensus was that Beth had been one of the lucky ones: happily married, with delightful, clever children and a lovely home. Tragedy had not hit her until now. Her children were successful, content with their families, but you never knew about the future.

She had wanted to write, wanted to act, wanted to travel, wanted to turn the world over, but she was at the end of it all content to be a GP's wife, a housewife—and how horrified the feminists would be to hear her say that!

Now, how could she face life without Geoff?

Don't think about it...

Chapter Two

They must have been living in Chantry Gate for five years when Gina arrived. Beth could see her now as though it was yesterday, the stocky Italian figure, the ubiquitous headscarf.

The wiring and plumbing and heating had been done and the house was beginning to look like home. There had been sporadic help from time to time but the cleaning ladies never stayed, none of them wanted old-fashioned drudgery when there were new houses that took hardly any effort, and they would rather work in the luxury of Chantry Park where there were tiled bathrooms and fitted carpets. They had looked askance at the huge Victorian windows and the rugs over the polished oak floors. No use telling them there was an electric floor polisher. They didn't want to know.

Beth was digging in the front garden, wrestling with the ground elder under the cedar tree, when a foreign voice said, 'Madam—a, *scusi*, please?' She straightened up, leaned on her fork and saw a small figure confronting her, a girl of about

23

twenty-five, dressed in black, with a square olive face, small bright black almond-shaped eyes under a headscarf.

'Madam-a, please-a, where this-a Grin Lowns?'

She handed Beth the slip of paper. The houses on the approach to Chantry Green had no numbers, so that they were always being asked where Twin Stacks was or April Cottage. Grin Lowns was a new one, however Beth looked down at the paper and read the address she smiled.

'Green Lawns?'

'Yes, Grin Lowns, where this-a place?'

'Go on farther up the hill and it's on the right-hand side, about a mile, I should say.'

The woman shook her head vigorously, folded the paper and put it in her pocket.

'Is too far,' she said.

'Oh, dear,'

'You want 'elp?' the little woman asked suddenly.

Beth looked at her, mouth open. Help she needed desperately, but from a stranger? Who was she? An Italian? The doubts flew around her head.

'Why is it too far—Green Lawns?' she asked.

'I work in 'ospital in Renton I get off bus and walk, I dining-room maid,' she said proudly. 'On my day off I work in

24

'ouse. You like 'elp?'

'Well...' Beth dithered, in for a penny. 'It is an old house—lots of work to do, not modern, you understand.'

'I not care 'ow 'ard I work.' She curled her lip. 'I work for you all day—two pun, eh?'

Her cockney co-workers had given her the most delicious accent so that her voice was a mixture of Italian, cockney and Irish.

'All day?' Beth cried. 'For two pounds?'

'You try. I come Tuesday, you see. If you not like, I go—all righ'?'

'Alrigh',' Beth said. 'All right,' she amended.

'*Madama*—I Gina Pagano,' she said, as though that explained everything. 'What you name?' she asked. 'Mrs Meldrum,' said Beth. 'My husband is the local GP, Dr Meldrum.'

And that did it. Gina beamed, showing her faultless white teeth, black eyes dancing like small shiny beads.

'I know 'im,' she said. ' 'E nice-a man. I see you Tuesday, madam-a.' And she walked off back the way she had come.

Unable to believe her luck, Beth eagerly awaited Tuesday, and there was Gina at eight o'clock, sweeping out the garage with a garden broom as she waited for the door to be opened.

Beth showed her the rooms and she seemed not at all put out by the amount of work to do, and endeared herself to the family immediately. They were used to people coming in and asking them how they coped. 'I say, those windows! Those terrible high ceilings—all those stairs—'

Gina just said: 'Is-a beautiful 'ouse, madam-a.' And they felt they could forgive her anything.

Armed with polishing cloths, pails of hot water and metal polish, she worked like a mad thing from eight until two o'clock, drinking her coffee as she did the stairs, and refusing lunch when Beth offered it to her.

'I not like-a food,' she said. 'I 'ave dinner tonight, I go on.' And did, like a whirlwind. At two-thirty she stopped and sat on the outside steps by the dustbin. 'Is-a too much-a,' she said. 'I finish now and come back next-a week. Al-righ'?'

'All right,' Beth said, 'and thank you, Gina.' Giving her more than she asked although Gina didn't want to take it.

Would she ever see her again? wondered Beth as she looked through the tidy house, the swept rooms, the gleaming brass and polished floors, or was she quite literally a new broom?

From then on Tuesday was Gina's day. She always arrived promptly, and after that first week, every chore was accompanied by an aria from an Italian opera, and Beth found there was nothing to compare with housework sung to the accompaniment of *Aida*.

They discovered that Gina had a mortal enemy, a Miss-a Potts, who was the supervisor of the dining-room maids. A simmering feud existed between them as Gina fought for the Italian girls' rights. And woe betide Miss-a Potts if she asked Gina to work on a Tuesday!

'I tell 'er,' she would say grimly, 'is-a my day off.' Her face was black whenever she mentioned Miss-a Potts. In fact all the family hated Miss Potts, sight unseen.

Beth discovered that Gina worked for two other households and that she could look as smart as a film star or the dumpiest little woman imaginable, depending what she wore. Invariably she wore a headscarf over her jet black hair, and sometimes Mrs Thingummy's voluminous tweed dirndl skirts and shirt blouses, or Mrs Whatsername's rather dressy dresses and cashmere cardigans.

It was not unusual to see Gina cleaning the bathroom wearing a royal blue georgette miles too long for her, an obvious Mrs Thingummy this one, or a cream-draped Courtelle from Mrs Whatsername. They felt they knew these other ladies of Gina's quite well, just by their clothes.

She was a treasure, and as the house took shape, and was decorated, and the garden was re-planned, Beth realised that they had made a wise move.

One morning she was due to go in for coffee, to the new house next door. Though in fact it was no longer so new, for the owners had taken possession just over three years ago: a very up and coming man in the American food business, Geoff said, and his Canadian wife, Bernadette, They had a daughter, the same age as Ian, who was at boarding school for they travelled a great deal on business—at least, Laurence Featherstone had to make several journeys a year to the States and Europe, and he was so handsome and so charming that Beth suspected that Bernadette liked to keep an eye on him, and who could blame her? Had she had the opportunity to travel, Beth would have done the same thing.

She wasn't sure she liked Bernadette Featherstone all that much, but one had to be neighbourly, and the children got on well together.

She walked down the drive and closed the high gates behind her, making her way to the large red brick pseudo-Georgian house with its neatly laid lawns and flower beds. Bernadette had ripped out all the old garden and had specialist landscapers to replan the whole thing. Everywhere was as neat and tidy as a new pin, for Bernadette was nothing if not a perfectionist. Everything grew for her. She had complete sway over the house and garden. For one thing—Laurence was hardly ever there, and for another he was too busy and only too happy to leave it in the hands of his capable wife.

There seemed to be nothing Bernadette couldn't do. An excellent cook and hostess, she dressed beautifully, kept her home immaculate, to say nothing of her sports achievements. She was an excellent swimmer, golfer, tennis player, and excelled at skiing.

'Well, I was brought up in Canada,' she would say with a complacent smile. 'It's second nature to us there.'

A French-Canadian with remarkable blue eyes, she had beautiful teeth, a lovely complexion, and just the merest touch of hardness around her beautifully shaped mouth. She adored her English husband, whom she had met on one of his Canadian trips. She had been his match in everything, she assured Beth. 'He was so impressed with me, he couldn't help asking me to marry him,' she said with a laugh.

'We had very strict training as girls,' she used to say, 'my sister and I. Although we had maids, my mother insisted that we knew how to run a house. I used to clean out the lavatories and scrub the kitchen—there was nothing I couldn't do by the time I was fourteen. My mother, you see, was a true Frenchwoman.'

Beth had never met anyone like her.

Now, seeing the Featherstones' roses in their true glory, each one perfectly pruned by the gardener, each shrub chosen for individual merit, the borders and specialist trees, Beth was overwhelmed.

'Hi—come on in,' Bernadette welcomed her, lovely blue eyes sparkling this morning, and dressed in a pale blue trouser suit and white polo jumper. Beyond the age for short skirts, which were all the rage, Bernadette compromised although she still had beautiful legs.

Through the carpeted hall, with its pale blue Wilton, and into the kitchen which was every woman's dream: painted in white, with every possible new piece of equipment—a washing machine, dishwasher, a small television on the counter, and simply acres of working space.

'Sit down,' Bernadette said, 'make yourself at home.'

On the counter was a magnificent pyramid of profiteroles, a foot high, covered in chocolate sauce, its golden cream-filled pastry a confectioner's dream.

'You didn't make it!' Beth cried.

'Sure—we've got guests for dinner from the States this evening and before I put it in the fridge I thought you'd like to see it. And—' she pointed triumphantly to a polythene-covered plate 'I made one each for us with our coffee!'

She really was amazing, Beth thought.

The newest design in coffee percolators was bubbling away. Bernadette always had the very latest gadget. Through the window they saw Bert the gardener in his shirt sleeves, mowing the lawn.

'He has an extra job this morning,' Bernadette said. 'Several enormous sacks of hyacinth bulbs arrived—gifts of Clarke's Bulbs—so of course we have to take delivery now.'

Beth could see the huge sacks, fat and lumpy with bulbs.

'There must be hundreds there!' she cried.

'I expect so, I stipulated only blue and white—can't stand the pink ones. Larry does a lot of business with Clarkes, something to do with fertilisers. It's wheels within wheels, you know.'

Yes, Beth did know—she had heard it from Bernadette before. It seemed that when you were as successful as Laurence Featherstone, the gifts and favours poured in.

'What do you think of this?' Bernadette picked up a sheaf of glossy car brochures. 'I have to choose my next car—you know I get a new one every year. What do you think? Pale blue with a dark blue trim?'

Beth, who drove a small ancient Mini, could scarcely stifle her envy and wondered what Bernadette did with her old one, but Geoff had explained: big business meant a constant turnover of cars, ploughed back and renewed. It was indeed another world.

'Come and see the dining room,' Bernadette said. 'I've laid the table and used my green Coalport—what do you think?'

Laid for eight, it looked wonderful. The silver gleamed the cutlery shone, the plates with their wonderful colours, the Waterford glasses...it was like a colourplate in a magazine. Pale pink roses sat in small glass flutes in front of each setting.

'So you have eight for dinner—I really shouldn't be here holding you up,' Beth said.

'Holding me up? Nonsense. I've nothing to do until this evening. Come up and see Annelise's room—I've had it re-decorated. I hope she'll like it. She'd better—it cost a fortune.'

Upstairs on a landing with the softest blue carpet and several pieces of antique furniture Bernadette unlocked the door to Annelise's room. She always went around with a bunch of keys to unlock the doors.

It was so different from Beth's house that she never ceased to be amazed. Immaculate, not a thing out of place. In the master bedroom, so-called, were white puffy eiderdowns and pale blue silk, yards of frothy curtains and a dressing room, while Annelise's room had been newly done over in yellow.

'She's grown out of that toy stage. Well, she's eleven now.'

Beth had seen the decorator's smart van going in and out.

Now the room was yellow and white check, curtains edged with frills and tied back, yellow checked bedspread and white-painted furniture.

'It's lovely,' Beth said truthfully. 'She'll love it.'

Poor little rich girl, she thought to herself. Everything and nothing. Probably the only time she's happy is when she's away at school, for at home she's so regimented, subjected to such a severe upbringing, her life can never be her own. An immaculate bedroom, and woe betide her if there is ever anything out of place! Her books stacked away in a cupboard, dressing table with only a silver hairbrush and a yellow tissue holder, and one doll on the bed. Four pictures of animals, and that was that. No wonder she liked to come around and play with Belinda. Her room was never tidy, even though Beth constantly berated the child and Gina did the best she could. She had so many bits and pieces—treasures she called them—that she couldn't bear to part with.

'And she had better keep it tidy,' Bernadette threatened. 'She is a very spoiled young lady. I tell her there are not many little girls who have a home like this and a lovely bedroom...'

Once, when little Annelise had been naughty, Bernadette had taken up the white fur rug in her bedroom to punish her.

Beth had told Geoff about it. 'What sort of woman would do that? It's hardly a punishment, is it?'

'Well, she's being deprived of something that she likes, is fond of.'

'Would it mean that much to her at that age—a white fur rug?' She tried hard to imagine Belinda's reactions and decided that she probably would not even notice it had gone.

'Perhaps the child was fond of it—saw it as a comfort? Still, it's not very kind, but then Bernadette is hardly my cup of tea. Her efficiency frightens me to death.'

'I know what you mean,' Beth had murmured, still thinking about that white rug.

Now, as she ate the delicious profiterole, which was as light as a feather, she licked her fingers and wiped them on the pretty napkin provided.

'Lovely,' she said. 'I'm my own worst enemy.'

'Oh, it won't do you any harm. I guess you keep slim, running up and down those stairs. Sometimes I pray that you will have a modern house one day with all mod cons—you deserve it.' She was a staunch Roman Catholic, was Bernadette.

'But I love Chantry Gate, I never want to move.'

And she could practically hear Bernadette's unspoken comment: Brave little soul.

'By the way,' she asked, 'how is your friend getting on—the one who came back from the States?'

'I haven't heard. I expect she's settling into her town flat.'

It was true, Beth supposed. Minna had been very quiet. She and Jimmy had come back from America anxious to settle down again at home. Minna and Beth had become friends when they'd shared a flat together in London while taking a secretarial course and afterwards while working, until Minna married Jimmy and eventually moved to Los Angeles with him. Jimmy worked in the film industry, and because British films were not doing so well, had gone to try his luck in America. He had had some success, but after three years they were coming back because they wanted their small son, Hamish, to be educated in England.

'I did enjoy meeting her,' Bernadette said, having been in Beth's house for coffee one day when Minna had turned up expectedly. She had thought her very glamorous.

'I expect you're glad she's back?'

'Yes, I am, I hope to see something of her—but of course, being in town and with the children at school...still, we'll see. Well, I must be off. I have a stint at the hospital this afternoon and a parents' meeting this evening.'

'Rather you than me,' Bernadette said. 'I couldn't cope unless Annelise was away at school.'

'No, but then Laurie needs you to be around so much—you've almost a full-time job.' Beth smiled.

'I tell you something, I don't know what he'd do without me,' Bernadette said, and Beth knew she meant it.

Bernadette suddenly jumped up. 'Where is that man?'

She looked furious and rushed out of the room, leaving Beth to wonder what on earth was wrong. She got up and stared out of the window but could see nothing. Presently Bernadette appeared with a shotgun and took aim at something in the rowan tree, which fell to earth with a soft thud. Bert appeared as if from nowhere and Bernadette shouted to him: 'Get rid of that!' and after putting the gun away, re-appeared as though nothing had happened to wash her hands at the kitchen sink. 'Ugh!'

Her face was as black as a thundercloud.

'What was it?' Beth asked, fearful that it might have been a bird.

'A bloody squirrel,' said Bernadette.

There was a strained silence. 'Oh. Well, I must go,' Beth said. 'Thanks for the coffee.' Her voice was deliberately cool although Bernadette probably wouldn't notice it. She was too thick-skinned.

Opening the wide gates, Beth walked up her gravel drive and preened as she always did at the sight of the old house standing there so proudly. It was as if it knew it was special.

New house indeed!

She unlocked the front door, and Gus the Labrador puppy got to his feet.

'So you knew it was me, you little spoofer,' she said, nuzzling him. 'You know, Gus, between you and me, I don't really like that lady. And don't you ever, *ever,*' she underlined, 'wander into that garden next door.'

Gus wagged his tail vigorously and looked up at her with shining eyes.

As if I would, he seemed to say.

Chapter Three

Beth opened one eye and thought: Monday, raising herself on one elbow to see clearly above the window boxes. The bedroom window nestled under a giant cedar tree, the spanned out flat branches giving protection against the weather. No need to look any further. The bedraggled petunias and blue lobelias were drenched and waterlogged. The roof of the house next door gleamed shiny and red in the steady grey drizzle.

Flinging her legs over the side of the bed, Beth pulled a dressing gown around her and made her way to the bathroom where she scrubbed her teeth and sloshed cold water over her face, finally brushing her hair vigorously.

Peering closely into the mirror, she pulled a face, then as an extra punishment peered at herself in Geoff's shaving mirror. She closed her eyes. She couldn't bear to look. She was forty and two days old...

Making her way to Belinda's room, she pulled back the curtains and shook her daughter gently. 'Belinda? Wake up, darling.'

The flushed little face lay partly buried in the pillow. 'Mummy? What time is it?'

'Seven-thirty, darling—'

She padded along the hall and pushed another open door. Ian, her younger son, lay there peacefully, a mound of jumbled clothes, trousers, vest, socks and pants all over the floor.

'Ian, it's seven-thirty.'

'OK, I'm awake.'

She made her way to Jon's room.

'Jon—seven-thirty.' Jon lay neatly, his bedclothes quite undisturbed, not a thing out of place anywhere. Every book stacked on the bookshelf, the cupboard a model of tidiness. Funny how different they were in so many ways.

She would leave Geoff for half an hour or more—he had been called out in the night and didn't return until three-thirty. A premature birth, not expected for another two weeks. She sighed. A doctor's life wasn't easy.

She took a pile of dirty washing downstairs, and looked at the hot-water gauge on the boiler, beginning to sort the clothes. Well, it would be a start.

She made the tea and slipped some toast into the toaster for herself, getting out the cereal packets and laying the table.

She collected the newspaper and letters from the letter box and read the headlines, turning the pages between pouring tea for herself and Geoff.

By the time the boys were downstairs and eating breakfast, the first load of washing was underway. She took up a cup of tea to Geoff, who was already in the bathroom. She poked her head round the door.

'Everything all right?'

'Yes thanks, Beth. Did I wake you?'

'Oh, I always go to back to sleep again. Is she all right?'

'Yes, a five-pound little girl—she'll be fine.'

Going into the children's bathroom, she collected another pile of clothes—coloureds and woollies—and took them downstairs, letting Gus out. No doubt he wouldn't be out long—he hated the rain.

Although the hedge and trees had made lots of headway, they could still see the house next door through the kitchen windows, but only its upper floor. She could see Gus, wet and disgusted, poking around the shrubbery. Bernadette she knew, was away somewhere in the South of France—Cannes, probably, she was very fond of Cannes. At some point Laurie would come back, leaving Bernadette there. Usually on his return he stayed a night or two in the house, then continued with his bachelor existence.

41

Sometimes he asked Geoff in for a drink or a game of billiards—the two men got on quite well considering how different they were. Geoff admired his business acumen, but they were poles apart.

'Come along, then—hurry. Daddy's dropping you off Belinda, on the way to the surgery.'

'Oh, good.' Belinda raised her face for a kiss—her pretty little round face and dark eyes—so like Geoff's—while Ian went to the cellar and got a huge hod of Coalite for the Aga. It would be Jon's turn tomorrow. A rule had been made when they moved into the house and they had always stuck to it. The central heating was a luxury even if it was solid fuel.

The old house settled down to silence. Beth always loved this time when she had the place to herself. The rain seemed to have stopped, and she could see small patches of blue in the sky. One load of washing was done and she went out into the garden to peg out the clothes, taking a chance that it would be fine now. There was nothing she liked more than seeing a line of washing, white shirts, school blouses, tea towels and undies, but the moment it was ready to iron she brought it in. By the same token, there was also nothing worse than washing left out.

The third load was underway as she

finished making the beds and hoovering the bedroom carpets. Gina would be here on Tuesday to polish and give it a good going over.

Geoff had left the gates open and she saw the white car coming up the drive as she hurried down the stairs. Minna...it could only be Minna!

Through the front door Beth saw her get out of the white convertible, and excitement gripped her. She threw it open. 'Minna!'

How wonderful she looked! A golden tan, cream shirt and slacks, gold bracelets and necklace, huge dark sun-glasses and that lovely hair, a sort of ashy blonde, wisped and flicked up to make a frame for her face.

Minna stamped out a cigarette on the gravel—typical Minna—and flung her arms round Beth.

'Hey, there.' The two friends hugged each other. 'Well, aren't you going to ask me in?'

How out of place she looked, Beth thought fondly. Exotic, glamorous, but wonderful too.

'Come on in! It's lovely to see you—I was wondering how you were getting on. Sit down, I'll make us some coffee.'

Minna looked around. 'Christ, how do you do it? You must be mad! All this work.

This kitchen! What do you see in it?'

Beth frowned. 'Oh, you know me. I love it, it has such character.'

'Yes, you could say that,' Minna said drily, opening her beautiful tan leather handbag and taking out a cigarette.

'Washday, is it?'

Beth nodded.

'Why do you do all this? Couldn't you send it to the laundry—shirts and sheets anyway? Besides, that thing is so antiquated,' she said, looking at the washing machine.

'Oh, Minna, don't keep on. These things cost money or didn't you know? After all, you haven't exactly had everything easy all these years, have you?'

'No, that's true.' Minna blew out a puff of smoke. 'Still, I've always set my sights high and so has Jimmy. I never intended to be a workhorse.'

'Good for you,' Beth said soothingly. 'And you aren't, are you?'

'OK. Pax,' Minna said. 'Well, I hand it to you—it looks nice everywhere. Not my style but you've done well. Do you remember the day you moved in and came out in a rash. I can see you now, sitting on the floor in the dining room, wondering how you were going to manage for curtains.'

Beth laughed out loud. 'Yes, I remember.

Well, it wasn't easy—there were so many windows and very little money.'

'And the curtains were too short! Still, you wanted it. Ciggie?'

'No, I've given up, about five years ago—you remember.'

Minna made a face.

'I don't intend to give up,' she said.

'Well, no one asked you to. It just seemed a good idea at the time. How's Hamish?'

'Fine. He loves his school, and it won't make any difference—'

'To what?'

Beth poured out the coffee and handed her the jug of milk.

'Black, thanks.'

Beth knew her of old, and knew by that air of suppressed excitement that Minna had something to tell her. Perhaps she was having another baby? But somehow she didn't think so. Minna was hardly the maternal type.

'I might as well tell you although it's not settled yet—'

'What?' Beth was all ears.

'I've found a house.'

Beth's mouth dropped open. 'What!'

'A house, dear, as distinct from a flat.'

'Oh. Well?'

'Aren't you going to ask me where it is?'

'No, where? Chelsea?'

45

'Now don't laugh—Chantry Green. Here, right under your very nose.'

'You're joking?' Beth said, unable to believe her ears. To have Minna and Jimmy living close by...

'It's true.'

'You wouldn't live in a place like this! You? Out in the sticks?—I don't believe it,' Beth said slowly.

'It's true. Jimmy made some money on his last picture and we've talked it over, and we think, well, it's only right that Hamish should be brought up in the country. Besides I like dogs, and we can't keep one in a flat in town, and Jimmy is fond of the wide open spaces—'

'You don't need to make excuses to me!'

'Well, it's not settled but we've made an offer—a low offer, but I think we'll get away with it because it is cash.'

It would be, Beth thought, they were the sort of couple who had their eyes and ears open for any chance of a bargain.

'Now tell me where it is.'

'Less than a mile from here, I'd say, an old farm house called Green Lawns.'

'I know it! It's the prettiest place. I had no idea they were selling.'

'Why—do you know them?' Minna asked curiously.

'No, but being a doctor, Geoff gets to hear things, and it is a very small community, you know.'

'Well, there was something about it,' Minna confessed. 'Sort of Tudory with beams, low ceilings, and of course a lovely garden. Eighteen hundred and something, I think.'

Beth was envious of the garden, certainly.

'Anyway, when you've finished your coffee, I thought we'd go to see it.'

'What—now?'

'What's the problem—the washing?'

'No, silly. It's just that—well—'

'Oh, come on, don't dither. The car's outside and we may as well go now while I'm down here. They're going to let us know by Friday but I'm pretty confident they'll take our offer.'

'What are they asking?'

'Ten thousand,' Minna said, 'with two acres.'

'Gosh,' said Beth locking the back door.

'We've offered eight,' Minna continued.

'Really? Well, I wish you luck.'

'Looks lovely from the outside.'

'But that hides a multitude. It hasn't been touched for years. We can't get in today, but it's empty. I thought we'd peer through the windows.'

Minna lit a cigarette—she always lit up before any proposed drive—and they roared up the lane where the houses became more sparse, stopping outside one

47

set back off the road.

Green Lawns was low and rambling, a typical farmhouse, with beams and a lych gate and a large thatched garage that had obviously once been a barn.

'Oh, it's so pretty!' Beth cried. 'Just look at those roses—and the rhododendrons down the drive. They're a picture in spring.'

They opened the lych-gate to walk down the gravel drive. The mullioned windows were dusty, and could have done with a coat of paint, and the beams were crying out for wood preservative while round the back stretched the two acres. Green lawns was right, for in the wet summer they had thrived but badly needed mowing.

'How long has it been empty?' Beth asked, peering through the window to the kitchen.

'About three months or so. The owner died.'

'I never knew who lived here,' said Beth. 'Look at those beams—you'll have to watch your heads.' She grinned, 'especially Jimmy. Has he seen it?'

' 'Course he has. We came down on Saturday—didn't want to say anything to you in case nothing came of it. Oh, I love it, Beth!'

It was unusual to see Minna so excited about anything.

The property was surrounded by fine trees, oak, elm and ash, with here and there a massive chestnut. There was a vegetable garden and rows of soft fruit bushes.

'Lots of upkeep, Minna.'

'No problem,' she said.

They wandered round the rose beds and Beth was fascinated by some of the beautiful shrubs.

'I shall have a swimming pool just here,' her friend said, pointing.

'A swimming pool!' Beth repeated. 'Really?'

'Yes, and you can all come and swim and we will have barbecues.'

A very different lifestyle from the previous owner, Beth thought, but Minna and Jimmy would certainly liven the old place up—and more to the point, spend on it.

'I can't wait to see inside,' Beth said, her nose smudged from pressing against the window. 'How many bedrooms?'

'Five—and a dressing room, and a simply super study for Jimmy, where he can write.'

'Write?'

'Oh, I didn't tell you—he's writing scripts now, television scripts. Had one accepted, and been asked to do another.'

'Then he's on his way,' Beth said

decidedly. She'd always known Jimmy was destined for a success.

They began to walk back. 'And this is the garage.'

'That'll take four cars,' Minna said.

'Mmm. Well, let's hope you get it—if it's what you want.'

'It is,' Minna said decisively. 'And we'll get it. Perhaps not for our offer, but we'll get it. Jimmy can be very persuasive when he likes—well, don't I know it? He persuaded me to marry him.'

They got into the car and drove back to Chantry Gate which looked huge after the low-built farmhouse.

'Stay and have some lunch,' Beth said. 'Just a snack.'

'Sure,' Minna said, 'then you can tell me some more about Chantry Green.'

She was peering through the kitchen window of the house next door.

'How are you getting on with her ladyship?' she asked.

'Bernadette? Oh, she's all right.'

Minna had taken against her on sight. 'Not my type,' she had said. Had she really disliked her, Beth wondered, or was it a case of one friend disliking another? Not that it mattered.

'She's in the South of France at the moment.'

'Lucky her. What's her husband like?'

'Dishy, I suppose you'd say. I suspect she has to keep an eye on him.'

'Oh, one of those,' said Minna, lighting another cigarette and picking up the newspaper.

Odd, Beth thought, preparing the lunch, how fond we are of each other, and yet we are so different. They had become friends on their secretarial course in London, and had shared a flat in Bayswater. They had taken to each other straight away, having the same sense of humour though Minna's could at times be much wilder.

Born Araminta, she was always called Minna. When her parents were killed in a plane crash on the way to Switzerland it was Beth who comforted her and went down to the family home in Sussex, helping her settle her affairs and sell the house, aided by Beth's own father. And when, after a time, Minna met Jimmy who was a film cameraman, and they married after a whirlwind courtship, Beth missed her very much. She and Jimmy had moved to another small flat until some time in the following year when he'd announced his intention of trying his luck in America. They kept in touch by letter, giving each other all the news, for by now, after three years, Beth had married Geoff and had a baby a year old, and Minna had a new baby too. When she announced their intention of coming back to England, Beth was delighted. She had read into Minna's letters her longing to be home again, so it was with a great deal of fellow feeling that she looked forward to her friend's return.

When they arrived, she couldn't believe her eyes, for Minna had changed from an attractive young woman into a casually dressed, elegant young mother, although for all the attention she gave the baby, Hamish, you would never have thought she'd given birth to him. They were accompanied by a Filipino nanny, who took complete charge of him. 'Don't look at me, sweetie,' Minna said to Beth. 'I haven't a clue—haven't an idea in this world what to do to him or for him. But don't worry—Sue Lily is a perfect gem. I'll probably look at him again when he's five years old.'

Jimmy seemed unsure of himself, as if the whole idea of being back in England was something of a shock, as indeed Beth supposed it might be. Perhaps he had not wanted to come home? His beautiful eyes rested on her for a moment as if assessing her reaction to their return before he shook hands with Geoff. The two men quite liked each other; Jimmy respected Geoff, while Geoff secretly saw Jimmy and his wife as an arty couple who had very little in common with him and Beth.

Minna and Jimmy rented a large flat in an expensive block in Chelsea. By now Beth was pregnant with her second child. Her life as a doctor's wife was a busy one and with a young family it was not easy to find time to visit Minna in town.

After Beth's second son was born, Minna and Jimmy came down for dinner to the small house Geoff and Beth then had in Windsor, before departing yet again for the States. Jimmy had had the offer of directing a film in Los Angeles, and was anxious to try his luck.

'I must say, it sounds jolly exciting,' Beth had said, for it did. Faced as she was with a life of surgery chores and nappy changing, even a working trip to the States sounded glamorous.

'Minna doesn't think so,' said Jimmy mildly. 'She hates the film crowd, don't you, Min?'

'You can say that again,' she said, lighting another cigarette. She was the only one of the four who smoked, and Beth could see the disapproval in Geoff's eyes.

'Come and see the garden,' she said. 'I've just planted some new roses.'

'How do you find time for gardening?' Minna asked querulously.

'It's surprising what you can do in a short time,' Beth said. 'Besides, it's therapeutic.'

'Why do you need therapy?' Minna asked.

'I don't really,' Beth said. 'I just love gardening. If I can put my hands in the soil and mess about with the earth...'

'Yes, I can see,' Minna said, looking down at Beth's hands with distaste, and she burst out laughing. 'Oh, I do wear gloves, honestly.'

'You could have fooled me.'

Minna looked around the small patch of garden that Beth had tried so hard to make a success, and Beth sighed.

Oh, she was going to miss Minna—she always made her laugh. And suddenly she frowned. She hoped Minna was happy. Odd, too, how she always forgot that Minna had a small son. He must be eighteen months old by now.

'You'll take Hamish to the States with you?' She had a sudden thought that they might leave him behind.

'Of course,' Minna said. 'I'm not that bad a mother.'

When they returned to the house, Geoff was on the telephone and Jimmy stood up.

'When are we going to see the latest addition?' he asked. 'Ian, isn't it?'

Beth was delighted. So pleased that anyone would want to see the baby. Minna had seen him before.

He followed her up the stairs, followed by Minna.

Beth tiptoed across the room and peeped into the baby's cot, but she need not have worried for he lay there, wide awake, six months old, his dark hair curling close to his head, his rosy face glowing, eyes shining up at them, arms flailing, legs kicking the clothes off. Jimmy bent down and took the small hand, the fingers clasping around his own. In the next bed Jon slept peacefully. Nothing would wake him once he was off.

'He's beautiful, Beth,' Jimmy said, not looking at her.

He likes children, babies, she thought, probably would have liked another, but he'll be lucky if Minna has anything to do with it!

Minna stared down at the baby, her face expressionless. 'He's like Jon,' she said.

'Do you think so?'

Beth tucked him in warmly and kissed him goodnight, hoping that he would stay quiet. So often a baby would cry after being disturbed. But all was well.

'A drink before dinner?' Geoff asked.

'Thanks,' Jimmy said. 'You're a lucky man, Geoff.'

'I am?' He grinned. 'One of my patients just died—but he was eighty-six.'

They all laughed.

'No, I mean that lovely baby—two sons. A man can't ask for more. I expect now you'd like a daughter?'

'Oh, please, not just yet,' Beth had cried with mock horror.

She'd been sorry when the visit came to an end. Goodness knew when she would see Minna again.

'An oddly assorted couple,' Geoff said, bolting the front door.

'Yes, I suppose, in a way,' Beth said. 'Jimmy is such a dear.'

'And she is a mass of contradictions. Taut—like a violin string.'

Beth stared at him open-mouthed.

'But she's so laidback—nothing worries her.'

'That's what she wants you to think,' Geoff said, yawning. 'Well, I'm for bed.'

'I'll be up later, I've just got to give Ian his last feed.'

Minna and Jimmy were away a long time before returning to London again and settling again in Chelsea. By now, Hamish was a sturdy small boy, more like his father than Minna. Jimmy's work constantly sent him off on different locations, but usually Minna went with him. She and Beth saw each other occasionally, when Minna surfaced in London but by now Beth had had her daughter, Belinda. Minna paid a flying visit when they moved into Chantry

Gate, so by the time they came back from Hollywood, this time for keeps, Minna said, they were well and truly settled in at Chantry Gate, and Geoff had his partnership...

Now Beth couldn't believe her ears. Minna and Jimmy living in Chantry Green? She couldn't understand it—didn't see Minna in a backwater like this. She was so sophisticated. Her background and life were so different. Wouldn't she feel stifled here?

Beth took a deep breath. 'Only one thing,' she ventured, putting plates and cheese and salad on the table, 'Won't you get bored here, Minna? I mean, it's hardly your cup of tea, is it?'

'I've had enough gallivanting around to last me a lifetime. Also,' she added, stubbing out her cigarette, 'what with the pool and the garden, you won't know me. I'll be a regular Gertrude Jekyll.' Which surprised Beth, who wouldn't have thought Minna had even heard of her.

'Shall we have a glass of wine?'

'Why not?' Minna said. 'There are no house rules, are there?'

'I mean, would you like one?'

'Give it here,' Minna said, 'I'll open it for you. So—tell me about the boys—oh, and Belinda. Is she still a little fattie?'

'She's not a fattie!' Beth remonstrated.

Minna raised her eyebrows. 'She's not? Oh, right.'

And they tucked into their lunch while she outlined what she proposed to do with the house.

Beth still couldn't believe it. It seemed so alien—the idea of Minna coming down here to live—yet she reminded herself that Minna's parents had lived in a lovely old house in Sussex. She had stayed there for a spell. Minna had after all been brought up as an only child in the Sussex countryside.

Still, they had fallen on their feet obviously. Jimmy was nothing if not a worker, and talented to say the least. As for Minna, she had the temperament to refuse to let things get her down. She was ever the optimist.

'Well,' she said now, lighting a cigarette and getting to her feet, 'I've got to get back. Hamish has an exeat.'

It was a strange thing, but it was easy to forget that Minna had a son.

'Keep in touch,' Beth said as she waved goodbye.

'Sure,' Minna called. Smoke drifted out of the car as she sped down the lane towards the village and London.

Beth shook her head, smiling. Minna would never change.

Chapter Four

There seemed to be an inevitability about Minna's move to Green Lawns, and once that was achieved, she and Jimmy were taken up with builders and decorators and carpet fitters. She had managed to find a daily woman from the village, a friendly soul called Mrs Bonnington who never seemed surprised at anything Minna said or did, and fitted into the household seamlessly. Minna too settled in as though she had always lived there.

The summer had been hot and dry, and already the leaves were falling off the trees. Belinda, who had been eight when they moved into Chantry Gate, was now almost fourteen, and already showed signs of the slim young thing she would become. Jon, tall and well-built like his father, would take his university entrance next year, and Ian was not far behind. Study seemed to be the order of the day, hours of homework for all, except for Belinda who had never lost her love of cooking. If she could get into the kitchen and cook, she was in her element.

'I shall marry a farmer and have lots

of children and bake bread and make scones—oh, and home-made soup. You should be grateful,' she said. 'It might have been horses.' Her best friend Rosemary was horse-mad, and only Rosemary's parents knew what hardship this brought about.

A year had gone by, and Minna had quite settled in. A newly fitted kitchen, dark blue fitted carpet throughout the house—which Beth thought quite wrong with the dark oak beams, but nevertheless added to the general air of luxury. The reception rooms had fat leather chairs and sofas, and doors were put into the breakfast room leading out to the garden where there was now an impressive swimming pool, rectangular in shape, and a summerhouse, with outside telephone and bar. Typically, Minnna had thought of everything. There were lots of birds and squirrels, and she had shown another side of her nature which Beth had not suspected, loving all the little animals and insects which roamed there, the birds and butterflies, and giving over part of the garden to wild flowers. She worked a lot in the garden herself, with help from a man called Rob. In fine weather she gardened in a bikini. Minna never dressed more than she had to, which accounted for her lovely golden tan.

One afternoon at half term she asked Beth round for tea with Belinda. They found her drifting on a raft on the pool, scraping potatoes. 'Just doing the veg,' she called out. 'Put the kettle on, will you?'

Hamish at twelve, and Belinda at thirteen, got on well together, although Belinda complained that he was so young for his age.

'Well, he's an only child—he hasn't had the benefit of two brothers to teach him.'

'Some benefit!' Belinda snorted, but she adored her brothers.

Beth watched Minna swim to the edge of the pool. How slim she was, firm legs and a trim figure, small-bust and a very flat tum—she was the epitome of the golden girl though Beth knew she never exercised. How she wished she herself could have been taller, slimmer, with a tan, even a pool—Minna seemed to have everything.

What a jealous old cat I am! she berated herself. Now, you wouldn't change places for the world. That was true. But just to have it a little easier, a little more help, a little more money—not a lot. And she broke off with a wide smile. How lucky she was, with three healthy children, and a husband like Geoff, and Chantry Gate.

'Right,' said Minna, staggering out with the tray. 'Tea up and lemonade for the kids.'

She put down the tray. 'I say, reminds me, I saw your neighbour—what's her

61

name, Bernadette? God! What a name! She was looking mighty pleased with herself.'

'Was she? Haven't seen her for ages.'

'Said she just got back from France, and would be asking us in for drinks. Can't bear the thought.'

'Oh, but you must go!' Beth said. 'You should see it—it's absolutely immaculate.'

'So what's the point of that?' Minna asked.

'Well, I mean, she sets such high standards.'

'And that would impress me?' Minna said, lighting a cigarette. She clicked her lighter shut. 'Oh, come on!' she laughed. 'I'm teasing. 'Course I'd go—wouldn't miss it for the world.'

But before that happened, soon after the children went back to school, Bernadette asked Beth in for coffee.

As she showed Beth into the kitchen, Beth could see that her blue eyes were sparkling, she looked radiant and so suntanned. And she had lost weight.

'Sit you down,' she said. 'I've some news and you're the first to know—outside the business, that is.'

Beth waited.

'Laurie has been made Managing Director for Europe!' she said, and waited for the impact to sink in.

'Bernadette! That's wonderful.'

'Isn't it, though? We knew two weeks ago—Laurie flew back from France to tell me, and of course, as you may imagine, our lives will change quite a lot. We will be moving.'

'Oh, are we going to lose you?'

Bernadette looked almost sorry—but not quite. 'We're looking for a new house and we shall have a town flat—company flat, of course—and the job comes with a Rolls and a chauffeur. Isn't it wonderful? I've sent off a telegram to my parents, they'll be so pleased. I haven't told Annelise yet—there's no need for her to know for a while.'

'Where will you go? Move to, I mean?'

'I'd like to go to Chantry Park—they have lots of beautiful houses there, and we shall want land, of course, a tennis court and swimming pool.'

Realising that she had really gone over the top in what it meant to them, she stopped short. 'I say, why don't you buy this house? You wouldn't know yourself. You could sell that old place and have this wonderful house with all mod cons.'

Beth could have hit her.

'Oh, you are kind, Bernadette,' she countered. 'But I'm sure we couldn't afford it. Besides, I do love my old house. Really, we're used to it. I don't think we could ever leave it.'

Bernadette shrugged. 'Well, there it is, I've given you advance warning.'

'So,' Geoff said, folding his paper after dinner. Thursday was his free evening, and he liked to relax and read the papers, and generally have a little gossip with Beth. 'Featherstone is on his way.'

'I should say he's already arrived,' Beth said. 'It's quite a position, isn't it?'

'Oh, yes, but then he's got what it takes. Of course, he'll have to work his noddle off to earn that salary.'

'How much will it be?'

'I've no idea. The American companies pay well, but they do want their pound of flesh. His life won't be his own.'

'Poor Bernadette.'

'Oh, she'll take it in her stride, she's a very competent lady.'

'I wonder where they will go?' Beth asked. 'They've already put the house in the agent's hands.'

'I don't suppose they'll waste much time now they're on their way.'

'And they can always move into the company flat.'

'Where's that?' Geoff asked.

'I'm not sure, Park Lane somewhere—after all, a prestigious company has to be in the best area.'

'That's true,' Geoff agreed. 'Well, I'm

just going to take a stroll round the garden. I thought there was quite a nip in the air this morning, but it is October after all.'

Three weeks later, after Beth had seen several people going over her next-door neighbours' place, Bernadette announced that they had found a new house. There was no doubting her pleasure and triumph. It was empty, and she had the keys.

'I'll take you to see it,' she said. 'It's absolutely beautiful—quite the best house in Chantry Park.'

It would be, thought Beth, trying not to feel unkind.

They went in Bernadette's new car, pale blue and gleaming, immaculate. Bernadette's slim strong hands gripped the wheel—she drove like a man. Her blue eyes reflected the colour of the car, her short cropped hair glinted in the autumn sun.

They arrived at the Park, with its houses dotted here and there, each one different. As the developer had said: 'No two alike.'

And there it stood in its own grounds, pristine white, with green shutters and a green roof. Completely surrounded by a clipped yew hedge, and across its wide wrought-iron gates a sign reading: SAN REMO.

'I'm not sure about the name,' Bernadette said. 'What do you think?'

'Well...'

But Bernadette was pressing the electric bell, and the gates slowly opened. 'Isn't that neat?' she asked, blue eyes like stars.

They drove in, and the gates closed behind them.

It was an asphalt drive, a semi-circular one, leading to marble steps which in turn led up to the front door. The house was immaculately kept in every way: gleaming windows, many of them, and quite uniform. Nothing odd about this house. It was a monument to someone's geometrical mind.

Once at the top of the steps, you looked back and down to where sloping lawns gave way to flower beds, past their glory now, and hedges cut with precision and—not a little topiary.

'It does look a little Italian,' Beth said, for something to say.

'It does, doesn't it?' Bernadette was greatly pleased.

Then came the bunch of keys. One thing, she'll have even more to put on her key ring now—it'll feel quite heavy, thought Beth wickedly. Now they were inside: white walls, polished floors, a couple of marble pillars, and a wide staircase.

Beth was impressed despite herself. For what it was, the house was a perfect example.

'You'll have a wonderful time furnishing it,' she said. 'What will you do about the floors?'

'I suppose we should have rugs, the floors are so nice, but I don't want any work. On the other hand, of course, I shall have to get staff now. I expect to be very busy as the MD's wife.'

'I can imagine,' Beth said. The drawing room was huge, with a marble mantelpiece and great windows opening on to the back lawns. There was a dining room to seat at least twenty-four, and a beautiful black and white kitchen.

'I shall probably rip that out—it's not my taste,' Bernadette said.

There was much more to the ground floor than that, but by now they were upstairs, inspecting six large bedrooms and three bathrooms.

'You're so backward in this country,' Bernadette said. 'Every bedroom should have an en-suite bathroom.'

She would have to start from scratch, Beth thought with horror, thinking of the acres of curtain material she would need, the linings, the fittings, the making up costs, the extra furniture...the mind boggled. Well, she decided at the end of it, Laurie's company was probably footing the bill. Money certainly wouldn't be a problem for Bernadette.

Outside was a three-car garage. 'Did I tell you a Rolls goes with the job?' Bernadette asked.

'Yes, you did actually.'

'And the chauffeur, of course. No more driving for Laurie—and I'm pleased too. Driving back and forth to London is no joke these days. Of course, he'll be flying mostly, but it does mean the car will be available for me.'

Well, Beth considered, what could you say? The house was quite splendid and you had to admire something so beautifully maintained, though she couldn't have lived there to save her life. But it was good for Laurie and Bernadette, there was no doubt about that. Great Foods, or whatever the name of his company was, had cause to be proud of him and his very efficient wife, who knew how to rise to every occasion. For Bernadette did. You had to hand it to her.

Loving every moment, she locked up behind them and drove down the drive. The gates opened slowly, and once they drove through, closed silently.

'I like that,' said Bernadette. 'Very efficient.'

She set the car in gear and they drove towards home.

'Any luck with your own property?' Beth asked. 'I've seen several people going in.'

68

'Yes, we think it's sold, although of course now that's not our worry. To a very nice couple, with two daughters—he seems to be a lot older than his wife.'

'What age are the daughters?'

'Oh, teenagers, I'd say. Pretty girls. They came with their parents the second time to look over it.'

That sounded interesting, Beth thought. Someone for Belinda to be friends with perhaps.

'Will you come in for a coffee?' Bernadette asked as they drew near home.

'I won't, thanks—Belinda will be home and I've something to do for Geoff. Thanks for taking me, by the way, I thought it was lovely.'

'Well, you're the first to see it,' Bernadette said, and took a deep breath and smiled, showing her beautiful teeth. 'It is, isn't it?' she said. 'The house of my dreams.'

Beth opened the white gates and walked down her drive thoughtfully. It was the first of the really grand houses she had seen in Chantry Park, although Geoff had been in quite a few. She couldn't wait to tell him about the Featherstones' new home.

Belinda, sitting at the kitchen table drinking her milk with a biscuit, absent-mindedly fondled Gus, who adored her.

'So what was it like, the new house?'

Coming back from the cloakroom, Beth stood still.

'Well—'

Belinda laughed. 'Not for you. You didn't like it?'

'You couldn't not like it, it was so beautiful. Whether or not I could live there is another matter but it was splendid, quite splendid. Goodness knows how much they had to pay for it, and it needs to be totally refurnished.'

'Not a problem, I would have thought.' Belinda was very practical for thirteen. 'Poor Annelise.'

'Yes, that did strike me, although I suppose there are people who would say she's a lucky girl. They will have a pool and a tennis court, and it is one of the finest houses in the neighbourhood.'

'Yes, but she's never there, is she? She's away at school, and she hasn't got a Gus, has she? Gus—booful, booful Gus!' And his eyes quite simply shone up at her, his tail wagging.

'Yes, I know, you want a biscuit,' she said, and dived into the tin. 'Just one,' she said, shaking a finger at him. 'Just one.'

'Don't get me wrong,' Beth said, afraid she might be seen to be carping, 'it really is lovely, and if anyone can tackle it, your Aunt Bernadette can.'

'Why do we always call your friends "Aunt"?' Belinda asked. 'Like Auntie Minna, Aunt Bernadette—'

'It's a form of politeness,' Beth answered. Belinda stared at her. You could see she didn't go along with that.

'So how was it?' Geoff asked when he came in.

'Ab-so-lutely magnificent,' Beth answered, drying her hands and giving him a kiss.

'Really?'

'Yes, honestly, it really is quite something. Not our taste, but very impressive.'

'Right up Bernadette's street then,' said Geoff, who didn't mince his words.

'Oh, definitely, she's like a cat with two tails.'

'You know who lived there?' he asked.

'No—but I wondered?'

'A member of a famous Italian car company—racing cars, that sort of thing,' he said.

'Really? That accounts for SAN REMO then. What happened to them?'

'The wife died and he went back to Italy, so I'm told. They were patients of Eric's, before National Health days, of course.'

'It was kept beautifully, not a blade of grass out of place, scrupulously clean inside—like a new house.'

'Well, they had an army of servants. I

suppose they'll all be out of a job now.'

'Not if Bernadette can help it! She's going to get "staff", as she calls it.'

'Any news about their house?'

Beth put down the lid of the Aga and took off her apron.

'Yes, she's says she thinks they've sold it to a couple with two teenage daughters.'

'Ah, that sounds healthy enough. Well, I'm going up to change.'

Gina arrived the next morning wearing an expensive two-piece jersey suit, and a stunning Aquascutum raincoat with the ubiquitous headscarf She looked, Beth thought, a little like the Queen walking round Windsor Great Park.

'Mmmmmm...' she sang, as she hung up the coat, obviously in a good mood. When Gina was in a good mood the whole world sang; in a bad mood, thunderclouds appeared on the horizon. But now she was all smiles.

'Where first, madam-a?'

'As usual, I think, Gina—upstairs. I'll just finish the vegetables and then I'll be out of your way.'

By the time she got down to the kitchen again, Gina was quite talkative.

'We 'ave-a new girl in-a dining room,' she said proudly. 'She so beautiful, madam-a.' She lowered her voice. 'Very smart, towl (which was tall), very blonde, and so nice. She smile, loverly smile, and she kind. She from Germany.'

'Oh, a German girl?'

'Yes-a, she German girl. She smokes,' said Gina, waiting for Beth to be impressed.

'Oh, does she?'

' 'Er name Renate, madam-a.'

'That's nice,' Beth said, and singing to herself, Gina went to the broom cupboard.

They probably have quite a good time up in that hospital, Beth thought to herself. It's another world, with all those foreign maids. So many foreign girls these days—but how would they manage without them? What had they done before they came? But there seemed to be no shortage of nurses, thank goodness. This afternoon she was due for a stint at the surgery because Ailsa, the Scottish receptionist, was away on holiday. Beth had often helped out in the old days, but now that the children took up so much time, and the house, only did the occasional stint.

She had promised Belinda that she could cook the supper this evening—and really the child was so good, no one minded when she put on a meal. Cooking was obviously going to be the love of her life. Still, Beth had done the vegetables, just in case, and now fell to thinking of Bernadette in her new house, and what the new neighbours would be like.

She was quite looking forward to new people. She had never really felt at ease with Bernadette.

Chapter Five

The New Year dawned before Laurie and
Bernadette Featherstone moved to SAN
REMO in Chantry Park, and strangely
Beth felt sorry when they had gone, for
they had been part of her life from the
time when she had seen the new house
take shape and the Featherstones move
in as the first buyers. One bitterly cold
morning towards the end of January, a
large removal van slid down the frost-laden
drive. The Rowlands had arrived.

Joe Rowlands was a large, bluff York-
shireman, some twenty years older than his
wife, Sheila, who was forty-two. They had
two daughters, Kate, who was seventeen,
and Francesca, usually called Fran, who
was fifteen. Bang went Beth's hopes of
companions for Belinda, but Ian lost no
time in showing his approval of Fran.

Beth decided they were the most
handsome-looking family, for Joe was
tall, with thick iron-grey hair, and dark
eyes behind the longest lashes she had ever
seen in a man, and both girls had inherited
these. Kate, who had started work in a
publishing house, had the same dark eyes

and long lashes, but when accompanied by long thick fair hair and a golden skin, the effect was devastating. Fran, on the other hand, had the same dark eyes and lashes, but dark hair like her mother, and was as pretty as a picture.

Sheila, too, was pretty, with lovely teeth and a ready smile, and the most efficient housewife if you discounted Bernadette, who was something else. Beth lost no time in getting acquainted with this new family, as different from the Featherstones as it was possible to be.

Sheila was a friendly soul, partly Scots, and had a direct manner and practical approach to all things. Out went all Bernadette's ideas on decor and in came Sheila's, which were basically white walls and white paint, plain curtains, and not a bit of nonsense to be seen anywhere.

'Can't stand a muddle,' she confided to Beth. 'I had the devil of a job getting Fran to throw out most of her things when we moved, she is the most awful hoarder I've ever come across. Of course, she's artistic, unlike Kate—or so they told me at school—so of course she collects everything. She's the bane of my life. I always think being artistic is an excuse for not bothering—these artistic people just get away with it, they've no organisation, no discipline.'

'Oh, Sheila!' Beth laughed. She liked this family, who were warm and friendly, despite Sheila's ruthlessness in sweeping everything away before her. 'I don't understand how you can find a home for everything in the kitchen,' she wailed. 'I've always got so many things about and nowhere to put them.'

Beth stood surveying the work surfaces, the table...it was like a show house. 'Where do you put everything?'

Sheila was puzzled. 'Well, cupboards, the fitments, I suppose. I don't know, I just have to find a home for everything.' And they giggled together.

The two women got on like a house on fire, and it transpired that Joe worked for a big cereals company and had known the Featherstones. In fact, that was how they had come to hear of the house.

'Did you ever meet her?' Sheila asked. 'I mean, was she friendly?'

'Oh, yes, extremely,' Beth countered. 'They were nice neighbours, but I always knew it was on the cards...'

'That he'd get on? Yes, we knew from the grapevine that he was down for the MD's job—these things get about. He's young, too.' She grinned. 'I'm afraid poor old Joe has long lost his chances of a big promotion—but then, he's not the type to be an MD. He's one of the boys. And he's only three years off retirement now.'

'Kate is going for an interview at a really large publishing house,' She confided. 'That's what she wants to do—publishing. She's already with a smaller company, and I think she'll go far. She's a tough nut, Kate, takes after her father.' And Sheila smiled fondly.

'Your Belinda's a nut case, too,' she went on. 'Knows exactly what she wants, doesn't she?'

'Yes—and she thinks Kate is the cat's whiskers.'

'People react like that to Kate. Either they're terrified of her or they adore her. It's odd, isn't it, to arouse such strong feelings?'

'Some people do,' Beth agreed, pushing her chair away from the kitchen table and picking up her handbag. 'Well, it has been very pleasant but it's time I got on—time for Gus's walk.'

'Oh, he's adorable!' Sheila cried. 'But he won't come near us when the girls call him over.'

Beth grinned. 'No—er—it takes a little time to...well, I'll see you.'

After lunch she received a phone call from Minna.

'Can you come round for a cuppa? Leave the ironing, I've got something to show you.'

'Sure, in about half an hour?'

Jimmy answered the door when she rang.

'Oh, Jimmy, I didn't think you'd be here.'

He smiled, almost apologetically. He was a tall man, slim and slightly built, with a mop of dark hair and rather beautiful golden eyes, Beth always thought. He closed the door and looked at her, almost as if he thought she might have something else to say to him. Beth took off her driving gloves.

'And how do you like living in Chantry Green?' she asked. She saw him so seldom. When she called he was usually working in his study.

'Love it, and so does Minna,' Jimmy said. 'It's a lovely spot. I just wish I didn't have to commute so often to town. For my part, I could stay here and never move out of the house—and if I play my cards right, I may do just that...'

'What do you mean?'

'Well, I'm writing my first novel,' he said. 'I've written scripts before, and been lucky with them, but this is a book—a thriller.'

'Oh, Jimmy, you'd do well with that!' Beth cried.

'I don't find it all that easy,' he said. 'Still, I'm into my stride now and it looks

79

as if it's going to work.'

'That's wonderful,' she said. 'I wish you all the luck in the world.'

He gave her a gentle smile. 'I'll let you read it when I've finished. Didn't you want to write at one time? I thought you—'

'Fat chance!' laughed Beth.

'You and Geoff must come and have dinner with us. I've been a bit lax—moving in and all—but we must celebrate the pool. Geoff will like that.'

'Wonderful,' Beth agreed. 'Where's Minna?'

'I think she's in the garage—sorting something.'

'I'll find her,' Beth said, making her way to the garage where she discovered Minna, in jeans and a headscarf, her face covered in streaks of paint.

'What are you doing?' Beth asked, intrigued.

'I,' Minna announced, 'am going to take up painting.'

'What?' Beth asked. 'Painting what?'

'Oh, not walls—I mean painting as in art. I'm going to be an artist. I think I'm a natural.'

'Oh!' Beth laughed. 'A hidden talent we knew nothing about.'

'That has nothing to do with it,' Minna said. 'I have a latent talent. In fact, I've painted one or two already—want to see them?'

She walked towards the house, and once inside the kitchen, picked up her cigarettes and lighter and lit up. She blew out a stream of smoke then made her way up the stairs, stopping outside one of the smaller bedrooms and opening the door.

'Ta ra!' she said. 'What do you think?' And against the wall stood two paintings. She had obviously painted over two original pictures and Beth didn't know whether to laugh or cry.

Minna frowned, looking at her. 'I can see you don't understand them, much less appreciate them, and that's a good sign.'

She looked hard at the first one.

'What do you see?'

'Well—'

'Don't you think that looks like a tree? The roots of a tree, I mean.'

'Exposed roots,' Beth said, suppressing a grin.

'It's not funny. In modern art you see what you want to see—and I see the roots of a tree, stark and bare.'

Beth bit her lip. 'Yes, well...'

'Honestly, can't you see them? A great tree, with exposed roots?'

'Certainly exposed,' Beth said. She wasn't sure whether to take Minna seriously.

'Anyway, that's what I'm going to call it.'

'Oh, it has a name?'

'Sure—ROOTS. That's what it's called.'

'Right. So what's this one?'

It was a jumble of colours, with nothing clearly discernible.

'Provence,' Minna said triumphantly.

'Really?'

'Can't you see the colours of Provence?' She asked, as though talking to a dim wit.

'Um, well—'

'Look.' Minna turned round earnestly. 'I think we should both take up painting seriously. It's about time you had a hobby.'

'Oh, but I can't—'

'No buts. Let's go down to Harrington's and buy some board and paints—we'll go in my car.'

'But—'

But she had gone—and Beth slowly followed down the stairs. She had been just like that at Secretarial school. Where Minna led, Beth would follow.

They raced through the town and pulled up sharply, Minna tossing aside her cigarette which was still burning. Inside Harrington's, a veritable artist's paradise, they browsed through the enticing shelves of rainbow-coloured tubes of paint and hardboard. Beth found herself with one piece of hardboard and a few tubes of oil paint, two soft-bristled brushes, some linseed oil and turps, while Minna had at least six pieces of board, dozens of large tubes of paint, a selection of brushes that would have done credit to Picasso, and all the requisite liquids. She must have spent a fortune. 'Bung them in the boot,' she said. 'We'll go home and make a start. Now, don't forget, you're to do a painting—anything, anything that comes to mind.'

'I have to get back,' Beth said. 'Belinda will be home.'

'OK, I'll drop you off. And don't forget, you're not to copy anything. I'll give you a ring tomorrow.'

'You don't suppose I'll have finished my masterpiece by then?' Beth cried.

'Why not? ROOTS only took me an hour or so.'

You couldn't help but laugh at her, Beth thought, carrying her board and materials to the front door.

'Do what you want to do, whatever comes naturally,' Minna urged. 'Anything —just what comes.'

Nothing, really, Beth thought, but she was fascinated enough to try.

The next morning, she left the house-work and went upstairs where she had hidden her purchases on the top floor.

Leaning the board against the far wall, she poured some turps and linseed oil on to a saucer and waited for the muse to take over. Something came back to her about priming the board. After five minutes no inspiration dawned, and hating to spoil the board, she went back downstairs and found a postcard of Lucerne.

She was absorbed in no time. Her tongue sticking between her teeth, she was totally enrapt until she glanced at her watch and saw the time. Twelve-thirty! God, where had the time gone? She rushed down to the cloakroom, cleaned her hands then made lunch ready. A strong smell of turps pervaded the house, so much so, that when Geoff came home to lunch, as he did sometimes, he twitched his nose.

'What are you painting? The little room?'

'No—just fiddling, cleaning up.'

She was vague, but he wasn't really waiting for an answer, knowing that she often touched up a skirting board or did a bit of painting, and when he had gone she flew back upstairs and looked at her effort again. Really, it wasn't bad but she was only a quarter of the way there. Nevertheless she felt quite pleased with herself.

'How did you get on?' Minna asked when she rang at five o'clock.

'Well, I have to say I'm quite pleased. I didn't finish it, though.'

'It? What—only one? I did four,' Minna said. 'Look, come round tomorrow morning and we'll compare them. Come early.'

'I'll be a bit late, Gina's coming tomorrow.'

'And of course we have to clean up before Gina gets there, don't we? All right, see you about ten.'

When Beth opened the door in the morning it was to a sad-faced Gina. Glum expression, dark shadowed eyes, there was something obviously wrong. Another row with Miss-a Potts, Beth supposed. She wasn't inclined to talk, or Gina either. She went about her business, banging things a little, and generally looking bleak.

'All right, Gina?' Beth asked after awhile.

Gina frowned. 'What-a you want? I do something for you?'

'No, that's fine. I'll be popping out for a moment to see Mrs Alders, but I won't be long.'

The house sounded quite sad without the usual Italian arias.

Holding her part-finished picture away from her because of the wet paint, Beth got out the car and drove round to Minna's.

Mrs Bonnington answered the door. 'Good morning, Mrs Meldrum—Mrs Alders is upstairs in the studio.'

Oh, the studio, so that's what it was now?

Beth held her picture gingerly as she made her way upstairs. Minna stood wearing a real artist's smock, kerchief around her head, surrounded by pictures and a strong smell of turps. The whole room seemed to be full of paintings.

'Hi, come in, let me see.'

Highly embarrassed, yet proud of her part-achievement, Beth exposed the picture. She saw Minna's frown.

'You've copied something!' she cried, disappointment in her voice. 'Oh, how could you, Beth! It's awful, disgusting—it's not even any good. Look what I've done!'

And Beth, annoyed with herself, with Minna and her own pathetic effort, turned to face the row of paintings along the wall. None of them made any sense. They were all of—well, nothing discernible.

'What are they?' she asked. 'I mean—what do you call them?'

'They're what you see!' Minna cried triumphantly. 'Aren't they good? Jimmy's over the moon, says I have real talent.'

'But to do so many in one day?' Beth asked. Really, even Minna could hardly suppose...

'Of course!' she cried. 'That's what makes them so good. They're childlike, primaeval, primitive—yes, that's the word. They're primitives.'

'Really?'

'Yes. Jimmy's talking about giving me an exhibition—he knows someone who has a small gallery.' Minna's myopic eyes were shining unusually brightly for her.

Beth felt she was dreaming, but she didn't put it past Jimmy—these two were apt to do the most unlikely things.

'Well, that's good,' she said, and thought it was really.

'Now this one I really think is good—I call it MEMORY.' Minna tilted her head to one side.

'Oh, why?'

'I don't know, it just came to me. You have to work on inspiration.'

Carrying her rejected painting, Beth made her way back to the car and home. Well, it wasn't so bad—and it did look a bit like Lucerne. She could touch it up. After all, what did you expect in half a day? But she would finish it some other time. She had lost the inspiration now, if she had ever had it.

She put the car in gear. She would hide it away, couldn't bear Geoff or the children to see it. And she giggled at the thought of what her husband would say. Well, what did it matter? Then she remembered Gina. Now she had to face her—something was wrong. Poor Gina... She seldom got into a tizzy these days but something was definitely wrong.

Gina was muttering to herself as she mopped the kitchen floor, her dark brows drawn together. She looked up to acknowledge Beth, but seemed far from pleased to see her back.

Beth didn't like to find her upset; she was a good worker, honest as the day was long, and conscientious.

Gina stood the mop by the pantry door and shook her head slowly at Beth.

'From-a the grass, madam-a, from-a the grass.'

'What does that mean, Gina?'

She curled her lip and spread her hands just above the floor. 'In Italy, madam-a, some-a girls, good girls, from Roma-a and Milan-a. Honest, work 'ard. Some-a girls, bad girls, like-a some-a girls from Naples, madam-a, very bad! Not educate, bad girls.'

The black eyes glowed at Beth, willing her to be shocked. 'They like animal,' she said, putting her hands down again. 'From-a the grass, madam-a.'

Oh, and enlightenment dawned. Needless to say, it became a scathing comment in the family from then on, from television personality to politician. 'From the grass,' they said to each other knowingly.

'That girl, Renate, madam-a, she from the grass. When she go back to Germany I give her three pun, madam-a,' And here the reason for Gina's misery began to become plain. 'For skirt, madam-a, very nice skirt, Renate 'ave, and when she go back, I say, you get-a one for me, eh? And the other girls. We give 'er three pun each, that make nine pun, alrigh'?'

Beth nodded.

'We not 'ear,' Gina said. 'We never 'ear from 'er.

'That Renate, she take our money. From-a the grass, madam-a.' And Beth knew if she had been outside, she would have spat.

'Oh, dear, but you may hear yet, Gina.' Beth didn't for a moment think she would. She could just imagine the gorgeous Renate with the little Italians' nine pun.

'No, I not 'ear,' Gina said, resigned.

'How long has she been back in Germany?'

'Six-a weeks,' Gina said. ' 'Ow I get this money back, madam-a?'

'Well,' Beth said, trying to give her a sensible answer, 'I don't think you can if she won't send it back. Perhaps she couldn't get the skirts?'

But disillusionment had set in.

'She not try, madam-a,' said Gina, black eyes bitter. 'She not try.'

Beth felt furious with the beautiful Renate. Not so much about the skirts, but because Gina had found that her idol had feet of clay.

'Madam-a, I write to this-a girl, this bad girl, and I take to the post office.' She waved an envelope clearly addressed to a place in Frankfurt in beautiful script.

'When you've finished, I'll drive you down to the post office and we will register it. I'll show you what to do,' Beth promised.

It was the least she could do.

Chapter Six

As she came to the end of the story, Beth laid down the magazine in disgust. 'Rubbish!' she said. 'I could do better than that.'

Geoff looked up from his paper.

'Then why don't you?' he asked mildly. 'You must get a bit of spare time to yourself, now that the children are older and you don't work in the surgery.'

'You're forgetting that the children are a full-time job at this age, and there's the garden.'

'But you like gardening,' he said.

'I know I do.' Beth was feeling cross with herself for being bad-tempered. She had been so irritable lately. Perhaps it was the start of the menopause?

'You know what I think?' Geoff asked, his eyes twinkling. 'You should get that old typewriter of mine from the loft, sit down at it and have a go. Isn't that what they say? Sit your bottom down on a chair and do it. You'll never know unless you try.'

She glowered at him, then couldn't help laughing. She didn't admit even to herself that her discontent was because Jimmy was giving Minna an exhibition and Beth was jealous of her, envious of the way things were always so easy for her friend. Even her painting which was, surely pretty awful, wasn't it? But Geoff was right. How would she ever know if she could write if she didn't try?

And she really wasn't envious of Minna, not deep down, just jealous of the way things came so easily for her. And she couldn't complain that Geoff gave her no back up for he was the first one to encourage her. It must be galling for a man to listen to a wife constantly saying she could do something then never trying to do it.

She made up her mind. As soon as Geoff had gone she would get the old Underwood out of the loft upstairs and clean it up. That would be the first step.

It took almost a morning to do that job, for having extricated the typewriter, Beth realised how badly the loft needed turning out and by the time she had finished that it was time for lunch and Geoff was coming in today.

She sighed. Oh, well, there it sat, looking sadly old-fashioned on the card table. She eyed it gloomily. It looked so depressing. Still, it was a start.

Her thoughts wandered from it for a few days, until she realised she was putting off the evil day. She was legitimately distracted when the Featherstones reappeared on the scene by the arrival of a heavily embossed invitation to their new home for a buffet supper.

Minna was on the phone straightaway.

'Have you got one? An invitation to Lulubelle's party?' she asked.

Beth knew at once who she meant. Minna could never remember Bernadette's name and called her the first thing that came into her head.

'Yes, on the thirtieth—are you going?'

'I wouldn't miss it for the world,' Minna said. 'Will Geoff be free to go?'

'Yes, he'll make sure he is—it's a Saturday and one of the others can do turn and turn about.'

Minna would look super whatever she wore, for she always chose the right thing, casual yet impressive. Perhaps they could afford for Beth to have a new dress, and not before time.

But what would she buy? Clothes had been so difficult for the older woman since the revolutionary mini skirts of the sixties. Once they'd arrived, nothing had ever been quite the same. Minna could get away with it, with that lovely golden tan and her fine legs, but for the average mum in her late-thirties or early-forties, buying clothes these days was difficult. It was a young people's world. For the first time the accent was on the young—they had the earning power, and once having got the world in their hands, they were not going to let go.

Thank God her three were all right, Jon having achieved a place at Edinburgh where he wanted to do medicine like his father. Beth would miss him when he left in October, the first of the three to flee the nest.

Well, then, she would write. She had been thinking about it for some time. But not a novel—she saw everything in cameo and was sure she could never extend to a full-length novel. Imagine writing *Gone With the Wind*—the woman was a genius!

And with her writing something, Jon's going, and Geoff's being made senior partner, things were looking up all round. Perhaps she would get someone else to stand in for the book round at the local hospital, and then there were the visits to the local nurses' home—but what to wear to Bernadette's do? She would talk it over with Minna.

Then her friend announced that her exhibition was to be put on at the Felix Gallery in Cork Street—and she asked Beth to go up to town with her to organise it.

More excitement! Oh, why did everything come at once?

Jimmy had packed most of the paintings in the Bentley and Minna and Beth set off, Minna with her usual cigarette, the radio blaring as they swept through the village and out on to the London Road.

Oh, Beth did enjoy days out like this! Minna always made everything so exciting.

'So tell me about this man who runs the gallery,' Beth said.

'Well, he hasn't been open long and he was looking for new talent, so when Jimmy told him about me, he was very interested and agreed to take six of my paintings. He came down to see them and said they were fantastic.'

No wonder she was excited, thought Beth.

'I've done four more since then, but I thought, well, I shall need some in reserve if they sell well and he's putting quite a high price on them. I hope you and Geoff will come to the opening? It'll be quite a do—lots of film stars and important people. You know what Jimmy is—I can't stand that crowd but they do have money to spend sometimes,' she said, throwing her cigarette out into the road.

'Minna, you shouldn't do that—it's dangerous.'

'Do you know, you sound just like my

mother?' She frowned. 'You're old before your time, sweetie.'

Beth sulked.

Minna turned to her, suddenly contrite. 'No, I'm sorry, you're quite right. I should stub it out first.'

And that was what made Minna so engaging: she could do a volte-face effortlessly.

The gallery certainly was small, but in charge was a tall young man, dark-haired and handsome, who fell over himself to please Minna, obviously noting the Bentley outside, and the fact that his client's husband was in showbiz as he put it.

Beth was quite fascinated. She had to admit this was another world, a world of money and patrons, as far removed from the life of a general practitioner's wife as it was possible to be.

Cedric, for that was his name, was certainly impressed with Minna's paintings —and Beth took a back seat while they discussed where they would hang, and how many, and could she do more, and what sort of reception they would have at the opening...yes, there would be champagne cocktails and interesting bits to eat.

Beth was totally ignored, but delighted to be there anyway, a part of this swinging London scene. She had never really believed that it would happen, but in no time flat here was Minna, about to be launched as an artist.

'So I thought about a hundred and twenty to two hundred for the Provençals, and ROOTS, of course, will be the *pièce de résistance*—I think five hundred.' At which point Minna turned to Beth and raised her eyebrows.

'Let's hope there'll be plenty of red Sold stickers' Cedric laughed, showing fine white teeth.

'So, we'll fix the exhibition for the beginning of December. I have a few other artists who will be ready by then, so if I take, say, ten of yours—what do you say?'

'That's before Christmas, is it a good time?' Minna asked.

'Absolutely,' Cedric confirmed. 'They'll make wonderful pressies. Any problems with that, Min?'

'None at all,' she said.

I don't believe this, thought Beth. I simply don't believe it, but it's actually happening.

They had lunch to celebrate and afterwards drove home.

What an exciting day, thought Beth. It did you good to break away from chores once in a while.

'You and Geoff will come to the exhibition, won't you?' Minna asked again.

'Of course,' Beth laughed. 'But we've got Bernadette's do first.'

'By the way, we'll pick you up for that—nothing like arriving in a Bentley,' said her friend.

'I've no idea what to wear,' Beth confessed.

'I thought you always made something on the day?'

Beth grinned. 'I used to—I don't know if I could do it now. Besides, this is somewhat special, but I don't want to spend the earth.'

'Oh, you always look nice,' Minna said.

Beth took Belinda shopping with her. At fifteen, she had her own ideas of what should be worn, but had quite good taste and was delighted to be asked.

They went up to town and had lunch, which Belinda found madly exciting, and Beth bought her a striped sweater which she wanted, knowing that she was really putting off the evil moment of choosing something for herself.

Walking through the materials department, her eye was taken by some navy French silk jersey—'You know, I could do worse than make a simple shift of this, with a brassy belt'—but Belinda pulled her away.

'Absolutely not. You're to get out of that habit of knocking a little something

98

up—it's quite ridiculous. Now you don't want to overdo it, do you? Something nice, but not over the top.'

They finally settled for a blue-green dress which was sleeveless and beautifully cut.

'Not a colour I've ever worn,' frowned Beth. 'Still, it's pretty.'

'And, it suits you,' Belinda said. 'It goes with your colouring.'

Beth had to agree it did. The colour accentuated her blue eyes and fair hair.

'Do you think Daddy will like it?'

' 'Course he will—that's if he notices it.' And Belinda pulled a face.

'That's true.'

'With your pearls. Now, let's find some shoes.'

'Oh, but my...'

'No, they won't. This is an outfit. You can always wear it for Ascot.'

'Ascot!' shrieked Beth. 'When am I ever going to Ascot?'

'You never know,' Belinda said, and dragged her off with her impressive package to the shoe department.

'Gold,' Belinda said.

'Oh, I thought—'

'Gold,' Belinda repeated. 'Strappy. You've got that pretty evening bag.'

'That's true.'

'Mummy, you are going to a special

do—you don't want to let Daddy down, do you?'

'Oh, well,' a resigned Beth said, not displeased with the whole thing but feeling guilty at spending so much money. 'It will do for Minna's exhibition as well.'

'Why do you have to justify every penny you spend?' Belinda asked with interest. 'It's your right, you've earned it—you work hard.'

When the evening came round, Jimmy's Bentley purred to a stop outside Chantry Gate.

'Looks good, sitting out there,' Ian said. 'We should get one.'

Beth sat herself beside Minna, who whistled.

'Ooh, a new dress!' she cried, and seeing Beth's face, 'It's pretty. Really suits you.'

Beth stole a glance at Minna who looked wonderful in a simple pale blue silk shift, knee-length, worn with gold sandals and not a scrap of jewellery. With her colouring, she looked fantastic.

The men were talking together as they drove through the Green on their way to Chantry Park.

They couldn't have had any doubts as to where the house was. SAN REMO was floodlit for all the world to see, and looked enormous.

'Gawd!' said Minna, overcome for once in a way, almost speechless.

Together with several other cars newly arrived, they went through the electronic gates and were told where to park by a man in uniform.

They walked up the marble steps and into the house, together with lots of other people, none of whom they knew.

'I suppose we're lucky to be invited,' Minna whispered. 'They're probably all food people.'

Inside, all was splendour. Women dressed up to the nines in fur wraps and lots of diamonds, the furs handed to the maid to be whisked off. Minna, who clutched a gold purse, had no wrap; Beth, her mother's ancient fur stole. Then they were led through the impressive hall and out into the newly built conservatory, where coloured lights swung in arcs and flowers were everywhere. At the enormous bar stood Laurie, handsome as ever, and Bernadette by his side in a black velvet trouser suit—she looked beautiful. Her hair was cropped short, and gleamed with blonde highlights, while her blue eyes shone with pride of possession.

'Jesus!' Minna said at sight of her. 'So this is Laurie?' she murmured in an aside to Beth.

He was handsome, Beth had to admit.

Tall, well-built, with amazing blue eyes, a fine smooth skin and small moustache, which when he kissed her briefly was unexpectedly silky. Champagne flowed and the noise was overpowering. 'Welcome to SAN REMO,' Bernadette cried above the din, and while Laurie busied himself at the bar, although there was no need, for there were waiters galore, Laurie held Minna's hand in his for a moment longer than necessary, approval in the swift glance that took in everything about her from top to toe. Afterwards he shook hands with Geoff, and held out his hand to Jimmy: 'I don't think we've met, old man.' They shook hands too, and Beth wondered what Jimmy was thinking. Laurie took down a bottle from the glass shelf 'Is this your brew?' he asked, and went to open the bottle of finest malt whisky.

'Here, let me,' Bernadette said firmly. She took the bottle from him and had it open in a second.

'As you can see, she's a whizz kid,' Laurie said, blue eyes twinkling. But behind that twinkle, Beth thought, his eyes are as hard as nails.

'Yes,' Laurie continued. 'My wife—the eighth wonder of the world. What would I do without her?'

Bernadette purred, showing her fine white teeth—she looked incredibly beautiful—while

Laurie smiled. Beth guessed that smile had gone a long way towards his success; it must hide a multitude of feelings.

'Do mingle,' Bernadette said, 'I'll introduce you to everyone in a moment—and I expect you'd like to see the house?' She came from behind the bar and thrust her arm through Minna's, taking Beth's hand at the same time.

Beth could imagine Minna's reaction. 'Well, this is the...'

It went on for half an hour almost: the kitchen, the drawing room, the library, the dining room, the upstairs rooms—until Minna could barely hide a yawn.

At the top of the stairs, seeing the crowd in the hall below, Bernadette clapped her hands imperiously.

'Will you all make your way to the dining room, where the buffet will be served?'

The throng made their way. Waiters and waitresses in black and white saw to their every whim while the wine flowed. The food was simply gorgeous and music played, all the hit songs from the latest musicals.

Laurie circulated amongst the guests, Minna nudging Beth once when he stopped to kiss a handsome woman in a red dress.

'Shouldn't think Bernadette has a dull

moment keeping an eye on him,' Minna declared.

'Good-looking, isn't he?' said Beth.

'Mmmm,' agreed Minna thoughtfully.

Beth took a deep breath. It was another world. There must be a short story in this somewhere.

Later, Minna and Jimmy went to Chantry Gate for coffee.

'Well,' said Minna, sinking into a low chair. 'At least the food was good.'

'She does everything so well,' Beth said, and went off to make the coffee.

Minna stretched. 'I've a busy week ahead of me too,' she said. 'Jimmy, I'm lunching with Cedric on Monday.'

'You are? Do you want a lift to town?'

'No, I'll drive up,' she said. She got up and followed Beth into the kitchen.

'I'm going to town on Monday—like to come?'

'Monday? My busiest day,' Beth laughed. 'No thanks, Minna.'

'I'm lunching with Cedric,' she said, and lit a cigarette.

'He's dishy, too,' Beth commented. 'Doesn't Jimmy mind that you're seeing so much of him?'

Minna laughed out loud. 'Darling, he's a poof!' She saw the rosy flush creep up from Beth's cheeks and down to her neck.

'You didn't realise it when you saw him?'

Beth shook her head. She was highly embarrassed, all sorts of conflicting thoughts going round inside her head.

'I don't remember meeting one before,' she admitted. 'I suppose I've never really thought about it.'

'You're blinkered, like a lot of people. Of course, being around the showbiz crowd, I'm used to them—once, when Jimmy was away on location, I lived with one for three months.'

'Minna, you didn't!'

'I did. It was wonderful. He used to do my hair for me, and was there to keep me safe without all the problems of a real male. Oh, yes, they have their uses, and like most of them, his sense of humour was terrific. I quite missed him when Jimmy got back.'

Funny, Beth thought, I really know nothing of Minna's life after we went our separate own ways, and yet we get on so well.

Late on Monday afternoon she surprised herself by going upstairs and taking the cover off the old typewriter, then sat down and wrote a short story that had been milling around in her head since the weekend.

105

Once finished, she read it through before writing a covering letter and sending it to one of the weekly magazines, enclosing a stamped addressed envelope for their reply.

Going down to the post office, she was in such a state of excitement—it was worth all the effort of writing it. And it hadn't been difficult. It just flowed. Perhaps that's what she was: a born writer.

Six weeks later, the day after Jon had left for his his first term at Edinburgh, and she was feeling particularly down the story came back—with a rejection slip. Beth turned it over. Nothing written on the back; no memo to say: too short, too long, well done. Nothing.

She hurried upstairs to the top floor and stowed it away in a drawer.

Well, she thought, I tried. But it might be a long time before she wrote another.

Chapter Seven

When Beth opened the door to Gina that morning, it was obvious that she had made a decision. Hanging up her Aquascutum raincoat and wearing her royal blue georgette with floating panels, she donned an apron, lips set in a straight line, and passed Belinda who was sitting at the kitchen table.

'Good-a morning, how you?' she asked Belinda. Gina was very fond of Belinda.

'I am missing Jon,' Belinda sulked. 'It's not the same. And when Ian goes...'

'Oh, by then you 'ave something else to do,' Gina said. 'You see.'

Belinda looked glum.

'Madam-a, *scusi*, *per favore*—I not 'ear from that girl Renate.' Her lip curled. 'But I get idea.'

'What will you do, Gina?' Belinda asked eagerly.

'I tell-a Miss Potts!'

'Oh, Gina!' Belinda said. 'You wouldn't!'

Gina shook her head vigorously. 'I would. I tell-a Miss Potts.' She withdrew a letter from her pocket triumphantly and handed it to Beth.

107

' "Now Renate, if you not send money (I not want skirt now) I tell Miss Potts and you know what that means!" '

The last sentence was heavily underlined.

Belinda grinned her approval. 'That's telling her, Gina!'

'Alrigh'?' she asked, folding the letter and putting it back in her pocket.

'Alrigh' ', Beth said.

And presently from the bathroom came the sounds of *'Nessun Dorma'*.

Beth smiled. Things were getting back to normal.

It was half term, and Ian and Belinda were home, although Jon had not come down from Edinburgh.

When the phone rang, Beth went to answer it.

It was Minna. 'Why don't you come round for a spell—bring Belinda? Hamish would like to see her—they could have a game of table tennis.'

'Give us half an hour,' Beth said.

When they arrived, she sent Belinda off to the games room, and made her way to the studio, where she found Minna surrounded by stacks of paintings.

'Pass me my cigarettes, will you?'

Beth hesitated only for a moment—then handed them to her, together with her gold lighter.

'So what've you been doing with

yourself?' Minna asked drawing on her cigarette.

'To tell you the truth, I tried a short story—actually, I sent it off—but it came back.'

'Don't give up,' Minna said. 'English magazines wouldn't recognise a good short story if they saw one, they're only interested in buying second-hand American ones.'

Beth managed to laugh. 'I just wondered if you wanted me to do anything about the exhibition—is it all arranged? All underway?'

'Yep.' Minna said. 'No problems. At least so far as I can see. The invitations go out on Wednesday—Jimmy's secretary is seeing to that.'

'Oh, it is exciting!' Beth cried. She was glad just to be on the fringes of it all.

'Oh, I know what I wanted to show you! Jimmy, bless his heart, has bought me a mink coat for Christmas. Don't say anything, I can't stand fur and I'll never wear the damn thing as it is, but I've had an idea. Go and ask Bonny to bring it for me—she knows where it is.'

Beth made her way to the kitchen.

'Mrs Bonnington, would you get Mrs Alders' new fur coat, please? She wants me to see it.'

'Yes, of course, Mrs Meldrum.' And she smiled at Beth pleasantly.

Back in the studio, Minna had stubbed out her cigarette and lit another.

'Of course, there's no way I'd wear it as it is, but I've had an idea—you know my old Burberry? Well, I've stuffed the mink into it and pushed it down the sleeves, and with a belt it becomes a mink-lined raincoat. That way, it's presentable and I can wear it. Of course, Jimmy doesn't like the idea—he wanted me to show it off, like he's the successful screen writer he is. But he'll get used to it.'

Mrs Bonnington returned, the coat held over her arm reverently.

Swathed in its cover, and satin-lined, it was beautiful, a lovely dark ranch mink. So soft...

'Put it on,' Minna ordered.

Beth's eyes were wide and luminous.

'Oh, no, I couldn't.'

'Oh, go on, I want to see what it looks like,' Minna said, so Beth did as she was told.

'Smashing coat,' Minna said, satisfied. 'He's got good taste—he often chooses my clothes.'

'What, Jimmy?'

'Yes, he taught me what to wear. Don't you remember, I used to wear the most godawful things?'

It was true. She now had a casual, elegant approach to clothes, which she

110

certainly hadn't had before. Minna had had outrageous taste when she was younger.

'Yes, that's what I'll do,' she said, pleased with the idea. 'It couldn't be easier, and it'll look rather nice underneath the raincoat—I'll wear it open so it shows.'

Beth took it off slowly, and folded it back into its cover.

'So, what news of Jon?' Minna asked. 'Has he settled in at Edinburgh?'

'Yes, hopefully, I think it's right for him. We shall have to see what Ian does.'

'I shouldn't think Hamish will make the grade,' Minna said, but quite cheerfully. 'One thing, I don't have to worry about him. His father will always find him a job.'

She looked at Beth through myopic eyes.

'Ask Bonny to put the kettle on, will you? I could do with a cup of tea.'

'All right,' Beth said, trotting off into the kitchen. I'm very obedient, she thought. Do this, Beth, do that. 'All set for Saturday?' she asked on her return.

'Yes. We drove up last night to check the gallery, and I must say, it's rather impressive. I'm glad Cedric has gone over the top. Everyone will be there.'

Beth found herself growing quite excited.

'Several film stars—you know how they like to be seen at arty dos—a producer

111

or two, some Americans over here at the moment.'

'What will you wear?' Beth asked.

Minna looked at her quizzically. 'What you really mean is, what should *you* wear?' she said. 'Wear that thing you wore to Bernadette's.'

'Really?' Beth couldn't help feeling relieved. They could ill afford a new outfit for her.

'Yes, it suits you. I'm wearing what I call my Marlene Dietrich outfit—you know, the silk pants and man's jacket?'

'Well, you always look super in that.'

'I wish now I'd invited Bernadette and that husband of hers—what's his name?'

'Laurie.'

'Mmmm. Do you think they'd buy? They've got plenty of money.'

'I don't know, she's not exactly into art,' Beth said, thinking, If that's what you call it. Still, it was an exhibition at an art gallery.

'Anyway, I didn't and it's too late now.'

Beth couldn't help feeling relieved.

'I tell you who will be there,' Minna said, stacking her paintings against the wall—there seemed to be no end to them, Beth noticed—'Gavin Lees and Jean Montrose.'

'Really?' Beth breathed. The newest

young pair of actors who had scored such a success in—?

'Oh, and that Frenchman—what's his name? He was in that thing with Brigitte Bardot.'

Minna was hopeless at names. No matter, it was all going to be very exciting.

Beth could hardly wait for Saturday to come round.

But in the event, she changed her mind about what she would wear. Guessing it would be a sophisticated affair, she decided to wear her old black dress. That was, if she could still get into it. Making her way to the storage wardrobe, she took it down and held it against her. Yes, she thought, it's plain, unfussy and suits me. The question is, can I get into it?

Standing in her slip in the bedroom, she pulled it over her head and eased the long back zip into place. Not easy but she had done it. It was a bit tight. She frowned. Perhaps she could let it out? Then she smoothed it over her hips, seeing the way the sleeves were cut narrowly, so flattering to the figure, that simple neckline—she would wear her pearls. You couldn't fault the combination. There was nothing like a little black dress. Of course, Geoff wouldn't like it, he didn't like to see her in black, but it couldn't be helped.

Better that, simple and plain, than being overdressed. Her new gold sandals, her pearls, and where were the pearl ear studs? Downstairs, she rummaged in her jewellery drawer. She fancied long drops, the lovely garnets that had belonged to her mother, but really, it would look overdone. Earrings like that weren't worn these days.

She brushed her hair until it shone, deciding she would put some rouge on her cheek on the night. She felt a bit guilty at spending so much time on herself, but goodness, it didn't hurt for once. She looked down at her hands. They were the trouble. Short nails, nothing glamorous about those. She thought of Minna's hands, large and capable but with strong filbert nails which she had manicured every week, and Bernadette's, with those long tapering fingers. Beth had an idea. What if she wore false nails? Just for once... She had seen them advertised and promised herself a trip to the chemist who was quite advanced for Chantry Green. He even stocked a small range of French perfumes.

She had known that's what she was going to do all along. After the grocery shopping, and the dog food, and the greengrocery and the corn chandler's—somehow she was eyeing the new counter display in the chemist. 'Perfect!' the advertisement said. 'Chipped or torn nails? Repair them, or treat yourself to fabulous new nails—you will be amazed.'

Beth got quite carried away.

After unpacking the shopping and putting it away, she hurried upstairs to the bathroom and examined her exciting new purchase. The nails were enormous, ten of them, and the instructions said 'cut to size, to your individual requirements'. Well, that shouldn't be difficult—they were only plastic. And then there was a tube of glue and she had some small sharp scissors. Oh, she was quite looking forward to it! She would rub lemon and handcream into her hands, and then for the varnish. Oh what a colour, not scarlet, that would be too much, but a jolly bright pink.

Humming, she stowed her package in the dressing-table drawer and went downstairs, smiling to herself.

Afterwards, getting ready for the opening at six-thirty, she wondered what she would have done if Belinda hadn't been home, for doing the left hand was one thing, but the right hand something else. Beth sat in her dress, having done her hair and made up her face, hands laced with cream, but dry round the nails (as advised). It was more messy than she'd realised. She'd just finished one hand when a gentle tap came on the door and Belinda entered. 'Oh, sorry, I didn't realise you weren't ready.' She saw the furious blush which flooded Beth's cheeks.

'What's the matter?' she asked, walking over to the dressing table, then saw Beth's left hand with its long pointed nails, unpolished as yet. Her eyes widened in disbelief, then horror, as she saw the glue and the uncut-as-yet right hand nails.

'Mummy! What have you done?' She took in the whole situation and began to laugh. 'Oh, you wouldn't? You haven't?' But she sobered up when she saw Beth's face.

'Why not?' Beth asked indignantly, secretly furious with herself for having embarked on the project at all.

Suddenly, she slumped on the stool. It did seem a bit ridiculous, over the top—but Belinda was quick to notice her disappointment.

'Well, the left hand looks great. Let's see about the other one, shall we?'

'Oh, would you?' Beth pleaded, and watched as Belinda dealt with her other hand. 'Now how does that feel?'

'Very odd,' Beth admitted. 'I can't imagine wearing them for any length of time.'

'Let's finish it, shall we?' Belinda said, by now carried away with the effect, and with straight deft strokes she painted each nail until she reached the desired effect.

Strange, really, Belinda had beautiful hands. It had been the first question Beth had asked when she was born: 'Has she nice hands and nails?'

'Yes,' the midwife sad. 'Two thumbs and eight fingers—she's all there.' But that hadn't been what Beth meant.

'Hold them out,' Belinda ordered, and had to admit her mother's nails looked stunning. But as to wearing them herself...ugh! She shuddered inwardly.

'Well, are you game to wear them this evening?' she asked.

'Of course,' Beth said stoutly. Wild horses wouldn't take them from her now.

'Well, you'll have to be careful holding things,'

'Of course,' she said again, as though she did it every day.

In the car, driving up to town, she saw Geoff do a double take as he noticed her painted nails.

'What?' she asked.

'New nail polish?' he asked. 'Nice colour.' And his eyes returned to the road. 'I like that dress,' he said, 'always did.'

Beth smiled to herself. Weren't men strange? He had always disliked it; didn't like her in black, he'd said.

It was a real gallery party, and Beth

was more than pleased that she had taken trouble with her appearance for even now she could barely hold a candle to the outfits the female guests wore. There were white mink coats and luxurious white fox furs draped over long satin dresses that clung to slim young figures, Minna looked wonderful in her pants suit, Jimmy by her side, and already there were red stickers on some paintings, denoting sales. The prices were there for all to see, hundreds of pounds, and Beth stared in disbelief. She recognised TV personalities, and several famous showbiz people, and there were lots of 'darlings' being bandied about. She gratefully accepted a delicious orange drink which was so refreshing that she automatically took a second one when they came round again. It was quite the best orange drink she had ever tasted.

The room grew hotter as more people arrived, for it was quite a small gallery, and she was introduced to girls and young men, and every time the tray came by, took another orange juice gratefully, then began to feel decidedly peculiar.

Minna was coming up to her with a famous drag star, and Beth thought how wonderful he/she looked with that tan, and false eyelashes an inch long, those splendid teeth, the long blonde hair...when she suddenly realised she must be excused, she could barely stand.

It was a considerable time afterwards, when people were making their way towards the door, that Geoff asked Minna if she knew where Beth was. 'She hasn't been around for some time and I wondered if she had gone to the ladies' room?'

Minna hurried over to the door and had some difficulty opening it for Beth was sitting on the floor at the other side, studiously easing off every painted nail—there was a small pile on the floor. She looked up, quite impervious.

'Come on,' Minna said harshly. 'Let's get your coat.'

'Oh, I do feel strange,' Beth moaned, and Geoff hurried to her side. Putting an arm around her, he made his apologies and led her towards the car. On the way out into the fresh air, she was sick.

She turned to him pale-faced. 'I feel much better now,' she said. 'I don't know what came over me.'

'How many of those champagne cocktails did you have?' he asked grimly.

'Champagne cocktails! Were they? Golly, I thought it was orange juice. They tasted so nice and refreshing and it was so hot in there.'

'I hope you realise we've missed dinner?' he said. 'Jimmy was taking us to the White

Elephant.' And he began to laugh. 'You are a nutcase! But you didn't really want to go on to dinner, did you?'

'No, not really,' Beth said. 'Do you mind? I'm sorry. It was as if they were from another world, wasn't it?'

'They were,' Geoff laughed. 'In more ways than one.'

He glanced at his watch. 'It's only half-eight—we'd be home by nine. Fancy trying for a meal in Windsor?'

'Lovely,' she said. 'I'm quite hungry now.'

She looked down at her hands: small, square hands with their few remaining painted nails. They looked so incongruous, she began to laugh.

'What are you laughing at?'

'I'll tell you sometime,' she said. 'Minna thought I should take up painting.'

'Don't you dare!' Geoff said.

'Still, I'm glad I went.'

Minna was on the phone first thing.

'Are you all right—you had us quite worried.'

'You weren't the only one,' Beth said. 'How did it go?'

'Sold every one,' she said. 'Not bad for a first effort, was it?'

'Wonderful,' Beth said. 'I'm sorry I got drunk.'

'You weren't drunk,' Minna said. 'Were you?'

'I was,' Beth said, thinking she would never touch another glass of orange juice as long as she lived.

Chapter Eight

The week following Minna's exhibition, Gina arrived wearing someone's rather moth-eaten moleskin coat which was a sight too big for her. She was in a state of great excitement.

'Madam-a!' she cried. 'I show you, I show you' and she brought out of her pocket a letter with a German postmark. She emptied it on to the table and out fell some German marks.

In the letter the beautiful Renate explained that she was sorry she could not write before, but she had been travelling round from place to place.

'Oh, well,' Beth said, 'if she...'

'She not travel around,' Gina said scathingly, 'she bad girl. She scared when I tell 'er I tell Miss-a Potts' and her black eyes shone with triumph. 'That Miss-a Potts, she terrible English lady. Renate not like I tell-a Miss Potts, Gina know that' and she laughed and laughed.

'Ow much-a mark-a in English money?'

'I don't know, Gina. Take them to the bank, they tell you.'

'Yes, I do that,' she said happily and Beth breathed a sigh of relief as, armed with bucket and mops, she crossed the hall singing 'Your tiny hand is frozen' in full spate.

Jon came home for Christmas and regaled them with stories of university life, while Ian and Belinda broke up from school. Bernadette had got into the habit of calling in for coffee on a Sunday morning after church, for the Catholic church was nearby.

On the Sunday before Christmas Day she arrived resplendent in mink coat and hat, accompanied by Annelise who swiftly disappeared upstairs with Belinda to her bedroom.

'What do you think?' Bernadette asked, twirling round. 'It's Laurie's Christmas present to me.'

With her very high-heeled patent court shoes she looked like a film star, and the matching hat was adorable, perched on her sleek hair do. Her blue eyes shone wide and ingenuous and on her wrists and fingers the bracelets jangled and the rings flashed. Beth couldn't help thinking of Minna and the differences between them.

'Laurie thinks the hat is too plain. He wants to buy a diamond pin for it. What do you think?'

Beth pursed her lips. 'Well, I don't think it needs it—but if Laurie wants to, who are you to argue?'

'Exactly,' Bernadette said peering at herself in the mirror. She turned to face Beth.

'I'll get the coffee,' she said, glad of something to do.

'Listen, we're giving a cocktail party on Christmas Eve. I didn't mention it before, I thought perhaps you wouldn't want to come but if you and Geoff are free and would like to join us...'

'Thanks, Bernadette, I'll see. Christmas Eve is such a busy time, with the children and all.'

'Yes.' Although Beth thought Bernadette couldn't quite see what the children had to do with it. What, she wondered, did little Annelise get out of Christmas, except eternal visits to church?

'We're taking Annelise over to Canada in January to see my parents, just for a week—they see so little of her, and she is the only grandchild—my sister has no children.'

'I didn't realise you had a sister?' Beth said. Surely there could only be one Bernadette?

'Yes, she's not in the least like me—doesn't even look like me, she's rather shy really. A goody-goody, you know. Nothing like her rumbustious, successful sister.'

Depends what you mean by success, Beth thought. I mustn't turn crabby, she reproved herself. It takes all sorts.

They were interrupted by the arrival of Jon in the kitchen, carrying his shoes through to polish them.

'My goodness! That's never you, Jon! How handsome and tall you are. Why, when I saw you last...'

'How are you, Mrs Featherstone?' Jon held out his hand and flashed one of his famous grins at her, grins that had swept most of the sixth-form girls off their feet before he left for Edinburgh.

Beth smiled. She supposed he was rather handsome, like Geoff, although he was fair haired like her. He was nice, good-natured and kind, that was the main thing. She was proud of him.

'And how is Edinburgh?'

'Cold!' He grinned. 'There's a saying among the faculty up there that if you haven't lived in Edinburgh, you haven't lived.'

'My goodness, you don't know what cold is! In Canada it's ten times colder. Mind you, its a dry cold, not damp like this. Ugh, I hate English winters!'

'What do you think Annelise will do?' Beth asked. 'She's sixteen now, isn't she?'

Annelise had grown tall and looked

125

a little like her father, with a lovely complexion and his attractive smile.

Bernadette sighed. 'I don't know—she's good at French, which she should be, of course, speaks it like a native—but she doesn't talk about anything she wants to do. They're so spoiled these days, Beth. What's Belinda want to do?'

'Cooking, without a doubt.' Beth smiled, sipping her coffee.

'Well, it's all experience.' Bernadette frowned. 'But as a career, I'm not sure.'

'Well, that's what she wants to do. Has done ever since I can remember.'

'I shall certainly send Annelise to a finishing school. I went to one so there's no reason why she shouldn't.' She stood up. 'I must get back. I expect Agnes has got the lunch ready—I said we wouldn't be late.' And she went into the hall.

'Annelise, I'm going. Hurry on down...'

Agnes, the new housekeeper—Beth had forgotten about her.

'You're pleased with her?' she asked.

'My dear, I wouldn't keep her if I wasn't. Oh, there you are. Say goodbye to Auntie Beth.'

'What is Belinda doing?' Beth asked Annelise.

'Sorting out recipes,' Annelise laughed. She really was a pretty girl, Beth thought, and went to the stairs.

'Belinda, come on down, Aunt Bernadette is going now.'

Belinda hurtled down the stairs two at a time, slowing as she reached the kitchen. She had no time for Bernadette.

'Hallo, Aunt Bernadette.' And her glance flicked over the fabulous coat.

'My,' Bernadette frowned, 'you've grown tall too. How's school?'

'Fine, thank you. So I'll see you again before Christmas, Annelise?'

'Yes, sure', she said. 'We're not going away until the New Year.'

'Do up your coat.' Bernadette frowned. 'And put your gloves on, it's cold outside.'

They walked to the door and saw Bernadette and Annelise outside, waving them goodbye.

'You know, Annelise looks like one of the royal children,' Belinda said to Beth. 'Prim little coat, gloves and hat—it's so old-fashioned. I'm glad you don't make me dress like that.'

'I have news for you,' Beth said, as laughing, she followed Belinda into the house.

'Was that coat real?' Belinda asked in disbelief.

'It was,' Beth said. 'Mink.'

'God!' Belinda said, and shuddered. 'Disgusting!' she went through the hall and up the stairs two at a time.

'Has she gone?' Jon said, emerging from the kitchen.

'Don't be disrespectful' Beth said mildly 'It's nice of her to call in.'

'Mother, you are far too kind,' he said on his way out.

Beth decided not to go to Bernadette's Christmas Eve party. It was such a special evening: going to Midnight Mass, putting up the tree and dressing it and the thought of meeting all those food ladies as she called them, was more than daunting. And by the time she got back from the local hospital where the doctors' wives did their share of brightening up the patients, there would hardly be time.

On Christmas morning the family stood in church, Beth's heart full of sadness for absent friends, her parents and the hospital patients, some of whom were so brave. But somehow, once they emerged, she felt better for it and with a lightened heart hurried home to see to the turkey and the rest of the Christmas dinner which was waiting for them in the Aga.

'Come on, old boy,' Belinda said to Gus who was sitting in the porch. 'Special treat today.' And his tail wagged nineteen to the dozen.

The presents were opened round the tree, and the old Victorian house came into its own—it was a perfect Christmas house.

The tree stood in the hall, brightly lit with coloured lights, visible from outside, lending cheer to the passers by. In the afternoon they listened to the Queen's speech, and ate nuts and fruit and sweets although no one really wanted them. Late in the evening, Geoff received an urgent call—when did he not? Beth asked herself, but that was what being a doctor was all about. And soon, she told herself, it will be New Year 1974, and what will that bring? How things have changed! But tomorrow they were all going in the morning of Boxing Day to the Rowlandses which should be fun.

Joe and Sheila were in festive mood, making a special effort, Beth realised. Both had paper caps on, and Joe's breath when he kissed her smelled mildly of whisky, his leonine head looking impressive even in a paper hat. Sheila wore a silver crown on her dark curls.

The drawing room was so unlike what it was in Bernadette's time with its chintz covered chairs and plain walls and curtains, a few photographs in silver frames. Holly and mistletoe were draped round the mantelpiece and the tree was so pretty with its small Chinese lanterns.

Kate, at nineteen, tall and elegant, was a beauty. No one could be unaware of her; there was something about her, a kind of magnetism, a special glint in the dark eyes, and she had that lovely low voice. You felt the unspoken passion behind it. Jon, not unaware, was already going across to her and her eyes laughed up at him. With her father's long dark lashes, she looked so sure of herself, so much in charge. Jon looked down into her eyes—Maybe...Beth thought. Ian seemed unaware of her charms, and began to discuss Joe's new tape recorder, while Fran and Belinda quickly got together. Fran was the quiet one, pretty as a picture, small and delicate-looking. Shy almost, though Kate was outgoing enough for the two of them.

They were all talking at once, two happy families, when the doorbell rang.

'I've asked Miss Evans,' Sheila confided. 'She's quite alone, and I thought she might like a bit of company.'

'How nice,' Beth murmured. Why hadn't she thought of that?

Miss Evans came in, a great beaming smile on her face, hand held out in greeting.

'We have met briefly, at a Friends of the Hospital do,' she said to Beth. 'Somehow I see so little of my neighbours. Because I'm working, I suppose.'

Beth knew hardly anything about her,

only that she worked in a government office and had an OBE. It was known that she did important work of some kind and was thought highly of in the Foreign Office. Beth guessed she must be around fifty something.

Sheila had a great bowl of hot punch, which everyone made for—hot wine and cinnamon—and it was seized on greedily. 'We always had this at home in Yorkshire, but I don't find people use it as much down South.'

And Sheila said as an afterthought, 'Kate has a friend coming in—a boyfriend,' she said in an aside. 'He works in the same office but I don't think there's anything in it. I hope not, she's far too young.'

Was she? Beth wondered. Minna was married at nineteen. Still, she couldn't see that happening to Kate, who was far too much of a feminist from what Beth had heard. She and Fran had lots of arguments about it, Sheila had said.

One Saturday afternoon, when Geoff and Joe had gone for a round of golf, Sheila and the girls and Beth and Belinda sat in the kitchen round the Aga, talking. The Rowlands girls were always such fun.

As they sipped their tea and laughed, Kate said to Sheila: 'Tell about when you were first married?'

'What especially?' her mother said.

131

'Well, you know, when you had to ask Daddy for money for your undies—your knickers. I didn't believe her, Auntie Beth.'

'Well, it's true,' Sheila said.

'Did you have to ask Uncle Geoff?' Kate asked Beth.

'Well, not really as it happens, because I had a little money of my own left to me by my parents. But had I not, of course I would have asked for a dress allowance.'

'A what?' And Kate shrieked with laughter.

'What's so funny?' Beth asked.

'That's what Mummy said she thought she was entitled to—a dress allowance. Belinda, can you bear it?'

'Well, you see, things were different then—we had housekeeping money, and I'm talking now about ordinary people, not people with money or really poor people. Ordinary people. The husband got his salary or wages, and the wife, if she was clever, managed to manipulate a bit out of the housekeeping.'

Kate was outraged and her dark eyes sparked. 'I think that's disgusting! That a woman should have to wangle the housekeeping in order to buy herself clothes!'

'That's why we wanted a dress allowance,' her mother put in.

'I find it incredible,' Kate continued.

'Catch me asking a man for money!'

'Yes, but it's different now. You'll probably go on working, as girls do after they're married these days.'

'That's *if* I marry,' Kate said grimly. 'Catch me being a man's slave.'

'Oh, I don't know,' Fran said. 'It depends how he is. I think if you played your cards right, you could do quite well out of it—being married, I mean.'

'You are disgusting,' Kate said. 'She's a real little horror, Auntie Beth. Catch me being beholden to any man.'

'You might change your tune when you fall in love,' Beth said.

'That's what I tell her,' Sheila agreed.

'It's not going to happen,' Kate said. 'I've learned my lesson watching your generation, tied for life—what a joke!—to a man who exploits you and makes a drudge out of you. That you actually have to ask for money for your clothes—I'd rather die!'

And Beth could see she meant it. Her nostrils flared most becomingly when she was angry, and those lovely dark eyes glinted and flashed. My word, I'd like to see the man who could tame that, she thought, and secretly hoped it wasn't to be Jon.

Now, on this Christmas Eve when the boyfriend eventually turned up, Beth was a little surprised. He was handsome, tall and well-built, and very sure of himself. She hadn't expected that somehow, imagining that Kate would choose someone whom she could order about, dictate to.

Kate, standing by her side, smiled wickedly. 'Could you fancy him, Auntie Beth?' she asked, causing her to blush furiously, not only at the girl's words but at her cheek.

'He doesn't know it,' Kate whispered, 'but I'm in line for promotion, and so is he. We're after the same job: assistant editor. Want to bet who gets it?

'David,' she said, going up to him and laying a slim white hand on his arm, 'come and meet my Auntie Beth and Uncle Geoff. My sister, Fran.'

As Beth shook hands, with him, Kate gave her an outrageous wink.

Oh, Beth thought, I'm glad Belinda wants to be a cook. I don't think I could bear it if she entered the rat race too.

Chapter Nine

Sitting in the window seat, the stacked boxes all around her, Beth didn't see them, too deep in thought. What a strange era the seventies had been. Men had worn tight-fitted shirts with huge collars, long hair, with sideburns sometimes, flared trousers. When you saw old films now, they looked so—well, sissy-ish, for want of a better word. Discos were everywhere and Indian restaurants and Chinese takeaways sprouted like mushrooms. Less and less one found small tea shops; instead coffee shops abounded and cooking was 'in'. Everyone was food-conscious and starting to take an interest in health. People were Yoga mad, and walked and jogged or trotted, whatever suited them. Good health was the order of the day.

Geoff's surgery was extended, due to a growing population, and they had taken on another doctor, a woman practitioner, bringing the total to four. It seemed to Beth that the seventies had been the start of a social revolution as the time when everything went over the top in every way, when the world changed—and not always for the better.

After the war, there were many references to the coming revolution—'Wait till the revolution,' people would say darkly—yet when it did come, the word was never used. It took place without anyone knowing it; the world changed, people changed, they wanted different things, and were determined to get them.

That decade saw Jon achieving his medical degree and Ian studying at university for an engineering degree while Belinda fully embarked on her chosen career as caterer.

She was absorbed to the point of obsession with all this, and barely had time for anything else; no time for boyfriends, she said, although there were always a few hanging around. And she had her skiing holiday every year, which had started after one Christmas when Bernadette asked her to accompany them to Chamonix. Beth still remembered the expense of kitting her out in skiing clothes, but she had had a glorious fortnight in the mountains and learned to ski into the bargain, an enthusiasm she had never lost.

'It was wonderful!' she cried to a relieved Beth on her return.

'You've gone such a lovely colour,' she cried, looking at her pretty daughter with her golden tan.

'Auntie Bernadette said that comes from the snow, the wind, the cold and the sun—it's not like a hot dry sun which burns,' she said knowledgeably. 'And can she ski!' she added with intense admiration.

'Who? Auntie Bernadette?'

Obviously Belinda's estimation of Bernadette had gone up by leaps and bounds.

'She really is magnificent, you should see her on the slopes.'

'Did Uncle Laurie ski?' Beth asked. She couldn't quite imagine it.

'Yes, but he went home after a few days. He doesn't get a lot of free time—business calls and all that. The phone goes all the time, not that Auntie Bernadette seems to mind. She just spends all her time out on the piste.'

Belinda's eyes were faraway, on the snow-covered mountain slopes.

'I think perhaps I had her all wrong,' she said thoughtfully. 'She's not the same person when she's doing her sports thing. She skates and she swims—gosh, she's terrific.'

'And what about Annelise—how's she?'

'Quite good. Not as good as her mother obviously, she's not that keen on winter sports. Not like me, I could live over there.'

How odd, Beth thought. No one else

in the family had ever skied, yet here was Belinda raving about it. 'What was the hotel like?'

'Oh, absolutely super! Plush, you know, and the rooms—well, such luxury. You can't imagine if you've never been. Of course, it's a world-famous resort. Good thing you bought me some clothes—lots of famous people staying there. I saw Audrey Hepburn.'

'Belinda! Really? What's she like?'

'So pretty and dainty, like an elf, with great dark eyes. She was walking across the hotel foyer the day we arrrived. Uncle Laurie whistled under his breath, and Auntie Bernadette looked daggers!'

Belinda's eyes were alight with memories. Beth hoped she would settle down after such a wonderful experience.

It was later, in the kitchen where they were clearing away and washing up, that Belinda, stacking glasses in the dresser, turned with dishcloth in hand and stared out of the window at the roof of the house next door.

'I suppose when you live close to someone, you really get to know them.' Beth knew further revelations were coming, but said nothing.

'Annelise is not quite what you think she is—not that I want to be disloyal,' she hastened to say, polishing round the tumbler fast and furiously.

'Oh?' Beth asked mildly.

'Well, she gives the impression that she's a bit of a puritan—you know, all that religious stuff, the way she dresses. Although that's Auntie Bernadette's fault,' she said accusingly, putting the glass on the tray.

'But, I mean, she's not exactly backward at coming forward. Has quite a nice line when you meet boys—sort of unexpected, you know. She seems so protected, but if she can get away from her mother, she'll—'

'Well, darling, I'm not surprised. Bernadette does keep her under lock and key. Besides, isn't that every young girl's wish—to be let off the lead at this stage? After all, you're only young once. Believe it not, I was too,' Beth laughed.

'You mean, she thinks she does—keep her under lock and key I mean, but Annelise has her own way of dealing with it. She's not above sneaking out. Some of the things they get up to in that convent are hilarious, and some of them—well, I'll leave it to your imagination. I can't help feeling I'm the one who has had a strict upbringing.'

Beth thoughtfully eyed the suds. Well, nothing was ever as it seemed. To young people of sixteen, seventeen or eighteen, the world was their oyster and they wanted to get at it as soon as possible. Confined as she was under Bernadette's eagle eye it was no wonder Annelise was a rebel, but if Belinda was right, that quiet shy approach the girl had was just a façade, and the wide innocent blue eyes not quite what they seemed.

There was more to this little revelation than met the eye, Beth thought, but Belinda obviously felt she had said enough.

'While you were away,' Beth said, changing the subject, deeming this a propitious moment, 'we thought it might be nice if you had a party—the boys and you and your friends. It was Ian's idea.'

'Oh!' And Belinda's eyes shone. 'Really? When?'

'Whenever you can arrange it between you, before the boys go back—I thought you could use the top floor, ask your friends to bring their records, and generally have a get together.' Belinda threw her arms round her mother.

'Oh, that's wonderful!' she said. 'Like Fran, Kate and Annelise?'

'Yes, it's just a question of getting a date to suit everyone. And Belinda, I thought if you would do the eats—you'll know best what everyone likes. The last birthday party for the boys, I remember making swiss rolls like trains and everyone shrieked with laughter—they wanted baked beans on toast.'

'Oh, I remember, yes.' Belinda laughed. 'Yes, of course I'll do that, and you can rely on the boys to see to the drinks.'

'Nothing wild,' Beth said severely. 'I've heard about some of these parties.'

Belinda grinned.

'And we shan't be going out,' Beth said. 'You can tell your friends that you have Victorian parents who insist on staying in while it all goes on.'

So the playroom, which was a good size and held the table tennis table, was cleared, and posters hung around the walls, giant photographs of the Rolling Stones, David Bowie, Stevie Wonder and the Eagles. Next to the record player stood a huge pile of LPs.

Apart from some school friends, they asked Fran and Kate, and Fran wanted to bring her new boyfriend Richard, then there was Hamish, and Annelise who was to stay overnight with Belinda.

Beth smiled to herself I always knew, she thought, that Chantry Gate would come into its own one day. And hoped that nearby neighbours wouldn't mind too much when the noise of the records came through the top-floor windows.

'Well,' she excused herself to Geoff, 'it doesn't happen very often, does it?'

'My dear, I'm so glad you are staying in to keep an eye on them,' Sheila with relief. 'According to the girls, some parents go out and leave them to it.'

'Not us,' Beth said firmly. 'They can have it on our terms or not at all, and I have to say, they didn't pressurise me at all—you have to do what you have to do, Sheila, and make a stand.'

In the event, quite a promising crowd turned up, Annelise one of the first, in a pleated skirt and white top under her navy coat. She looked quite demure, Belinda told Beth later, until she asked if she could change in Belinda's bedroom. When she emerged, Belinda whistled. Annelise looked stunning. Her hair was brushed out all over her head, she wore pale pink lipstick, and her eyes were made up heavily which made her look much older and very sophisticated. The mascara made her blue eyes seem enormous.

'Where did you get that dress?' Belinda asked.

'I bought it in the village—that little shop, you know, the trendy one. I was supposed to be buying tights for Mother.'

It was a full length tight fitting dress, black, very low-cut, sophisticated and showed off her young slim figure and her lovely creamy skin.

'Wow!' Belinda said, envying her, and

142

wondering what her own mother would have said. Annelise looked about twenty-one. 'Has your mother seen it?'

'You must be joking,' Annelise said.

'You'll knock the boys cold when they see you.'

'That's the general idea,' Annelise laughed. My, but she was pretty, Belinda thought.

'Let's go on up.'

There was no difficulty finding the way, for the music blasted down as both girls made their way up the stairs.

'Jon's gone to the front door, just to be sure there are no gatecrashers,' Ian said. 'You know what happened at the Pilkingtons' party. 'Cor!' he said, turning and catching sight of Annelise, his face reddening. 'Does your mother know you're out?' He grinned at her.

'Not like this she doesn't, silly,' Annelise said, dimpling.

'Well, come on over. Did you bring any records?'

'No, didn't realise you wanted any,' Annelise said, Belinda knowing full well that the only records she would have been allowed were the hits from the current musicals that her mother had bought.

'No matter,' Ian said. 'We've got plenty.'

And suddenly Jon returned with some newcomers and the room was full. Two or three girls they had known at school, four

143

young men, Fran looking lovely, escorted by Richard who looked so young and fresh-faced, in his dark suit. Kate, her dark eyes warm and lively, was easily the most magnetic of the girls. She made a beeline for Jon. He bent his head and kissed her lightly. He always enjoyed talking to Kate—she was different, sexy, but not very feminine. She could bowl a man over if he let her, thought Jon, but she wasn't his type. He admired her, though, and wished, how he wished, that Laura, the girl he had met in Edinburgh in his last term, could be with him tonight. But she had a further year to go, when hopefully she would get her degree and come South again. His family hadn't met her yet, would say he was too young to get serious, but he knew he was not. There was no doubt in his mind whatsoever. No doubt at all.

He smiled warmly at Kate, and handed her a drink.

'So, how's life treating you?' he asked.

'Well, I got promoted,' she said, dark eyes looking up into his.

'I knew you would.' His glass clinked against hers. 'I don't think there's any holding you, Kate Rowlands.'

'I think you're right,' she said, smiling and showing her beautiful teeth.

'And how is the boyfriend—what's his name?'

'Oh, I chucked him. He became too—what shall I say?—too possessive, if that's the word. Because I went out with him once or twice, he thought he owned me.'

'Silly man!' Jon said.

'No, seriously, Jon, why shouldn't we women have as much freedom as men?'

'You're off on your hobby horse again,' he said, 'and it's only...' He glanced at his watch.

'Well, it's always nice to talk to you anyway,' said Kate. 'You're one of the few people I can talk to man to man, as it were.'

He looked down at her and grinned. 'I don't quite see it like that.'

'Oh, you!' she said, and walked off to talk to the others.

'You're Hamish, aren't you?' she said to the very handsome young man standing on his own, knowing she had met him before. His name had stayed in her memory.

'Yes,' he said. 'Who are you? I've met you somewhere.'

'Here, I expect,' she said. 'Your mother paints, doesn't she?'

'Yes, well—er—' He was young and rather shy. Pity to tease him, she thought.

'I understand she's having a great success.' Kate smiled, knowing that when she did, she could charm the birds off the trees.

He relaxed. 'She is,' he said. 'And what do you do?' He suddenly summoned courage from somewhere to deal with this older, very attractive, undeniably sexy female.

'I'm in publishing,' she said. 'Assistant Editor, no less.'

'Oh. My father's a writer.'

'Now I've got you!' Kate cried. 'You're Jimmy Alders's son—I remember now.' He was a handsome young man, she thought, with a mop of unruly curls, wonderful eyes, tall and well-built. Pity he was so young. She was beginning to feel like a man eater. He'd be useful to know, too.

'Let's go and meet my sister,' she said. 'Do you know her? Fran?'

Anything, she thought, to get her away from drippy Richard.

Ian couldn't take his eyes off Annelise. Who would have thought it? The girl who came in sometimes from church on Sundays, butter wouldn't melt in her mouth. Just showed, once they were let off the hook. He'd bet her mother didn't know what she had on!

He went over to her. 'Hallo, there, Annelise.' His eyes ran over her dress and back to her face again. 'You look fantastic.'

Not unaware of the attraction she held for the opposite sex, Annelise dimpled. He

146

put his arm around her and they began to move together to the music. He had set the lights so that they dimmed and flickered on and off, and by now a lot of the couples were smooching round the floor or talking while listening to the music.

Belinda found Hamish, still unable to believe that he had grown so much, into a strong-looking, handsome young man. Pity he was a year younger. Difficult to believe he was only seventeen—a year made such a difference, especially to boys.

Hamish liked Belinda. He felt at home with her. 'How's the catering course going?' he asked.

'Great,' she said. 'I'm enjoying it. In fact, I've been trying out some of my experiments for us this evening.'

He groaned.

'Come on, you know they'll be good,' she said. 'You can come down with me later and we'll look to see how they are.'

The bowls and dishes of dips and crisps and tiny cheese biscuits, shredded vegetables and assorted nuts, were fast disappearing, while Wings and other new groups played on.

Downstairs in the sitting room Geoff yawned and Beth put down her embroidery.

'Darling, if you want to go to bed, I'll stay up.'

147

'Good Lord, no!' he said. 'I'm just getting my second wind. Are we in for many of these, do you think?'

Beth grinned at him. 'It's not that bad,' she said. 'Could be worse. They could be out somewhere on the town, and us not knowing—I hope the neighbours won't mind?'

'I bet Sheila's having kittens,' he said.

'Why should she? She knows they're safe enough in here. Better than being in some awful dump where you don't know what's going on.'

'Yes, you're right.'

At midnight, she opened the door and made her way into the kitchen where she found a crowd of young people gathered around the Aga. Belinda's efforts sat on the kitchen table, the dishes quite empty. It smelled so good, Beth felt hungry.

'Good thing I made another lasagne,' Belinda cried, taking it out of the oven. 'No good giving them bits, Mummy,' she had said. 'Young people get hungry.'

She was a born mother, Beth decided.

They all greeted her. 'Hallo, Mrs Meldrum, hello—good to see you.'

They were a nice bunch, she thought, going back to Geoff.

'Well?' he said, and she smiled broadly. 'You'll never guess. They were all in the kitchen eating pasta.'

'What's that?' he asked. 'Oh, you mean lasagne, spaghetti, that sort of thing—Italian stuff. Give me good old English food every time.'

'The young ones like it, and it seems to be coming fashionable. Anyway, they're all enjoying themselves.' She frowned. 'I must say, I thought Annelise...I hardly recognised her. I hope Bernadette—'

'What?' And he yawned again.

'Nothing,' she said, and despite herself grinned.

Chapter Ten

Walking round The Cedars, an old Georgian house just outside Chantry Green, which had recently been sold, Beth clutched her auction catalogue. There were lots of things she would have liked, such as the round Georgian dining table and set of chairs, to say nothing of some exquisite small pieces of furniture and lovely carved mirrors, but she knew she stood no chance with those. Though she might, if the bidding was not too high, go for the grey-painted mirror with its lovely bevelled glass and important surround. It would look so right above the shelf in the hall on which stood the old ormolu clock which had come from Geoffrey's home.

But it was the curtains she would be bidding for: twelve feet in length, even longer than she needed though she could easily shorten them. She was carried away already by her plans to tackle the job, before she even knew if she stood a chance of getting them.

She sighed. Ah, well, it was the luck of the draw quite literally, and Wednesday morning would see if it was going to be her day or not. She looked at them once more. They were heavy glazed cotton, lined and interlined, but of such fine quality and design: a pale creamy colour with lover's knots and bows in pale blue, and here and there a yellow rose, somewhat faded. They would be just right for her and Geoff's bedroom which she had wallpapered in yellow self-stripes. She had waited a long time for suitable curtains, knowing that she could never afford to have them made, so much yardage was needed. And these curtains had swags and tails and tie backs—they were just what she wanted. If only someone else didn't want them even more.

Back home, she made a tour of the house, imagining the lovely old mirror in the hall though she felt there would be a lot of bidding for that. It looked quite valuable. Geoff was always pleased with her efforts round the house, leaving it all to her and approving of whatever she did.

In the big drawing room she had papered the fireplace wall a lovely Venetian red, one papered wall being fashionable that year. The eighteen-inch skirting boards, gleaming white, made a lovely contrast to the dark paper, and the other walls were painted ivory which formed a good background for her pictures, most of which she had picked up at auctions when she found she had a liking for watercolours. Privately she thought the room lent itself better to oil paintings but she had an eclectic collection, and they were all very personal to her.

The comfortable furniture, now loose-covered in flowered chintz, looked well against the background of dark red, and when the fire was lit on winter evenings, Chantry Gate really came into its own.

Geoff's study she had painted dark green. The dramatic colour made it seem smaller and more cosy. She had bought him a desk at auction and a huge chair, so that with his books and a couple of rugs, it was now a highly comfortable room. Someone had told her that originally the study and the drawing room had been one before being divided—heaven knew how large that room must have been! The gleaming white paintwork in this room, and wonderful panelled double doors, were set off by the dark walls. She could do with new floor-length curtains in here, but would bide her time. She couldn't do everything at once.

The dining room she loved best of all. It had a window seat which opened up to store all sorts of things for the family, and to either side of the marble fireplace were white-painted shelves. That was where Beth had decided to arrange her teapots. So far she had six and one of the chief joys of going out searching in auction rooms was to find a teapot to add to her collection. Of course, it was impractical, as Bernadette always told her with a shudder, to have them exposed to dust and dirt.

'Never mind, one day I'll have it glazed,' Beth said, knowing that day was a long way off. 'It will look like the collection at Waddesdon.' She'd smiled, but Bernadette was never amused.

'You make work for yourself,' she complained. 'You're your own worst enemy—all that dusting—and I don't suppose Gina gets around to it?'

'Of course she does, flicks the occasional duster,' Beth teased.

Who could explain to Bernadette why someone wanted to collect old teapots, or anything else for that matter?

The room had a Regency-style wallpaper, and thinking about it, Beth decided she had become quite an expert at paper hanging over the years. At first, standing on a step ladder with yards of folded, pasted wallpaper, it had been difficult, unless one of the boys was at home to give her a hand. But usually she had done it herself, and had become so accomplished she now thought nothing of decorating a room. Sanding down paintwork, undercoating, then one, two or even three topcoats to get the finish she wanted. In the dining room were the nicest curtains of all. She had gone to a sale out in Oxfordshire and bought ivory silk curtains lined with pale blue. She never tired of admiring them. They were somewhat worn, but she didn't mind that.

Beth was philosophical about her auction buys. Getting things at a fraction of their cost, things which had originally been top quality and expensive, more than compensated her for her trouble.

On the way home from the viewing, she stopped and bought a pretty little teapot, obviously Viennese for it was a darling little shape, and fluted, painted dark red with Cupid and some roses on the front. It had a fine little spout, and a pretty finial. She withdrew it from its tissue paper and, after washing it gently, added it to her collection, standing back to admire it.

Seven now, she thought. Roll on Wednesday.

On Wednesday, she staggered home under the weight of the curtains which she had managed to buy. Straight to the cleaners with them. And not only that, she had secured the mirror. No one had seemed too interested in it, probably because it looked rather dirty and the carved surround was faulty in many places, but that never worried Beth. She was good with her hands. Altogether a successful day, and there was nothing she looked forward to more than a job like that to tackle.

Wednesday saw the meeting of the local hospital committee which she chaired, to discuss the hospital fête.

The usual women ran the cake stall, the tombola and the raffle, the market produce and craft stalls. It never ceased to amaze Beth how everyone rallied round for a good cause and helped to make it the success that it always was.

She ran the bric-à-brac stall, and loved doing it. People brought out all sorts of things, and the fête-goers usually made a beeline for it. She had many helpers, needed for sorting, and on the day there was a mad scramble to find the best bargains. Most of the volunteers asked Beth's advice over pricing as she was becoming quite an expert on antiques.

On leaving the committee room, she decided to call in on Minna on the way home. She found her in the studio, covered with paint, while Jimmy was working downstairs in his study. Beth made her way upstairs, noticing the strong smell of paint pervading the house and wrinkling her nose.

'Go on up,' Jimmy had said. 'She'll be pleased to see you, Beth,'

Minna was, turning round to greet her enthusiastically.

'I'm glad you called in—I wanted to show you my new painting. I've done four. I'm in my green period,' she said. 'Sit down, make yourself at home. I'll get Mrs Thing to make us some tea.' She lit a cigarette and showed Beth the first canvas.

It was larger than usual. 'What do you think?' Minna asked eagerly.

Beth tried not to show her ignorance, for it seemed to her to be just a jumble of bright green and white.

'Well,' she began.

'Oh, I know, you're not into art,' Minna said. 'But it's unusual, isn't it?'

'Certainly is,' Beth agreed.

'It's called Greenwich Park,' Minna said.

'Oh, well, I love the vivid green.'

'So do I,' Minna said, pleased at Beth's approval.

'Now this one—I had a devil of a job with this.'

She turned it round to face Beth: a red background with strong green lines down it.

'Poplars,' Minna said.

'Really? What's the background?'

'Storm,' Minna said impatiently. 'Red sky.'

'Oh,' Beth said. 'Of course.'

'Now this one...' She stood it against the

wall. 'This is the best, I think. It's called FLOTSAM.'

Against a background of what might have been sand, were ragged balls of green.

'Like, you know, in the desert—in Arizona. Great tufts of dried sagebrush, you know?'

'But it's green, not dried, and is that sand?' Beth asked, quite genuinely curious. 'The background, I mean?'

'No, love, it's not Arizona,' Minna said patiently. 'It's the seashore.'

'Ah.'

'And this one I haven't finished yet. I'm not sure about—'. She stubbed out her cigarette on the floor and took another one. Her face was streaked with paint, she wore a headscarf and her tunic was all shades of green. 'Let me just wash my hands and we'll go downstairs and get some tea.'

'What've you been doing?' She enquired once they were in the kitchen.

'Not a lot,' said Beth. 'Buying some curtains at auction—I managed to get just what I wanted. They really are super, beautiful quality.'

'And do they fit?' Minna enquired.

'No, I've got to shorten them.'

'Of course you have,' She said. 'I can't think why you...'

'And a mirror—a really lovely mirror.'

Minna showed a little more interest in that.

'Nice?'

'Really. It's for the hall. They're going to deliver it tomorrow—I couldn't get it in the car.'

'Jeez!' Minna said, examining her nails.

'What I really came about,' Beth said, 'was wondering whether you had anything for my stall—the bric-à-brac stall for the hospital fête?'

'I might have,' Minna said. 'You know,' she added seriously, 'I could donate one of my pictures—that would bring in the money. On the other hand, no, perhaps not.'

'It's up to you,' Beth said, 'we're grateful for anything.'

'I'll have a look. When is it?'

'Three weeks' time. You might like to give me a hand?'

'You must be joking!'

'It's fun,' Beth said doggedly. 'Honestly.'

'Really? I'll give it some thought then, but I won't promise.'

'Thanks, Bonny,' She said as Mrs Bonnington brought in the tea. Minna yawned noisily. 'I seem to spend all my spare time painting.'

'Have you sold any more?'

'From the exhibition, yes, all except two. Cedric wanted more, but it's bloody exhausting, standing all day, you'd be surprised. Also, strangely, you run out of ideas—it's like Jimmy and writer's block.'

'Oh, I never thought of that.'

Minna lit another cigarette. 'You pour.'

'How's Hamish?'

'Doing well.' Hamish had a place at Durham now. 'I don't know how long he'll stick it out, though. It was Jimmy who wanted him to go—wanted him to have what he'd never had. But Hamish says he wants to get cracking. There's a great big world out there, he'd like to have a go at it.'

Beth handed her a cup of tea. 'Well, it's not for everyone, university,' she said. 'What's Jimmy doing?'

'Another film script. They're going to make it at Pinewood, so at least he won't be off on location. Not that it worries me—I usually go to France when he shears off. Have you seen anything of our friend Bernadette?'

'No, she's been in Canada. She went in the spring and I think she's back now, but she's always busy. When Laurie's at home they're continually out somewhere. I don't see her so much now that she's moved away.'

Minna pulled a face.

'Well, what about this fête then? Shall I go and look now?'

'No, any time in the next two weeks. I'll collect it if you like?'

'What sort of things?'

'Anything—mine isn't the only stall. There are clothes stalls, vegetable produce —you can make a cake if you like?'

'What? Oh, I thought you meant it for a minute!' Minna protested.

On the day of the fête, Minna became quite enthusiastic when she saw the piles of things that had been donated.

'Some of these must be worth something,' she said, picking up a very pretty plate. 'Fancy giving away something like this.'

'Oh, yes, people are very generous, and it is for a good cause.'

The stall was now loaded with glass, china, brass and porcelain, some pieces quite good, others rubbishy. Each piece had a sticky label on it, giving its price, and as all the lady helpers stood by their stalls, waiting for doors to open and the rush to begin, Minna was infected by the enthusiasm around her.

Then the double doors were opened and a horde of women rushed in, making a beeline for the stall that interested them. There was no doubting the popularity of the bric-à-brac stall, closely followed by home-made cakes.

The sale was fast and furious, even Beth was surprised by the speed of it, and the money mounted in the tin box. At the end of the afternoon there was nothing left—except for a few pieces of rubbish which, even then, someone bought up as job lot.

'You know we could do something like this for a hobby, a money-making hobby?'

'What?' Beth couldn't believe her ears. What on earth would Minna want to do that for when she already made so much money from her paintings?

'Well, why don't we do an antiques fair? They have them once a month, don't they?'

'Yes, but—'

'We could start off buying things, getting them together, and it would be fun to go around collecting. Oh, come on.'

'I would like to,' Beth said. 'But it's so time-consuming, trying to find things.'

'Why do you put so many obstacles in the way?' Minna protested. 'Find out when it is, and if you're not doing anything on that day.'

'It's on a Thursday—once a month.'

'And you're not booked on that day?'

'No.'

'Well, we could go around collecting whenever we had a moment—it would be fun,' Minna said, now quite enthusiastic.

'We could share the price of the stall, and keep the profit on our own things. How about that? Don't tell me you'd want to give some of it to charity?'

'No, but—anyway that wouldn't matter to you, would it? And I suppose I do have quite a few things I could start with. I can never resist a bargain.' What, she wondered, did Minna know about antiques? Not that it mattered, she would soon learn if she didn't sell them.

'All right,' said Beth. 'I'll enquire about it.'

'That's the spirit,' Minna said enthusiastically. 'I'll see what I have at home, and then we'll go around buying. Do you know who runs the market?'

'Yes, Joyce Darbell, I think—I'll give her a ring. Of course, she may not have a stall available.'

'Now, now,' Minna said. 'Think positive.'

So, it was put underway, and after trawling round the auctions and small antiques shops, they had quite a collection with which to start their stall.

It was a fine Thursday morning and they got there before eight o'clock, setting out the goods and waiting for the market to open at nine.

Beth was interested to see what Minna had found and her eye fell on an attractive clock set, a garniture of a clock and two side ornaments.

'Oh, that's so pretty—where did you find it?' Beth asked.

'Well,' Minna said airily, 'I've brought it along today, but it's too good for the stall, I paid forty pounds for it, and I think I shall take it up to town and get a good price for it. Those antique shops in Church Street are very good for that sort of thing—'

Beth bent over and picked one of the side pieces.

'It's spelter, Minna,' she said. 'It looks like ormolu, but it's spelter—'

'Yes, that's what he said it was, ormolu,' Minna said. Then she looked at Beth suspiciously. 'What do you mean, spelter?'

'Well, just that's it's not ormolu—'

'How do you know?'

'Well, you get to know after you've knocked around the auction rooms as long as I have. It's a kind of metal, used extensively to make these sort of things—' she recalled many such sets bringing next to nothing at auctions.

'What price have you got on it?'

'I've doubled up—eighty,' Minna said. 'If they don't like it they can do the other thing—it's too good for this market—'

In the event, no one bought it, but they did have a good day and lots of laughs. After paying for the stall, they made enough money to invest in buying more stock and went home well satisfied.

'Ready for the next one?' Minna said, packing up her car with the unsold items.

'Of course,' Beth smiled, she really had been delighted with the day's takings.

But she never saw the clock set again.

Chapter Eleven

'Come and have a coffee with me—you must see the tulips,' Bernadette said one May morning. 'I've been getting Annelise ready to go back to finishing school in Switzerland tomorrow, and I haven't had a moment. Laurie is in Canada.'

It was some time since Beth had seen Bernadette and she agreed with pleasure. Driving through Chantry Park, where all the houses stood in beautiful gardens, she realised there was none quite so impressive as Bernadette's.

Behind the handsome railings which Laurie had had made to Bernadette's design the view was beautiful, for the house stood on rising ground and the lawns, so well-tended, looked like brilliant striped green velvet, lines standing out like an advertisement for a lawn mower. Beyond, simply thousands of tulips bloomed, like an army on parade. Red, yellow, pink—it was quite a sight.

The new massive wrought-iron gates, which had also been designed by Bernadette, now stood high and wide, embellished with the huge initials LBF entwined and painted in gold. As Beth arrived, the gates silently opened and she drove in, parking the car round by the garages out of sight of the house then making her way to the front door. Agnes the housekeeper opened it to her, immaculate in her navy blue nylon uniform. She looked, Beth thought, like an elderly Norland nurse.

'Good morning, Mrs Meldrum,' she said in greeting, although there was a certain stiffness to her smile that Beth hadn't noticed before. 'Pleasant day.'

'It is lovely,' Beth agreed.

'May I take your jacket?'

'No, I'll keep it on. I expect we shall be going into the garden.'

'Very well. Mrs Featherstone is in the study. Ah, here she comes. Mrs Meldrum, Madam.'

'Thank you, Agnes.' Bernadette descended the stairs, lovely legs in their high-heeled shoes treading delicately.

'Beth, my dear, long time no see.' She bent and kissed Beth's cheek.

Everything was pristine. Furniture glowed, huge candelabra shone, each droplet like a diamond in a golden setting. The carpet was so thick, Beth almost sank down into it, and there was a hushed air about the place. Great bowls of beautifully arranged flowers stood on flower pedestals—white lilies, pale pink rosebuds. Bernadette was an excellent flower arranger.

'Let's go into the garden before we have coffee—I want you to see the tulips. They've been wonderful this year.'

She led the way through the conservatory, filled now with exotic plants and white-painted furniture, and taking from her pocket a huge bunch of keys, unlocked the door to the garden.

It looked unreal to Beth, it was so perfect, but she couldn't fail to be impressed by the magnificence of the show, which resembled nothing so much as the Dutch bulb fields in full bloom.

Her eyes shone and she gasped with pleasure, quite overcome by the sheer drama of it all.

'It's magnificent, Bernadette. My goodness, what a sight!' she murmured.

'Yes,' sighed Bernadette. 'It is nice, isn't it? It was suggested to me that I open it to the public. My dear, can you imagine?' She turned horrified blue eyes on Beth. 'Hordes of people walking all over the place.' She shuddered.

Suddenly she hurried over to the bed of scarlet tulips and bent down. Beth saw her furiously pick a rogue tulip—a pink one among the reds. How dare it? thought Beth, quite shocked. Bernadette came back to her, crumpling it over and over in her hand.

'Perfection again,' Beth said.

'Well, that's what we strive for.' Bernadette cast an eagle eye over the other beds to see all was well. So might an officer have inspected his troops, thought Beth.

'Your gardener is good,' she said presently. 'He must work very hard to keep it in this condition.'

'That's what I pay him to do,' Bernadette said. 'I'd sack him if he was no good.'

They wandered happily round the rest of the formal garden, exclaiming from time to time and admiring the close-cut hedges and the grass whose edges looked as if they had been cut with nail scissors. Beth couldn't help comparing it with her own garden, which was as unlike this as a garden could be. And yet you had to admire this—it was so over the top—and if people had the money to do it, why not? The pity of it was that so few people saw it.

Bernadette led the way back to the house, closing and locking the door carefully behind her and pulling down the white sunblinds.

'We'll have coffee in the kitchen, then you can tell me all that you've been doing. It's ages since I've seen you.'

The kitchen seemed to go on forever, with fitments and built-in cupboards, and Beth went over to stand by the windows overlooking the fabulous garden and terrace, the stone pots filled with flowering bulbs, soon to be discarded in favour of summer flowers. There were huge pots and Versailles green tubs with clipped yew topiary. Was this all really one man's work?

'Do you do anything yourself in the garden, Bernadette?' she asked now.

'I advise—he'd be hopeless if I didn't tell him what to do—and I keep an eye on him, as you can imagine.'

Coming back to sit down, Beth wondered what the finish was on all the fitments for it looked like opaline glass, everything in white, with a blue-tiled floor. The lighting was beautifully done, concealed, and Bernadette seemed only to press a button here and there for something to pop out or pop up, or tell her something was ready. It really must be a pleasure, working in a kitchen like this.

Bernadette's slim white fingers briskly prepared coffee and biscuits. Everything she did seemed effortless.

'When we've finished our coffee, I must take you upstairs and show you what I've bought for Annelise. The most lovely tweed suits and silk blouses.'

'How does she like Switzerland?' Beth asked. Annelise had already been at the finishing school for almost a year.

'Loves it—and I like to think they're doing her good. So far, she has done deportment, languages, flower arranging... it's a very comprehensive course. Keeps her on her toes and out of mischief, I'm happy to say.'

Beth studied her as she talked. Her face was flawless, smooth as ivory, eye lashes perfectly mascara-ed, small straight nose just sprinkled with freckles. The one rather endearing thing about her was the perfectly shaped mouth with its strong teeth—until it occurred to Beth that there were one or two new lines about her mouth which gave her a rather discontented look. She hadn't noticed them before.

Going over to the door, Bernadette listened then came back to sit down.

'I'm going to have to get rid of Agnes,' she said suddenly.

'Oh,' Beth said, surprised. 'Why?'

'Well, for one thing I can't stand her, and for another—well, she spies on me.'

'Spies on you! Oh, Bernadette, surely not!'

'Well, you may not believe me, but I think she listens when Laurie and I—you know?'

Beth waited, genuinely puzzled.

'When Laurie is home, he's inclined to be a bit—well, boisterous if he has had anything to drink and he—well, he would think nothing of—'

Beth was intrigued to say the least.

'He's very masterful, doesn't like to be thwarted, you know.' And the blue eyes looked straight into Beth's. She began to see what Bernadette was getting at.

'Oh, I see what you—'

'And he doesn't give a damn if she is within earshot or not—do her good, the old bat, give her something to think about, he says.'

'You mean, when you're in your bedroom?' suggested Beth.

'Not only then, my dear!'

'But she sleeps on the top floor, doesn't she?'

'Supposed to,' Bernadette said grimly, 'but you can't tell me she doesn't come down to see what's going on.'

'Oh, you're imagining it,' Beth said.

'No, I'm not, and Laurie gets furious with me because I can't relax. I know she's there, outside the door, listening.'

'Bernadette!'

'You think I'm joking? Well, one night I got out of bed and there she was with her ear to the keyhole.'

Beth frowned. 'Are you sure?'

'Of course I'm sure. Why would I imagine it?'

'What did she say when you found her there?'

'Pretended she was passing on her way downstairs.'

'What does Laurie say?'

'It makes him worse, and—well, I just can't relax. It's not the same. We had a housekeeper and maids at home but we never saw them after dinner, they lived down in the basement and on the top floor—just never saw them. I hate her, Beth.' And Bernadette's eyes filled with tears. She took a scrap of fine lace out of her pocket and dabbed at them.

'Oh, Bernadette, you've got yourself into a tizzy over nothing, I'm sure,' said Beth, striving for commonsense.

'Yes, but sometimes—now that Annelise is away—when Laurie comes home, if I'm still up, he grabs me, and even in the hall or halfway up the stairs he simply...and he's strong...it's as if he can't wait to have me, and I know she—'

What a melodrama was unfolding, Beth thought. You never knew what went on in other people's lives. It was beyond belief Laurie Featherstone, tycoon, smoothie, insatiably pleasuring or not pleasuring his wife, as the case might be. She really didn't know what to say.

'Well—'

Bernadette had recovered. 'Beth—you won't mention this to anyone, will you? Not even Geoff.'

172

'Bernadette, of course not!'

'Good, because you can see what a state I'm in. I mean, wouldn't you want her to go?'

'If I were sure.'

'Well, I'm not imagining a thing like that. Laurie banged out of the door this morning because he was so mad at me, and it's all her fault. Ugh, she's revolting!'

She sniffed, and pulled herself together. 'Come upstairs and see Annelise's clothes.'

They hung on neat silk-covered hangers, each one matching the dress or suit: beautifully cut tweed suits and blouses, all fit for any middle-aged woman, and obviously expensive. Did Annelise really wear these things? Beth would take a bet that she never did, probably never even tried them on.

'Is she here?' Beth asked.

'She stayed in town last night with her friend Lulu Partington—you know, the daughter of Lady Partington. Such nice people, and I know she's safe up there.'

Not, Beth thought, if Belinda is to be believed. She had suggested that Lulu Partington's reputation left a lot to be desired.

While she was looking at the clothes, almost absentmindedly Bernadette was dusting everything with a soft cloth, and flicking around the fitted cupboards with a feather duster.

What a life, thought Beth.

Annelise's underwear and sweaters lay folded on the bed ready for packing, her shoes neatly laid out in rows and polished.

'This is such a pretty room,' Beth said sincerely.

'Yes, it is,' Bernadette sighed! and Beth wondered. Was there any kind of happiness in this house?

'Well,' she said, 'I think your garden is lovely—it takes such a lot of effort to keep up your standards, Bernadette.' Somehow, she had a sudden feeling of pity for her.

'Well, thank you, Beth. It is a full time job, as you may imagine. Now, we must go up to town sometime and have lunch—when you've a free day,' she said, 'when Annelise has gone back to school—is Belinda still enjoying her course?'

'Loves it, she just has got her second diploma, so she's away now, and could get a job at any time, but we are leaving it to her. She seems to know what she is doing—'

Bernadette walked with her to the door, unlocking it with great ceremony, as Agnes appeared in the hall.

'I'm sorry, Madam, I thought—'

'You may go,' Bernadette said frostily.

Ugh, Beth thought once outside, making her way back to the courtyard and starting up the car. I wouldn't have Bernadette's life for all the tea in China. As she approached the gates, they opened slowly and let her through.

She enjoyed the rest of her drive through the park and reached home just in time to see Gina putting on her navy silk coat over a filmy dress.

She was in full voice this morning. Everything at the hospital was going well apparently.

'A letter for you, madam-a, it come by second post,' Gina said. 'From Mr Jon.'

'Oh.' And Beth went to get it from the hall table.

He was going down to Wiltshire for the weekend and would like to come up for Sunday lunch. Could he bring a girl with him? One he had met in Edinburgh, a fellow student. Her name was Laura, and she now lived in Marlborough with her father and was back home before finding a job.

'He's coming down for Sunday lunch, and bringing a girl with him, Gina,' said Beth.

'Oh.' Gina's small almond eyes glittered. She loved a romance. 'Madam-a, maybe she the girl he marry?'

'Oh, no, I shouldn't think so,' Beth

said hastily. 'I expect he has lots of girlfriends.'

'But this one he bring to lunch,' said Gina.

Belinda was delighted that her brother was coming. 'I wish Ian could be here too,' she said.

That evening, when they sat in the drawing room, Geoff going through the papers, Beth knitting, he said, 'So you saw the tulips?'

'Oh, Geoff, that garden is spectacular. You can't imagine—the colours!'

'So what does she do—Bernadette? Sit up in her castle with her bunch of keys.'

'No.' Beth found herself flying to Bernadette's defence. 'She works jolly hard to keep it to that standard, I can tell you.'

Later, he said, 'What are you smiling at?'

'Was I?' Beth didn't know she was. She had remembered what Bernadette's story had reminded her of. Was it the Duke of Wellington who after returning from battle and being greeted by his wife, pleasured her in the hall with his boots still on?

Imagine, she thought, Geoff coming home from a busy evening in the surgery and chasing me up the stairs...

'May I cook the Sunday lunch?' Belinda asked.

'Of course,' Beth agreed. 'Roast lamb, roast potatoes. Nothing fancy, mind, no garlic—you know your father doesn't like it.'

'I know, redcurrant jelly, mint sauce. And two puddies?'

'I want to make my apple tart,' Beth said.

'Then I shall make something rich and cold and creamy,'

Beth wasn't so good at that sort of thing.

'You haven't had my old French cookbook, have you?' she asked with a frown, searching among the shelves.

'Now why would I do that? I have a perfectly good collection of my own.'

'Ah, here it is. Twelve ounces of flour...'

'I can't think why you need that. You must have made it a hundred times.'

'I know, but I like to check the recipe. And I like this one because the pastry says three tablespoons of water while most pastry recipes say "water to mix".'

She tied her apron round her still trim figure. 'Besides, I'm not a natural born cook like you. You can taste something and know just what's missing. I can't do that. I have to have the recipe, just to check.'

'Well, the table's laid, fresh flowers in the dining room. She didn't give you a bunch, I suppose?'

'Bunch of what?'

'Bunch of tulips,' Belinda said.

Beth was shocked. 'Oh, you couldn't cut them!'

'Why not?'

'Well, it would look like missing teeth.' And they both began to laugh.

They were all in the drawing room waiting for Jon when he put his head round the door.

'Mother.' He was holding a girl by the hand. 'I'd like you to meet Laura.'

Beth looked up into a pair of smiling brown eyes, and knew without a shadow of doubt that this was the girl Jon was going to marry.

Chapter Twelve

Minna and Beth sat side by side behind their stall at the antiques fair. They had done well this morning, had had plenty of customers and sold quite a few things that had hung about for some time.

'There's no market in August,' Beth said. 'It starts again in September.'

'Oh, well, I couldn't have done it anyway because we're going to France at the end of next week.' Minna gave a deep sigh.

'How's your painting going?' Beth asked curiously. Her friend never seemed to talk about it now.

'Finished with that,' she said. 'I got bored to tears with it.'

'But all that money!' Beth cried.

'I can always take it up again if I'm short of a bob or two.'

'But you don't make a fraction here of what you'd make on a picture,' Beth said.

'No, but it's more fun. I enjoy it.'

'How long will you be in France?'

'Month or so. Hamish isn't coming this time, he's made quite a few buddies in Durham.'

179

'Did I tell you Belinda is doing a cookery course in Normandy? She goes next week for a fortnight, it should be jolly interesting.'

'Where does she get that from? Cooking? I mean, you were never mad about it.'

Beth laughed. 'No, but she's always been interested in food, ever since she was quite small.'

'I couldn't do that to save my life—all that work, all that preparation, and then it's eaten in a flash, gone. What a waste of effort!'

'She doesn't see it like that—she enjoys it. And you like to eat well, don't you?'

'That's different. I couldn't do it for other people.'

Beth glanced at her watch. 'Well, I supose we'd better start to pack up. It's almost four.'

'How's the romance going?' Minna asked, wrapping china in bubble paper.

'Oh, Laura comes to see us quite often at weekends.'

'Where does she live?'

'Wiltshire, with her father. Her mother died years ago, but she's a really nice girl.'

'Do you think they'll marry?'

'Well, I think they're going to wait for her to get her degree—although they are unofficially engaged—'

'Sweet,' murmured Minna.

'Is Jimmy going with you to France?'

'I don't suppose he'll stay more than a few days—he's not that keen on the South of France. He'd rather be at home working. Me—I could live out there. Sun, sea, no need to dress. I suppose I'm a beach bum at heart.'

'Well, you like the sun. I could never do that. Can't sit in the sun.'

'Poor you.'

She was right, Jimmy was back after a week, leaving Minna out there to soak up the sun. He called round to see Geoff, and they all had a drink together on Sunday morning.

'Stay to lunch,' Beth said.

He grinned. 'That would be great.' He was obviously delighted not to have to go home and cook for himself. The housekeeper had Sundays off.

'You'll meet Laura, Jon's girlfriend,' Beth said.

'Oh, I didn't know it was a definite thing.'

'Oh, yes,' Beth said darkly. 'We think it's the real thing, all right.'

They spent a pleasant day, lazing in the garden afterwards, chatting, while Jon and Laura went off for a walk.

'Nice girl,' Jimmy said.

'Yes, it seems to be serious, but you can

never tell,' Geoff said.

'Minna says she given up painting,' Beth said.

'Well, you know Minna, easily bored,' Jimmy said. 'It's always a five-minute wonder.'

Is it? Beth thought. She had never realised that about her friend. Jimmy made it sound as if he were used to it.

Late in August, Minna was back, calling on Beth in a state of great excitement.

'I've got some news for you!' she announced, her grey eyes, usually devoid of expression, now alight with excitement. 'Guess what?'

Beth was slicing beans.

'How can you sit inside doing that job?' asked Minna. 'Bring them outside in the garden and I'll tell you all about it.'

They sat round the tiny pond where the goldfish swam.

'I don't know how you could have bought this place with half a garden,' Minna said crossly.

'Well, we did, because I wanted the house,' Beth said equably. 'Anyway, you can't see the join.' And she laughed. 'What is this all about?'

'Well, there's this village—a hilltop village, derelict almost, with a tower. It's absolutely fabulous.'

'Where's this?'

'Not far from Fréjus. And the mayor, you know how French mayors are, wants to restore the village, develop it so that it's just like it used to be. There's an old church, fifteenth-century, with a mummified saint in it, and a tower with a bell that they ring in case of fire.'

She was quite breathless. 'All the houses are empty now, most of them falling down, and the mayor wants to create a living village and is prepared to give, Beth, *give* the house and the land it sits on to anyone who will develop it and rebuild, providing they are someone of importance.'

'Famous, you mean, or have money?'

'Yes, that's it! He would like to deal with an artist or writer, an actor or director. He wants to create an artistic colony, centred round the tower and the church. Don't you think that's a marvellous idea?'

Minna was breathless with excitement.

'Sounds like it,' Beth said. 'So?'

'Well, I want Jimmy to build, then we would have a permanent home in the old S of F. And this is where you come in...'

'Me?'

'Yes, I want you to convince him that it's a brilliant idea. You know he thinks I'm full of harebrained schemes, but for some reason he thinks you're level-headed, so if you tell him...'

'Hold on, hold on! I don't know what I think yet.'

'Now what would you know about it? Have you ever been to the South of France?'

'Course I have—with your parents, when we were about sixteen.'

'Well, then. But you know he thinks you're sensible, and honestly, Beth, it's a smashing idea. Imagine being *given* the plot. The mayor already has some people interested from Paris.'

Beth could see there'd be no stopping her.

'But don't drag me into it, Minna, it wouldn't be right. You'll have to convince him yourself.'

'No, you will. Come round this afternoon and have a chat with him.'

'Oh, I don't think...' But she knew she would. Why was she so weak where Minna was concerned? If they were to build a house in France it should be because both of them wanted it, not because Minna did, backed up by Beth. Still, in for a penny...

That afternoon they sat by the pool in Green Lawns, Minna in a bikini, for the sun was hot, and Beth with her face smothered in sun cream, wearing shorts and tee shirt, taking advantage of the blissful setting.

Jimmy came towards them, frowning, a worried look in his eyes. His hair was curling damply in the heat, the long lashes cast shadows on his face. He sat himself down on the edge of the pool.

'You know she's gone mad,' he said, nodding to Minna.

'I haven't,' she said frostily, not looking up. 'Beth thinks it a good idea, too.'

'Minna thinks I'm made of money.'

'Oh, you have enough. And, imagine, having a permanent home in the South of France—what an opportunity.'

'Do you have any idea at all what it'll take? This place has already cost us an arm and a leg, the pool, the grounds, the staff.'

'Oh, stop moaning,' Minna said. 'I could paint out there,' she said, and sat up, brimming over with enthusiasm. 'I can't think of anything more wonderful than painting in France, like Picasso and Cézanne. The sun and the scents...'

'And whatever happened to *that* five-minute wonder?' Jimmy asked. 'Besides, there's the business of actually owning it—just how long do you think you'd want to be here in England? Once we got that, you'd be off in France all the year round.'

'Oh, don't be ridiculous,' Minna said, but Beth knew he was right. She would

185

never see Minna once she had a home out there.

'You could come and stay, with Geoff and the children—well, Belinda at any rate—and Hamish.'

'He'll have his own life,' Jimmy said. 'Already since he's been at university he's made his own circle of friends. He won't want to come with us.'

'He will when it's the South of France,' Minna said smugly. 'He'll want to take his girlfriends there.'

She lay back and closed her eyes, and Beth looked at her.

Her body was perfect, not an ounce of superfluous fat anywhere: firm legs, strong, concave tum, small breasts, and that lovely golden tan. Beth sighed. She'd get her house in the South of France, she thought, just because she was Minna. She always did what she wanted. Beth felt slightly aggrieved. Why did some people have it so easy? Then she remembered all those who didn't. And would she change places? Not likely!

'And' Minna was running on, 'what an investment. Can you imagine? We could let it for an astronomical sum.'

'That's likely, that is.' Jimmy said. He knew his wife only too well. 'You wouldn't let your house out to strangers.'

'Well, friends then, and we would charge

them. Oh, I know a good thing when I see it.'

'Where exactly is it, anyway?' Jimmy asked.

'Well, drive out of Fréjus on the way to Draguignan, about halfway. You must have seen it on the old road, like a big sandy hill, all the houses clinging round the clock tower. It's a derelict village actually, but when everyone rebuilds and gets a community going, can you imagine? The mayor said you would be just right, a screen writer and director. He already has an architect, and artist, a retired French general—'

'I am impressed,' Jimmy said, and Beth wondered if he meant it or whether he was being sarcastic.

'He's a good businessman, I can just see it, and we would be given the land.'

She would keep it up, Beth thought, pressurising him until he gave in; not yelling, not screaming, just a gradual wearing down.

'What do you think, Beth?'

'Oh,' she said hastily, 'don't ask me. It sounds wonderful, a dream, but after all, it's not my money.'

She saw Minna's expression as she closed her eyes in disgust. 'I thought you said it was a good idea?'

'Well, it is. I mean, it would be lovely.'

'Nothing ventured, nothing gained,' Minna insisted. 'If you don't put yourself out in this world, you get nowhere.'

'You mean, if I don't put myself out,' Jimmy said, and Minna sat up suddenly. She was furious.

'Didn't I do well with my paintings?' she asked. 'Didn't I make some money at that?'

He was immediately contrite.

'Darling, of course you did! Of course you did—and I hand it to you. Look, leave it with me, I'll give it some thought.' And he walked away.

And where some women would have flung their arms around his neck to thank him, Minna slyly closed one eye. 'I'll get my house in France,' she said. 'See if I don't.'

Yes, Beth could see she would.

A week later, Minna and Jimmy were off together, flying out to France, already planning how to go about it—and to hear Jimmy you would have thought it was his idea in the first place. How does she do it? Beth wondered.

'Minna' she called after her when they parted, 'how about September—do you want me to book?'

'What? The antiques market? Oh, count me out—I won't have time for that.'

Typical, Beth thought. So she would

have to go it alone—that's if she kept it up at all.

When Minna and Jimmy returned it was late-October, and then they were back only for a couple of weeks since Minna was returning to France to check on the building work, leaving Jimmy to work.

'You won't want to do the antiques fairs up to Christmas, then, Minna?' Beth asked her. 'Shall I try taking some of your stock?'

'If you like,' she said casually. 'I don't suppose I shall be doing it again, I just won't have the time.'

No, Beth thought. It had been another five-minute wonder. But she missed her, just the same.

The long vacation was over, Ian back at university, Jon at his hospital, and Belinda about to take a hotel and catering course which would keep her away from home until the New Year.

How things changed, Beth thought. Once they grew up and moved away from home, life changed drastically. Minna was away, and Bernadette whom she had hardly seen all summer was in Canada. It was time she flung herself into her social work again.

The yew hedge had been cut, all the deciduous trees had lost their leaves, and a sharp frost covered the rhododendrons whose leaves hung down, shrivelled with misery. They hated frost. But the mahonia buds shone yellow in the sunshine already, and bulbs were coming through in the front garden. It was always good to see them, a sign of spring, and she remembered Bernadette's tulips. But there was winter to get through first, and providing it wasn't too severe, it brought its own interests. Especially Christmas.

She met Sheila Rowlands in the village early one Monday morning, it seemed ages since she had seen her. They had been away during the summer, renting a house in Italy, and apart from hearing that Kate had secured a very good job with a famous public relations firm, Beth had had little news of them.

Now, Sheila suggested that they go into the Old Green Door for coffee. 'I must tell you,' she said. 'Fran has this new boyfriend. My dear, she's quite serious—you should hear Kate on the subject.'

It made a nice break as they seated themselves in a corner and ordered coffee and home-made scones.

Sheila looked set for a comfortable gossip.

'Well, this boyfriend of Fran's—his name is David—is Jewish,' she said, waiting for the news to sink in.

Beth felt that Sheila expected some reaction from her.

'Do you like him? Is it serious?'

'My dear, yes! She's mad about him.'

'What's he like? What does he do?'

'Handsome young devil, a real whizz kid apparently. Takes over failing businesses and turns them round, making huge profits. Joe explained to me. But I didn't quite follow. He's a very wealthy young man apparently, and Fran—well, she's over the moon. I needn't tell you what Kate has to say about it, though!'

'Why is she so against it?'

'She sees Fran as a silly little thing, spoiled, just waiting for a rich husband to take her over, to look after her and cosset her.'

'That's not such a bad idea, is it?' Beth laughed.

'But you know it's against all Kate's principles. No woman should become subservient to a man, in her book. He buys her lovely presents too. Yuk! Kate says. Aren't they funny?'

Beth laughed. 'Young Fran knows a good thing when she sees it?'

'Yes, she may look sweet and simple but honestly, Beth, I think she's as tough as old boots. She knows just what she wants, where she's going—and is going to get it, just by being her sweet self, staying feminine, pleasing David.'

'I can imagine Kate's feelings. But they're so different, Sheila.'

'And who's to say who's right? I can understand Kate's being against it. It's nothing to do with David's being Jewish, it's just that she thinks Fran is making a fool of herself. Whereas *I* think Fran is being exceedingly clever.'

'But you say she adores him?'

'Seems to, but who knows?'

'And she's only—what?'

'Nineteen,—almost twenty.'

'What does Joe say?'

'Thinks she's far too young to know her own mind.'

'It'll work out, as they say,'

'Yes, but they want to get engaged at Christmas.'

'Oh!'

'Apparently he's taken over a chain of restaurants and turned them into a roaring success—he's quite brilliant, Joe says.'

'How old is he?'

'Well, that's just it—about twenty-eight.'

'Still, there's a lot to be said for an age difference.' Beth pushed back her chair. 'Well, keep me posted. I've got to fly—the man's coming at twelve to service the boiler.' And she hurried back to her car.

'Hallo, there,' she said to Gus who was

in the porch and got up to greet her.

'How about some lunch, eh?'

His golden eyes looked up at her, tail wagging.

She was his absolutely favourite person.

Chapter Thirteen

So there it was, that Christmas, for all to see in the national newspapers: the announcement of the engagement of Frances Rowlands to David Greenman. The Meldrums were asked over to meet him.

'Well!' Belinda said. She had been out of things for a while and the announcement had come as a surprise. 'She hasn't known him long, has she?'

'No, but he seems to have swept her off her feet, as they say.'

They made their way across to the Rowlandses the day after Boxing Day, treading over the brittle frosted drive, the conifers shining like stars with the reflection from the outside lights. Ian was with them but Jon had gone down to Laura's for the weekend.

The atmosphere was especially Christmassy: a large tree stood in the hall decorated with red lanterns and coloured lights, and holly festooned the stairs and the wall lights.

'Come on in,' Joe boomed, as they divested themselves of their coats. They could smell warming Christmas pies and mulled wine.

Sheila came out to greet them, looking pretty in her red dress, her dark curls shining.

'Oh, I'm glad you could come. We so wanted you to meet David.'

Fran stood by the fireplace, a picture in a little pink angora sweater and pleated skirt to match, her wonderful eyes luminous as stars. Beside her stood a tall, well-built man with a mane of dark curly hair and a neatly trimmed beard. His eyes were so dark they might have been black.

Fran came forward. 'Oh, Auntie Beth, it's lovely to see you.' And she kissed Belinda, and gave her a special hug. They could not help noticing that on her engagement finger she wore the largest diamond they had ever seen—a solitaire which blinked and shone under the lamps, almost blinding them.

'I say!' teased Belinda, taking her hand, while Fran blushed prettily. She took David's hand. 'I want you to meet David—David Greenman. David, this is Belinda, my special friend, and her parents, Dr and Mrs Meldrum from next door.'

They all felt their hands seized in a firm grip. He had the nicest smile, Beth thought. A warm character, she decided, and by the way he looked at Fran, there was no doubting his feelings for her. He treated her as if she were a fragile piece of china, which compared to him she was.

Ian shook hands with him, adding his congratulations. While out of the corner of her eye, Beth could see Kate who looked magnificent as she always did when she was in a tizzy or angry, her dark eyes flashing fire and her nostrils dilated. She was like a young filly being held on a tight rein.

She came over to them and kissed Beth briefly then Belinda who went to admire Fran's ring. Geoff had made his way over to join Joe, glad to get away into a man's company.

'Well, Beth,' Kate said, and she noted the lack of 'Aunt', that they were now on an equal footing, 'what do you think? Let me get you something to drink. Daddy, some punch for Beth.'

She returned with a glass of steaming punch, handing it to Beth. The lovely scent of cinnamon and cloves wafted under Beth's nose.

'To the young couple,' she said, sipping the hot toddy and smiling at Kate. 'I understand I have to congratulate you too? You seem to have landed yourself with a pippin of a job.'

'Thank you,' Kate said. 'Yes, I'm

delighted, it's a fabulous appointment and a marvellous salary.'

'Then you have what you want. And apparently,' she nodded towards Fran, 'so has Fran.'

Kate shook her head. 'Honestly, Beth, she's only known him five minutes.'

'A bit longer than that,' laughed Beth.

'Well, you know what I mean. It's as if she jumped at the first man who came along with a bit of know how and able to keep her in luxury.'

'Now you're being unfair,' Beth said coolly. 'She's probably madly in love with him, and he seems to be awfully nice.'

'Have you seen the ring? Well, you could hardly miss it. That's going to be how her life will be—showered with gifts to make her way easy, waited on hand and foot while she sprawls at his feet.'

Beth laughed. 'But, Kate dear, if that's the way she wants it...you're different, more independent.'

'You can say that again!' Kate glowered.

'And does it matter, really? As long as Fran loves him and your parents approve?'

'Well, I don't know that Daddy does really—he sees it as a good marriage from a financial point of view, his little girl won't have to pinch and scrape, but she *is* so young, Beth, she's never really had many boyfriends.'

'I don't think that matters,' Beth assured her. 'Tell me about your new job?'

Kate moved away and returned with a tray of delicious canapés, which she offered to Beth.

'Well, I meet the most wonderful men,' she said, and now her eyes were like twin stars. They became a lighter brown, and twinkled. 'Dishy men, Beth—TV personalities, pop stars. Mostly married, of course.'

'That's a pity,' said Beth.

'Doesn't worry me,' Kate said coolly. 'I prefer it. Saves entanglements, you know? I go along with it all, and enjoy their company. It's not my fault if their wives can't hold on to them.'

'So that's your philosophy—it's the wives' fault?'

'Basically, if their husbands are bored with them, they're bound to stray.'

'Perhaps if the opportunity presents itself?' Beth asked.

But Kate ignored that. 'I have met some wonderful people, famous men—you'd be surprised. And I've learned a lot,' she said, a cynical little twist to her mouth. 'It goes with the job—it's a rat race, but I love it. I like all the intrigue and the schmaltz. You have no idea what goes on in that world.'

'I'm sure,' Beth said drily. 'Your mother

198

says you would like a flat of your own in town?'

'Yes,' Kate said seriously. 'Well, it's a must really. I can't keep commuting back and forth and I work late hours—I expect she's told you I often stay in town?'

'No,' Beth said, for Sheila hadn't mentioned it.

'Well, I do—by the time I've finished and sometimes have a late dinner engagement. You know how it is.'

She suddenly looked much older than her years, and Beth was relieved to see David Greenman coming towards them, a smile on his face.

'So pleased to have the opportunity of meeting you,' he said to Beth. 'You live in that lovely old house next door—Victorian, isn't it?'

'Yes,' Beth said, pleased that someone else appreciated Chantry Gate.

He looked at Kate, and she returned his look unblinking. There was no love lost between them, that was obvious, but while David kept up his pleasant smile, Kate's was sickly sweet—Beth was reminded of a kitten she had once had, pretty but with sharp little claws...

And then Joe was asking everyone to be quiet while they opened champagne, and the corks popped, and the wine was poured, and the young couple were toasted, and Beth thought she had never seen such a happy-looking pair.

I hope, she thought, they will be happy. They seem well matched to me. And wondered: What would I feel if it were Belinda?

I would want her to be happy, she decided, but how could one be sure? In the end Fran and David had to take their chances like everyone else.

After the champagne came turkey sandwiches and mince pies. Beth sat with Fran and Sheila.

'David wants them to be married next June,' Sheila said, and looked worried.

'Why not?' Fran asked.

'Well, darling, we would have liked you to wait until you are twenty-one,' her mother said.

'That's so old-fashioned—what's the point?' she asked.

It did seem a bit odd when you thought about it, Beth realised. What did a few months matter?

'You see, David has seen a house,' Fran explained to Beth. 'Its Georgian, set in farmland down in Sussex, and he has the opportunity to buy it. He's very keen on old houses—that's why he liked yours. He thinks it's beautiful.'

'So do I.' Beth smiled.

'Well, there's nothing to stop him buying it, is there?' Sheila asked. 'Then, if and when you marry—'

'*When* we marry,' Fran said.

'Well, when—'

'Where does he live now?' Beth asked.

'With his parents. They're a very close family, living in Mill Hill. He has a brother and a sister at home too.'

'Where did you meet him?'

'At a party in town,' Fran said. 'Excuse me.' And she went off as Joe called her over.

'What do they think about it?' Beth asked.

'Not best pleased,' Sheila said grimly, 'although they're not orthodox and will do anything to keep the eldest son happy. Still, so far as they're concerned Fran's not exactly what they'd hoped for.'

'Mmmm,' Beth said.

But the die was cast, and from that moment David became one of the family. His sleek dark green XJ6 Jaguar was more often than not in the Rowlandses' drive.

'It won't take long for that to be changed into a Bentley,' Ian said. 'See if I'm not right.'

Things settled down again, except for an outbreak of Asian flu which kept Geoff and the other doctors and the local hospital on their toes, so that he would arrive home to snatch a few hours' sleep if he was lucky, looking dark around the eyes and quite exhausted, and Beth found herself as busy as she had ever been, helping out at the surgery and the hospital.

One morning when the flu epidemic seemed to be dying down, a telephone call from Minna announced that she was home and would call in for coffee. Beth was pleased, she had missed her friend.

Her white sports car drew up outside, its convertible top up against the weather. Minna slid out in cream pants and cream sweater, her fair hair brushed carelessly on top of her head, all dark sunglasses and gold chains. She looked very pleased with life.

She sat at the kitchen table watching Beth make coffee.

'I think you were doing that when I left,' she said.

'I probably was—life doesn't change much round here,' Beth said. 'So, how's the house?'

'Oh, fantastic. Those French workmen— well, I have to say they're mostly Italian— but do they work! Put the British to shame. They've dug out the foundations and put up the brickwork and the roof, and it's going to be a super kitchen. There are three bedrooms and two bathrooms, of course. It's quite small, really. Oh, and lovely tiled floors—I can't wait for you to see it.' She paused for breath and lit a cigarette.

'When do you think you'll come over?' she asked eventually.

'It's not finished yet, is it?'

'No, but you could get away for a couple of days.'

'On my own?' Beth asked.

'Oh, I shouldn't have asked. Busy doctor's wife and all that.'

'We'll come when it's finished—I'd love to see it.'

'Two of the neighbours have moved in. The one next door is a barrister. He practises in Paris and only comes down for weekend. Then there's a couple from the French Embassy: young, good-looking. Most of the residents will only be there for weekends and holidays. There's another couple too—they came once to see how things were going. He's Yugoslav or something like that, she's English, and they deal in antiques.'

'That's interesting.'

'Oh, not your kind of antiques, Beth—solid iron, early Stone Age, you know the sort of thing. Stuff they've dug up, thousands of years old, real antiquities. So what's new on the home front?'

'We had a flu epidemic.'

'Yes, I heard, glad I missed that!'

'And Fran next door is engaged. She had an engagement party.'

'Oh, fun! And who is she marrying—the local garage owner?'

'No, Minna, he's a very successful young businessman, David Greenman.'

'Oy, vey! So what did Joe have to say about that?'

'Oh, I think they've accepted it now.'

'So would I, if I had a daughter,' Minna said.

'I sold one of your boxes. I've made a note of the amount.'

'Oh, good.'

But no mention was made of her doing the antiques market again, so Beth kept quiet about it.

'Is Jimmy pleased about the house?'

'Well, you know Jimmy—it's not really his kind of thing. The only snag is the small plot of land that you get isn't big enough for a swimming pool. Still, there's a big one a mile away, although I expect we could have a portable pool—Jimmy saw some in Paris.'

February brought an invitation to Bernadette's annual party, postponed because of flu and the severe weather. Beth and Geoff and Sheila and Joe were to join the elite crowd of foodies, as Sheila called them, and one very cold night they all made their way to SAN REMO. There was no danger of missing it because it was now floodit with dozens of little trees loaded with fairy lights. 'Good lord!' Geoff said. 'What an extravaganza.'

But they were delighted to be there. Fur wraps and velvet cloaks were taken by two uniformed maids and whisked up the wide staircase.

Bernadette looked wonderful: suntanned after her winter sports holiday in Colorado, in a white pants suit, her cropped hair glossy as silk, large blue eyes not missing a trick.

The huge conservatory was full of flowers, and waiters whisked about with trays of drinks and canapes. You could hardly hear yourself speak, there were so many people there.

Beth was surprised to find how much she had missed Bernadette. Somehow, she seemed part of the scenery of Chantry Green.

'How is Annelise?' she asked when she got close enough to speak to her.

Bernadette's eyes darkened. 'Oh, Beth— I've had such a time. I must tell you about it.'

'Is she here?'

'No, she's gone to Canada to see her grandparents, she usually goes this time of year. Come round one morning, we'll have a chat. You know, I put on a good show, but underneath, my heart is often breaking.'

Beth thought this sounded ominous.

Laurie Featherstone looked more handsome than ever. He stood out in any crowd: tall, broad-shouldered, with his thick fair hair, small silky moustache and open smile. A man to inspire confidence. No wonder he had gone such a long way. But he was nice, too, kissing Beth and seeming genuinely glad to greet Geoff. 'Nice to see you again,' he said, and acknowledged Jimmy, then turned his attention to Minna, holding her hand for a fraction longer than necessary as she looked back at him, face expressionless.

Jimmy seemed almost mesmerised. Beth always suspected that he was making notes for characters in his books and scripts. He wandered around, seeming to listen to bits of conversation, and she had to admit, if you caught snippets of it, it was a bit of a giggle.

Later, in the dining room, they saw the great table simply loaded with wonderful dishes of all kinds. The table had been covered in mirror glass, and the decorative motif was a pond with dozens of napkins made into swans, seemingly floating round the table.

'Oh, Bernadette, how clever!' someone said.

'Not at all.' And Bernadette took a snowy napkin from a pile, and with deft fingers turned it into swan in a matter of seconds.

Most of the women were fascinated—she was incredible. Was there anything she couldn't do?

'Try some of that,' she said to Beth, 'it's new and delicious. I got the recipes from the States.'

'By the way,' Beth whispered, helping herself to salad, 'did Agnes go?'

'Oh, my God, yes!' Bernadette said. 'I now have an excellent daily woman who comes every morning, and she's a great worker, I can tell you. Well, I've trained her. How I lived through that time... Hallo there, Sandy, have you had some dressing? There are six kinds...'

Looking around, Beth couldn't fail to be impressed. Out of the corner of her eye she saw Minna, plate poised, talking to Laurie Featherstone.

A lethal mix, she thought irreverently.

The food was superb, no doubt about it. Everyone was impressed. At the end of the evening, when they stood at the stop of the steps, seeing everyone on their way, Beth thought what a handsome couple the Featherstones made.

Bernadette took Beth's hand and in an aside murmured, 'Why don't you call round one morning—say Tuesday or Wednesday.? I've so much to tell you.'

'Wednesday then, and thank you both for a super evening.'

'Our pleasure,' Bernadette said, showing her lovely teeth in a wide smile.

'Christ,' Minna said when they got back in the car. 'I just don't understand women like that—I think she's bonkers.'

'Did she really prepare all that stuff herself?' Jimmy asked in wonderment. 'She should open a restaurant.'

'Well, don't look at me! I can't boil an egg, and I don't intend to try,' Minna declared.

'Dear one, I know,' said Jimmy. 'Still, not bad, eh, Geoff? Be nice to come home to a dinner cooked by Bernadette, wouldn't it?'

'But how often *does* he come home?' Minna said, taking out a cigarette.

'Not in the car, please, Minna,' said Geoff, who was driving.

Minna, cigarette halfway to her mouth, couldn't believe her ears.

'Sorry,' she said. 'Get him,' she muttered to Beth.

But Beth was secretly pleased.

Good for you, Geoff, she thought.

Chapter Fourteen

Just time for an hour in the garden before going to see Bernadette, Beth thought, making for the rockery, Gus following close behind.

She was delighted to see all the bulbs coming through. The scillas had long gone, but the daffodil spears and the narcissus were well up, and great clumps of perennial alyssum and aubretia made a splash of colour. It had been a good idea to make use of an awkward corner by building a rockery. All the plants had thrived, instant gardening, she thought now, and it had quickly become such an attractive feature, especially when you thought how many wonderful pot-grown plants you could buy at garden centres these days. She seldom went out without coming back with something or other for the garden.

Gus kept scrabbling about desperately in the soil, looking up at her appealingly now and again with his large golden eyes.

'You won't find a rabbit there, Gus,' she said sympathetically. 'Never mind, you tried. When I come back we'll go for a walk in the woods.' His tail wagged back and forth. 'No, not now—later.'

She scrubbed her hands at the sink, and put on her raincoat—it looked like rain. She got the car out and drove through the village to Chantry Park. The gates to SAN REMO were open, surprisingly, and as she drove through to park in the courtyard she saw two large builder's lorries there. Outside the house sat the Rolls; obviously Laurie had not left home yet, for the chauffeur sat in the driving seat reading his newspaper. Perhaps she had arrived at an inopportune moment? But her finger on the doorbell brought Bernadette at once.

'Oh, glad you could come,' she said. 'I still have some last-minute packing to do for Laurie, he's off to New York, but you won't mind waiting in the kitchen for me? I won't be long. Let me take your coat.'

Beth went through to the kitchen and walked over to the window where an extraordinary scene met her eyes. The enormous terrace of York stone was being lifted by four hefty workmen, stone by stone. The pieces were huge and quite a weight, she suspected. They had done about a quarter of it, making a huge pile in one corner, and she wondered why. It had been beautifully laid and was as perfect as if it had been there since the year dot.

Well, there had to be a reason. Perhaps

they were dispensing with the terrace? But that didn't make sense for they loved to sit out there in the summer. The huge pots and urns had been stacked in a corner, and it was quite fascinating to watch the men going about their task.

When Bernadette returned, Beth was sitting at the table, impressed by the way the men were doing their job.

'Ah, that's done,' she said. 'Sorry about that—last-minute rush.'

She was followed by Laurie who poked his head round the kitchen door. 'Hallo, Beth, sorry about this—have to fly. Keep an eye on them, Bernadette.' And he nodded towards the garden. 'They'd better do a good job, or they won't get paid.'

'Darling, of course I will. I won't take my eyes off them.'

'Well, cheerio then. Cheerio, Beth.' And he was gone. She didn't even go to the front door with him, Beth thought. People lived such very different lives.

'What a drama out there,' she said. 'What's going on?'

'The terrace has to be relaid,' said Bernadette, blue eyes clouding over.

'But it looks perfect as it is.' Beth couldn't believe it.

'You don't know Laurie,' Bernadette said moodily. 'He's such a perfectionist—had them go over it with a spirit level.'

211

'Really?' Beth asked faintly. She had thought it was Bernadette who was paranoid about things. Was it really Laurie who demanded perfection?

'They're taking it up and will re-lay it but they can't seal it until May, when the threat of frost is over.'

'I see. Won't it get muddy out there with the winter rains? Even snow,' Beth asked, realising she sounded like a Job's comforter.

'They'll cover it with polythene sheeting,' Bernadette said. She knew all the answers. 'Anyway, let's have some coffee—I've got it ready. I've been dying to see you.'

Having poured the coffee and set the tray with biscuits and cream, she sat down herself.

'Of course, I haven't seen you since before Christmas.'

'Except for the party,' Beth said. 'It was a wonderful evening, Bernadette.'

But Bernadette was no longer interested in past events.

'Listen,' she said confidentially, 'and you won't mention this to anyone, but Annelise has been expelled from her Swiss finishing school.'

'Oh, Bernadette, I am sorry,' Beth said, and she was.

'Well, they asked me not to send her back next term—let's put it like that.' And

Bernadette bit her lip. 'I can't imagine what my parents would say if they knew. Of course, I haven't told them. I just said she'd finished her course. But Laurie was furious.' And her large blue eyes looked tearful.

'He blamed me, said I wasn't strict enough with her.'

'Oh, surely not?' Beth said. 'Did the school give a reason?'

'For smoking—and I bet she wasn't the only one! Also they said she was a bad influence on the other girls, led them astray—can you imagine, Annelise? She wouldn't say boo to a goose. She hasn't got half the spunk I had when I was that age.'

Beth sat, remembering Belinda's words. Was she a dark horse, pretty little Annelise? Still, it was rotten luck for Bernadette with her standards—but then, why was the girl like she was? It seemed only natural she would rebel once she got away from home, from Bernadette's watchful eye. Which all went to prove something, Beth thought, except that she felt a little sorry for Annelise too. It was the sort of situation when it would be better once she had really grown up and married, or was free to do her own thing. She would always rebel under Bernadette's watchful eye.

'What will you do now?'

'I don't know. She'll stay with my parents for a while—there's plenty to keep her occupied over there, and I can rely on my father to keep an eye on her. He did on me,' she said grimly. 'They were so strict, you can't imagine.'

'I should think when she gets back here, you might like to let her train for something. Is there one particular subject she likes? Is she artistic? Perhaps she's brainy like her father, has a business head?' Beth suggested, more out of politeness than anything else.

'She might be like him in more ways than one,' Bernadette said sourly. 'She doesn't seem to take after me at all.'

'Well, you mustn't let it worry you,' Beth said kindly. 'Sometimes high-spirited girls like Annelise turn out the best.' She thought she sounded like her own mother, but suddenly Bernadette's eyes filled with tears and she dabbed at them with a hankie.

'Oh, you are nice,' she said, suddenly blowing her nose, 'have some more coffee. And tell me what you've been doing, all the news?'

They were interrupted by her cleaning lady, a large young woman with a rosy face and a nylon overall to match, as different from Agnes as chalk from cheese.

'Excuse me, madam,' she said. 'I'll just give them banisters a wipe over on the top floor, then I'll do the study.'

'Righto, Concepta,' Bernadette said. 'You carry on.'

'Is that her name?' Beth whispered when she had gone.

'Yes, she's from my church,' said Bernadette. 'Now tell me about Jon—and Laura, isn't it? How's the romance going?'

'Pretty serious,' Beth said. 'She's such a nice girl.'

'And would you be pleased if he married her?' Bernadette asked.

'Oh, yes, and I'm sure they will get engaged soon, as soon as she hears the results of her exams. And by the way,' she went on, 'Fran Rowlands is engaged.'

'Yes, I heard,' Bernadette said. 'I saw it in the *Telegraph*.'

'We met him at Christmas.'

'How's Sheila taking it? Does she mind?'

'His being Jewish?' Beth guessed that was what Bernadette meant. 'No, I think they accept that, they just wish she would wait until she is older.'

'Well, I can't talk,' Bernadette said gloomily. 'I've done my best for Annelise, and look what's happened.'

'Look on the bright side,' Beth suggested. 'At least she's a bit of a rebel, which is usually a good sign.'

215

Bernadette's face brightened. 'You think so?'

She was naive in some ways, Beth thought, despite her sophistication.

'Why don't we go out to lunch one day?' she suggested. 'A Wednesday would be good for me. I've just embarked on a new venture—working at fund raising for the Red Cross. We need all the help we can get if you've a spare moment?'

'You must be joking!' Bernadette said with horror. 'Keeping this place going takes all my time!'

'Well, you set such a standard,' Beth said. 'It's positively immaculate.'

'I don't know any other way,' said Bernadette. 'And it's too late to teach an old dog new tricks now.'

And, thought Beth, driving home, there was only Bernadette and Laurie occasionally, sometimes Annelise. What would she do if she had a large family and dogs and toys all over the place? And she laughed to herself. She couldn't imagine it.

Beth was glad though that she had taken on extra work. Although there was always plenty to do in the house, despite Gina's regular help, and always work to do in the garden, nevertheless with the family away, Beth had more time to herself now. She thought of Minna's painting and her own effort at that. Well, she was no artist.

Then she thought wistfully of the rejected short story. One day she would write. One day. Somehow this didn't seem to be the time.

But she missed Minna, missed her wisecracks and her sense of humour. She always made Beth laugh, even though some of her shots were barbed. They had always been such friends, and yet since she had come to live nearby, they had not been as close as Beth had thought they would be. She sighed. They had seen nothing of Jimmy either, but then he was often involved in some production or other.

Gus was waiting for her, eyes eager, tail wagging.

'Booful Gus, good boy,' she said, patting him. He was ecstatic. 'Did I say I would take you walkies?' and his tail wagged even more furiously. 'I believe I did. Let's go and find your lead.' And she unlocked the front door and went into the house.

Later they walked up past Green Lawns, and saw that the house was shut up. Gus looked at Beth.

'No, not today, Gus,' she said. 'We're going to the woods.'

By midsummer, Jon and Laura were engaged, and Fran about to be married to her David. Sheila was quite philosophical about it.

'Doesn't seem much point in waiting,'

she said. 'David has bought the house, and the workmen are almost finished doing it over, so why wait? The only disappointment, of course, is that it won't be a big wedding. They're getting married in a Register Office which I suppose is the best way round it, but you know how it is—you imagine your daughter in full bridal white and all the trimmings. Still, I'm getting used to the idea now. It will be strange, Beth, because Kate is seriously looking for her own flat, which will mean that Joe and I will be alone after all these years. It'll take some getting used to.'

Beth knew it would. After Jon and Ian and Belinda had gone, even though temporarily, it seemed very strange, and had taken some getting used to, which was why she had flung herself into new things to do. But at least they had not actually left home, not yet anyway. Their rooms were still there for them to come back to and she took comfort from that. Of course, Jon would soon be gone for good but still...

It was a quiet wedding, just a family affair, although Joe and Sheila gave a small dinner party to celebrate afterwards. Sheila was more interested in Beth seeing the house, which she said was out of this world. 'I can't wait for you to see it—we have an invitation to go over soon after they get back from their honeymoon which is being spent in the Bahamas. Isn't she a lucky girl?'

Beth looked forward to that. She loved seeing strange houses.

It was a lovely day in July when they set out, Sheila driving as they made for the Sussex countryside. Some of the journey was familiar, with pretty scenery. England at its best, thought Beth, seeing the country houses set amidst the trees, immaculate lawns and impressive driveways. There were cottages too, not to be outdone with their gardens, roses spilling over walls and trellises, neat flower beds carefully tended.

The house was quite a long way down into Sussex, not far from Midhurst, and at first sight of it, Beth gasped. Large wrought-iron gates stood open to an avenue of lime trees, and the drive wound on and up until they reached the house. Sheila stole a glance at her, and grinned when she saw Beth's face. 'Not bad, eh?' she asked. 'Clever little thing, our Fran.'

She was indeed, Beth thought, as Fran appeared, as pretty as a picture, looking so youthful you couldn't believe she was a married woman. She was still starry-eyed, though, and there was no doubting that she was happy.

'How lovely to see you, Mummy, and

Auntie Beth too.' She kissed them both. 'Come in.' And they were inside.

A magnificent hall with polished wooden floors and rugs, a huge window on the landing sending shafts of sunshine down while the fireplace of gracious white marble was filled with flowers.

'Come on, let's see what you've done,' Sheila said, so proud she could hardly contain herself.

Fran put her arm through Beth's. 'The house dates from 1793,' she said. 'Not, I might add, unaltered since then. David has spent a fortune on it.'

It was obvious where he had spent the money. Everything had been restored in perfect taste. Beth, who knew a little about such things, realised that every lock, every door, every window, was in keeping with the house's period. He must have searched the country for what he wanted. No wonder it had taken a long time.

'And, Mummy,' Fran was saying, 'it came yesterday—the dining table. It took us ages to find it.'

She opened the door of a large cool room of beautiful proportions, walls covered in an old French wallpaper—Beth could only guess at the price a roll. And there it sat: a Regency mahogany dining table with D-shaped ends. 'It extends to nine foot six,' said Fran. 'We expect to do quite a lot of entertaining.'

'The chairs are lovely, too,' Beth said admiringly. They were so elegant, and there were ten of them.

'Early George III. We found them at a sale in Midhurst.'

She must have learned a lot since she had known David, Beth decided. How lucky she was to have this at such an early age. He must have a great deal of money to be able to afford all this.

Fran took them through the rest of the house, first into the main bedroom, which was in pale colours with an enormous bed and a French dressing table on which reposed lots of silver-encrusted bowls, brushes and mirrors.

'Presents from David's family, it's family silver,' said Fran.

'Lucky girl,' cooed her mother.

Then the other bedrooms, all lushly fitted out, bathrooms, a grand drawing room—quite the prettiest Beth had ever seen. Elegance was the operative word. Even Sheila was silenced after a time by the sheer luxury of it all.

'David knows an awful lot about antiques,' Fran said at last. 'I'm only just learning, but it's quite fascinating.'

They were making their way to the kitchen, a dream of modernity with French windows opening on to the garden.

221

'That was David's idea,' Fran said. 'Would you like lunch outside?'

'No, let's have it in,' Sheila said. 'I want to look at all your gadgets. She's got an au pair, too,' she went on. Even she seemed envious.

'Well, that was David's idea. He doesn't like the idea of his wife soiling her pretty hands,' Fran laughed, and Sheila made a face.

'Not that it would do for me,' she said. 'I'd go mad with an au pair under my feet.'

'Oh, she's not under my feet, Mummy,' Fran said. 'I see to that. I keep her busy.'

She served the lunch expertly. Even Belinda would be impressed, Beth thought. Cold Vichysoisse, smoked salmon and a light salad, strawberries and raspberries with cream, and coffee to follow.

It was a lovely day out. Beth thoroughly enjoyed it.

Who would have thought just over a year ago that this would happen? And she wondered what Kate thought about it all now.

As if reading her thoughts, Fran looked up.

'Kate's coming down to lunch on Sunday with—well, perhaps I shouldn't say,'

'Oh, go on!' urged Sheila.

'Well, Matthew Orion.'

'No!' gasped Sheila. 'She didn't say anything about meeting him.'

'Well, she wouldn't, but I can tell you, they're going strong at the moment. Not a word—don't tell her I told you.'

'As if I would!' Sheila promised.

Beth wondered what his wife would have to say about that? She was a well-known actress. They probably had what was called an 'open marriage'.

They strolled round the gardens after lunch and sat outside for a while before going home.

'What news of Belinda?' Fran asked. 'I quite miss her.'

'She's working as assistant chef in a rather well-known Scottish hotel,' Beth said. Well, she had to have something to brag about.

'Good old Belinda!' said Fran. 'And Jon?'

'About to announce his engagement to Laura, I think,' Beth said with a twinkle in her eye.

'Oh, I'm glad—I like Laura.'

'Yes, we do too.'

'Well, we'd better be getting back, I suppose. Hard to leave all this luxury and this beauty spot—and my little girl,' said Sheila, coming over quite sentimental which was unusual for her.

'Oh, Mummy!' Fran said, and threw her arms around her.

No tears from her though at her mother's departure. She's as happy as a sandboy, thought Beth. And why not? The man she loves, and all this.

Sheila was quiet on the way home.

'I still can't believe it, Beth,' she said finally. 'It all happened so quickly—like a dream. Now she's gone with a home of her own, and even gets on with her in-laws like a house on fire. They adore her—and she's happy enough, isn't she? Joe misses her.'

'Of course he does, it's only natural,' Beth said. 'But it happens, Sheila. Life's an endless circle.'

Which was trite, but true. You never knew what was round the corner.

Chapter Fifteen

Beth could remember saying that to Sheila all those years ago as if it were yesterday. 'Life is an endless circle', for it was true, and you realised it more and more as time went by. Surrounded now by the relics of her past, jumbled possessions that could matter only to her, boxed and wrapped and ready to move on to the next stage—the last lap? When the children were young you thought it would go on forever, especially if you were fortunate enough to live a happy life. You would do all the things you wanted to when they had grown up, you told yourself. But instead life seemed to become more complicated, with ripples spreading ever outward as when a stone is thrown into a pond. There were in-laws and grandchildren who grew up in their turn. How lucky that Geoff had lived long enough to see his beloved grandchildren! Only now did she fully realise how fortunate they had been as a family. Not everyone was so lucky.

She looked outside at the dark green Provençal pot standing in front of the cherry tree on the drive, the tree that year after year had spread its great umbrella of white lace followed by tiny cherries that were inedible. The large green pot held at the moment a clipped box tree which she had planted when the summer flowers were over. She had given it to Minna as a moving in present when they moved in to Green Lawns. She and Geoff had spent a week's holiday in Annecy by the lake, had driven down into France and stayed in such a pretty hotel, wandered by the lakeside with its medieval timbered houses, seeing the reflections in the water of the scarlet geraniums that spilled over the railings, watching the boats drifting by. It was a glorious week. Then they had driven down to spend a few days with Minna and Jimmy.

Making their way precariously down into the Gorge of Gondo, they had lost their way somewhere between Minna's village and Draguignan but found it eventually. When they saw it for the first time, Beth gasped. It was enchanting. They parked on the small plateau and went on by foot to find the house locked with the shutters secured. Minna was out. Thankfully a neighbour came to their aid, rescued them and asked to make themselves comfortable in her small atelier while they waited for their hostess.

'I am Madame Descamps, please call

me Solange, and this is my husband Paul. Please come in and a wait for Minna—I am sure she won't be long.'

The Descamps explained that they came from Paris, that he was a retired police official and she an artist who hoped to sell some of her paintings in order to boost Paul's retirement pay. They talked, and she showed Beth her paintings which Beth thought very good, and the time went quickly until Minna arrived (with no apologies) but a thank you to the Descamps for looking after them.

'See you later,' she called, leading the way across the small plateau beneath the clock tower. 'Follow me,' she said, unlocking the great oak door which led into the cool flagged kitchen, shutters closed now against the heat.

'Oh, Minna, it's lovely!' Beth exclaimed, looking round.

'Nice, isn't it? By the way, I expect she showed you her paintings—well, watch it, before you know it, she'll have sold you some!'

'Not very likely,' Beth laughed. 'I thought they were very good, but a trifle expensive.'

Minna showed them into their bedroom which had French pine furniture and curtains and bedcovers in blue and white—such a pretty room—with a bathroom en-suite to match.

Jimmy was off somewhere, it seemed, Nice or Cannes, to see what he could find by the way of a portable pool. 'Unbearable to think of living here without one,' Minna said, clad now in a minute bikini and looking devastating, a golden tan all over.

'Do get changed, you two, you look overdressed. I'll unpack the shopping,' she said.

'Didn't she know we were coming?' Geoff asked when the door closed behind her.

'Of course she did, but you know what Minna's like.'

But Geoff wasn't easily mollified. His principles would not allow him lightly to accept bad manners.

Opening the shutters, Beth was entranced by the view. The little village seemed to cling to the side of the cliff, a sheer drop below, while in the distance lay the blue hills of Provence. The scent of thyme hung all about them. The little houses all looked restored, and the splendid clock tower with its great bell had been recently renovated. No wonder Minna had fallen in love with it all.

'There's a tiny path down there—I wonder where it leads?' said Beth, leaning out of the window. 'Oh, this is heaven, and so warm, and the air is scented with lavender and thyme.'

Geoff turned and looked at her. She deserved this break, although none of it was exactly his cup of tea. He would rather be back in Annecy by the cool lakeside.

He put his arms around her and hugged her tightly then kissed her eyes, her nose and her mouth.

Beth raised startled blue eyes to his.

'Oh, I'm not just a handsome English doctor,' he said, going into the bathroom to shave.

Beth found Minna in the kitchen slicing tomatoes and dressing them in olive oil and basil, tearing lettuce and green stuff apart.

'Solange is giving a buffet this evening—we usually share the chores. You can give me a hand with this if you like. Oh, I tell you what you can do—would you mind going down to the village for the bread? They save it for me if I don't collect it and I forgot—Jimmy usually does it.'

'Love to. Which way do I go?'

'Out of the front door, past Solange's atelier, down the sandy path until you come to the village—it won't take a moment —Geoff might like to go with you?'

He had come into the kitchen, newly shaved and wearing white slacks and a striped tee shirt. It was nice to see him so relaxed.

'Yes, I'll come,' he said.

They walked hand in hand down the path, which was steep, seeing the tiny ruins of a church on their way down, and its massive oak door.

'Must be hundreds of years old,' said Geoff. 'Look at that woodworm.' The stout doors had been almost eaten away. 'We must take a look round later.'

And then the path flattened out and they were on the edge of the village where there was the unmistakable scent of the *boulangerie* which had just opened again after being closed for the afternoon.

The proprietress, a large stern lady, greeted them with the distinctive stare the French reserve for strangers, but when Beth explained that she had come for Madame Alders's bread, her face broke into a smile of welcome.

'Ah, Madame—merci, merci. Bon appetit!'

'Oh, the smell of this bread!' Beth said as they came out of the shop with four long loaves and made their way back up the steep path.

'No wonder Minna wanted to live here,' she said, as they opened the door and went into the kitchen.

'What time do we have to be there tonight?' she asked, putting the loaves on the kitchen table.

'Six-thirty—drinks first,' said Minna.

They were the first to arrive, carrying plates and bowls of salad, Solange coming out to greet them, looking very much the artist. She wore a long silk skirt which fluttered in the slight breeze as she walked, a vivid shirt with gold chains, while her hair was loose and tied back. She came towards Beth with hands outstretched.

'*Bon soir,* Elizabeth,' she said warmly.

Her husband Paul was a round fat man with a balding head and a jovial smile. His eyes were very blue and alert, observant eyes.

'We will speak English,' said Solange. 'It is better. Paul pretends he cannot, but he does very well. Come, my dear, sit here, it's cooler.'

Geoff was seated next to Paul.

Minna, who had on a pale pink silk shift and gold sandals, followed with the trays of food. 'Jimmy will be along later.'

'There is no hurry,' Solange said. 'We have all the time in the world.'

They were soon joined by the couple from next door, the architect, and the handsome Yugoslav and his English wife. Soon she and Beth were talking antiques. Presently more friends of Minna's arrived— a couple holding hands. Max was a handsome man surely approaching sixty, thought Beth, and his companion, Aimee, was a young woman in her thirties, with long black hair and large lustrous eyes. He was devastatingly smooth, and bent low to kiss Beth's hand. What a charmer, she thought, and realised that Minna and he were really old friends.

'She's his fifth wife,' whispered Minna, 'and she won't be the last.'

Beth laughed. 'He *is* terribly good-looking—a bit like Omar Sharif.'

'And an absolute rake! But women can't resist him,' she said. 'You can see why. Ah, here's Jimmy.'

'Well, how did you get on?'

Jimmy, always polite, came forward after greeting his host and hostess to welcome Geoff and Beth. 'What sort of a journey did you have down, Geoff? Not too troublesome?'

'No, fine,' he said. Good thing he got on with Jimmy, Beth thought, for this was not his sort of crowd. He hated small talk and having to make light conversation, though he did get on well with Paul.

Another couple joined them: a pretty girl called Nadia in pale blue silk pyjamas and her husband, an Italian called Massimo, who were renovating a house farther down the hill.

Beth loved it all: the sophistication, the banter, the other worldliness that she never saw at home, the jokes between them all, many of them way above her head.

As it got darker, and the crickets came out, everyone having eaten and drunk the superb wine, she noticed that Max and Aimee were closely entwined and exchanging kisses, but no one seemed to mind, and Minna's jokes and asides became even more risqué as she exchanged badinage with Pepi, the Yugoslav. They certainly seemed to understand each other very well, while his wife, who looked like Brunhilde with her long golden plait, sat quietly listening.

Even Jimmy said, 'Pack it in, Minna,' at one of her remarks until she turned on him. 'Why don't you go home to bed?' she said. 'You must be tired after the long car journey into Nice.'

Somehow the evening lost its charm, the night air grew chill, and Beth was glad when Nadia said it was time they got going. With a sigh of relief, everyone got up to leave.

'Where are you all going?' Minna asked. 'It's only—'

But Paul stood up and took charge.

'Thank you for coming. *Bon soir, bon soir.*'

'What about a nightcap?' Minna asked, once indoors.

'Not for me,' Geoff said. 'I'm for bed—we had a long journey today.'

Beth sighed, backing him up. 'Yes.

Thanks, Minna.' And they made their escape.

Downstairs she could hear Minna and Jimmy arguing.

Once in their cool soft bed, Geoff turned to Beth. 'Want to read?'

'No, too tired,' she said. What with the journey and the red wine, they were asleep in a few minutes.

In the morning, Geoff was up and about early as always.

'It's lovely out there,' he said. 'Best time of day. I could do with a walk.'

Beth rubbed her eyes. 'Gosh, I slept well.'

'Umm' he began. 'How long are we staying?'

'Presumably as long as we like. No, seriously, I said a few days.'

'Until Friday perhaps? We could leave early and make our way back slowly.'

Beth knew what he meant.

'Yes, why not?' she said. It wasn't going to work. Minna's world plainly wasn't theirs.

She wondered at what point they had grown so far apart, she and Minna. They had always been such friends and got on like a house on fire. Shared the same sense of humour, giggled at the same jokes, but somewhere along the way they had changed. Was it marrying the men they had? Or her living such a domestic life as a doctor's wife? At all events, the estrangement seemed to have started since Minna had come to live at Green Lawns. When her friend had first told her she was coming to live nearby, Beth had been wildly excited. Now, it seemed the whole thing had gone sour.

The next day Jimmy drove them to Nice and Cannes, ending up in a super fish restaurant, and on Wednesday Geoff took them out to dinner at a favourite restaurant of Jimmy's in St-Paul-de-Vence. On Thursday, after a day at the local pool, Minna did a return buffet to which they all came except Nadia and her Italian husband.

The warm air surrounded them like a cocoon while Minna chatted to Pepi and Geoff talked to Paul, whose English turned out to be remarkably good after all.

'There—what did I tell you?' Solange said.

'Jimmy, go into the kitchen and get some more pistachio nuts. You'll find them in the—'

'I know,' he said, going inside. 'We need some more wine anyway.' He had been unusually quiet all evening.

He had not been gone a moment before Minna had thought of something else.

'Beth, ask him to bring out the catalogue

of my paintings. I promised to show it to Pepi. He'll know where it is.'

'Sure.'

She found Jimmy standing still by the kitchen table, both hands flat down on it, as though trying to remember something.

'Pistachios,' she laughed, 'and Minna would like the—'

But the smile died on her face, and she had no time to finish before he caught her hand in both of his.

'Beth, I have to talk to you!'

She felt her face go a fiery scarlet, and the touch of his hand holding hers was electric. Was this about Minna?

'Jimmy—'

His golden-amber eyes searched her own, and she felt her strength drain away.

'Beth—don't hide it. You must know—' And suddenly his lips were on hers and, forgetting everything, she drowned for an instant before breaking away, shocked at herself, at her weakness, at his revelation.

'Minna wants the catalogue—her exhibition catalogue,' she said almost all in one breath, and hurried to the door with the bowl of pistachio nuts, standing outside for a moment to take a deep breath and regain her shattered composure, feeling empty, drained, and as if she was on fire.

Beth would remember it for a long time: the dark warm night, the stars overhead, the sound of crickets and cicadas and the scent of French perfume, heady French wine, good food. Most of all the undercurrent of things left unsaid, only hinted at...

For the rest of their stay, she and Jimmy avoided each other's eyes.

'Jimmy's going back on Sunday,' Minna said when they announced their departure. 'You could have given him a lift if you'd stayed until then.'

'Sorry, Minna,' Geoff said. 'I have to be back for Saturday. But he's welcome to drive back with us tomorrow.'

'Oh, no, he wants to go on Sunday,' she said. 'Something to do with a meeting on Monday.'

What a relief! Beth thought. How could she? she asked herself? How could she feel like this about a man who was not her husband? And Jimmy—how long had he felt that way? As long as...no, she must put it behind her, that way madness lay. Think of anything: the children, Geoff, Gus, the garden.

They took their leave and drove home, making an overnight stop at an hotel on the way, reaching Chantry Gate late on Saturday evening to be greeted by Belinda who was busy cooking in the kitchen.

Beth was surprised to see her. 'What are you doing home?'

'Telephone message from Jon to the

hotel saying he was coming home—he's bringing Laura to Sunday lunch, they have some news for us. We all know what that means! So I caught the first train down.'

'Oh!' And Beth's eyes danced. 'You think...'

'I'm sure of it,' Belinda said. 'I didn't want to miss it. So how was it? France?'

'I'll tell you when I've been up to change,' Beth said. It was good to be home.

And good it turned out to be. Jon and his pretty girlfriend were engaged at last, Laura sporting a small single diamond on her engagement finger, and constantly looking up at Jon with adoring eyes.

Geoff too was pleased, because he liked Laura, although Beth knew he had not wanted Jon to tie himself down too soon.

'They're right for each other,' she said when they got into bed.

'Let's hope so,' he said.

And so the circle turns, Beth thought.

By late-summer, Fran was pregnant with her first baby, and when in March she gave birth to a son, both families were over the moon. Sheila hastened down to be with her, and Kate was asked to be godmother, which surprisingly she was delighted to do, taking her forthcoming duties very seriously.

She was overjoyed with the baby, filled with a sense of wonder that she couldn't hide. 'Isn't he tiny?' she said, looking at him with awe and holding his hand.

'You'll have one of your own one day,' Fran said, looking as beautiful as she would ever look.

'Not me,' Kate shuddered. 'You'll find I make an excellent aunt and godmother, but mother, no.'

Minna returned from France in September. She had been away the whole summer. Bernadette was in Canada with Annelise before returning home to take up her social duties once more.

Minna sat at Beth's kitchen table, smoking, her white slacks and pale blue shirt setting off the golden brown of her skin.

'Did you get the portable pool?' Beth asked.

'Yes, it's not bad—takes up all the garden though. Still, it's better than nothing.'

She didn't look all that overjoyed with life, Beth thought. Perhaps she was not too pleased to be home? She did so adore her life in the South of France.

'Did Hamish go down to see you?'

'No,' Minna said, stubbing out her cigarette. 'He's gone to Kenya, doing some project or other. I'm not sure what.'

'So you haven't seen him for some time?'

'No. By the way, you know where that patch of lawn is on the far side-over by the birches?'

'Yes.'

'I'm having it made into a rose garden—an Italian rose garden,' Minna said. 'The landscapers are starting next week.'

'Really?' Beth was surprised. Did this mean that she was growing tired of France? She had done no work on the garden at Green Lawns for some time.

'Will you go back to France at Christmas?'

'No, I don't think so. Christmas at home this year, I think. Well, you know, Jimmy wants it at home.'

It was unlike her to give in to Jimmy's wishes on anything.

'His mother, poor old soul, she must be eighty odd, I think she's on her last legs.'

So that was it. The old lady had money, that much Beth knew. There was a sister involved too, whom Minna hated.

So that explained that.

One morning in November, quite a pleasant day, Beth stood at the kitchen sink looking out onto the next-door drive. Fran's car was outside, Sheila had said she was calling in on her way to London, and

Beth saw Fran put the baby in its little chair in the back and set off waving.

She envied Sheila. Beth herself was looking forward to having grandchildren.

It was later in the day, after lunch, when she saw the police car outside Sheila's house and wondered what was wrong.

She decided not to ring, after all, it was none of her business, but it was a little odd. Presently a policeman knocked at her front door, and after identifying himself, asked her if she would like to accompany him to the next-door house, as Mrs Rowlands had asked her to go in if she could spare the time.

'Of course,' Beth said. 'I'll get my coat. Is something wrong?' Oh, surely it wasn't Fran and the baby?

'Mrs Rowlands has had some bad news,' the policeman said. 'Her husband—'

Beth's hand flew to her throat. Joe?

'What happened?' she asked as they walked across the asphalt drive.

'Mr Rowlands dropped dead on the golf course,' the policeman said, and Beth's heart lurched.

Oh God! What would Sheila do now?

Joe was sixty-five, young to die, and Sheila so much younger than him.

Sheila stood white-faced in the hall, her cheeks drained of all colour. She looked unsteady, as though about to topple over.

'Sheila, my dear.'

Beth put both arms round her and led her back into the drawing room. Sheila was like a zombie. 'He didn't know Fran was coming—didn't even see the baby,' she kept saying through stiff white lips. Beth sat her down and went into the kitchen to make a strong pot of tea.

'Someone will have to go to the hospital,' the policeman said. 'To identify him. Are there any children, madam?'

'Yes, a daughter who lives in Sussex but who's in London today, and the eldest daughter who works in London. I have her telephone number.'

'Would you like us to telephone her, madam?'

'It might be better if I did it,' Beth said.

She took a strong cup of tea into Sheila, who was shivering as if she had flu.

'Sheila, dear, drink this and afterwards we'll go to the hospital. If you feel up to it?'

'I must see him—I want to see Joe.'

Beth bit her lip.

What a dreadful shock for them, how ghastly, and with no warning.

It was a good way to go for Joe, though. Just so awful for those left behind.

Chapter Sixteen

How bare the shelves looked without the teapots! But they now reposed, safely wrapped up, in her car, forty-two of them. Beth had decided to take them herself, to bear the responsibility. She had never had the shelves glazed in—Gina had dusted the teapots every week and they had come to no harm. Poor Bernadette had had kittens at the thought of them being exposed like that.

Beth got up and walked around the dining room. Strange to think that someone else would be living here next week, after all this time. All the wonderful family meals and celebrations and Christmas lunches they had here...but it was no time to look back, just to be grateful for what she had had.

Chantry Green had changed, but Chantry Gate had not, or so she liked to think. Chantry Green had moved on. The village now had no grocer's shop where you sat on high stools and gave your order—and that had been only twenty years ago. Nowadays a very smart sort of supermarket sat there owned by a handsome Indian family.

Looking much like Fortnum & Mason's or Harrods outside, it was very smartly maintained and well run, and nothing was too much trouble for them. They kept every kind of bread and delicious croissants, strange teas, and all sorts of nuts and herbs and spices. The old chemist's shop had gone upmarket too and stocked expensive merchandise besides dispensing.

Beth glanced at her watch. Soon time for bed. She would have to be up early in the morning for the removal van would be here at eight-thirty, but she was an early riser anyway.

Even though it was dark now, she could see the dried green flower-heads of the hydrangeas peering at her through the dining-room window like babies' faces. Originally a lovely deep blue, they dried to a delicious green. Bernadette had given her a root, and she had propagated them until there were six great clumps under the window. She had given lots away—everyone admired them.

Bernadette had had a bank of them, and they made such a picture in summer, all a vivid blue—well, she wouldn't have tolerated an interloper. At the first sign of a pink one it had been rooted out. Beth usually salvaged it from the compost heap. She was never fussy where she found her plants. Her pink hydrangeas were planted by the pond where they grew as a foil for the pale blue lobelias.

She had been an artist in her way, Bernadette, and her sister...now what was her name? Angélique... Beth had been there in the kitchen when Bernadette said she would be coming over in the summer for a visit.

'Is it her first visit to England?' Beth asked. She was looking forward to meeting her, bearing in mind that Bernadette had said she was so different, a retiring character, a good woman.

'Yes, it will be—she is bringing Annelise back. I can't wait to see my daughter again—she's been over there almost the whole summer.'

It was a little hard on Bernadette, Beth could see that, the girl seemed to spend more time in Canada than in England.

'It's very exciting for you,' she said, for she thought it was, but Bernadette didn't appear to be best pleased. Perhaps she didn't get on with her sister?

'The only snag is I shall have to take her everywhere—as if I don't have enough of that with visiting Americans. I must have seen every London show at least three times if not more. Still, can't be helped.'

Beth tried to imagine having to go to shows so many times that you were bored, and failed.

'Fortunately, I shall have the car because Laurie will be away most of the time, and Jack can drive us sometimes, say to York or Scotland—she'll be bound to want to go up there.'

Bernadette sounded really depressed at the thought.

'Is she coming with her husband?'

'She's not married,' said Bernadette, and Beth wondered why she had got the impression of a hardworking little woman way out on a farm in bleakest Canada. She was so different, Bernadette had said.

'She was,' Bernadette continued, 'but the marriage was annulled. You can always pull a few strings if you know the right people—and my father does.'

'Oh.' There seemed to be no answer to that. Beth had thought the sister was a shy little woman, diffident and nothing like Bernadette. It didn't sound that way now.

'Anyway, I shall give a luncheon for her, just us girls, and ask a few friends—we shall have to show her we know how to do things in England,' Bernadette rattled on. 'You must come, and Minna, and I thought I'd ask Sheila—she could probably do with a bit of cheering up. It was a terrible thing, Joe dying like that, my heart bleeds for her—I've sent up a little prayer. What about the eldest daughter—Kate, is it? I suppose she would be working?'

'I imagine, still you could ask her.'

Beth looked forward to it; not only the luncheon, but meeting Angélique.

'Bernadette, your house plants always look so wonderfully fresh and green. Mine seem to wilt a bit in this weather.'

'Well, I do them with plantshine every week. You'd be surprised how glossy it makes the leaves.'

It was a July day, warm and sunny, when Beth drove up to SAN REMO in her car. She had brought Sheila, and Kate who was taking a few days of her holiday at home, mainly because her mother didn't want to go away. Minna was in France, so unable to come.

The gates swung open and they sailed in, much to Kate's amusement, and parked alongside three other cars in the courtyard.

'Look at it!' Kate said. 'Immaculate. All the flowers standing to attention.'

'They'd better!' Beth laughed.

'So what's so special about this sister?' Kate asked.

'It's her first visit from Canada and Bernadette wants to impress her,' Beth explained.

'She'll do that all right!'

A new maid Beth hadn't seen before led them into the conservatory where Bernadette stood beneath the trailing overhead plants which were a riot of colour. Beside her stood the most beautiful woman Beth thought she had ever seen.

She was a mite taller than her sister, slimmer, with beautiful legs and figure, her hair more glossy, her eyes even more blue, but with a lovely expression and a ravishing smile—whereas if you caught Bernadette off guard she could look quite sulky. Beside her Bernadette looked like the twin who had not quite made it.

No wonder she'd been slightly on edge! But she smiled brightly and came towards them.

'Angélique, I'd like you to meet neighbours and my dearest friends, Beth, Sheila, and her daughter, Kate—my sister Angélique.'

Beth was quite bowled over. It was the last thing she'd expected to see, such a radiant beauty, and so sure of herself.

'How very nice to meet you—I've heard so much about you.'

Even her voice was low and husky, with the slightest French accent, whereas Bernadette had hardly any.

Angélique turned. 'Don't keep your guests waiting, Bernadette.' And she smiled sweetly. 'What will you have? Sherry, a cold drink—a dry martini, perhaps, with ice?'

Her beautiful blue eyes were trained on them.

Beth and Sheila chose dry sherry while Kate opted for a dry martini. 'With lots of ice, please!'

Looking at her, Beth could see the light of battle in Kate's eyes.

'Is this your first visit to England, Angélique?' she asked coolly.

'Yes, I hope I will not be disappointed—Bernadette has told me so much about it.'

'Well, we must see if we can show you the delights of our country,' said Kate. 'I should be happy to show you London—that is, if Bernadette has nothing planned?'

'Oh, I expect she will have made a full itinerary,' Angélique said, looking round for Bernadette. Beth almost expected her to click her fingers.

Bernadette returned with the tray of drinks.

'Oh, darling, not enough ice. Let me,' Angélique said, and disappeared to return with the ice bucket.

'There,' she said triumphantly, taking cubes out with the tongs. 'Three, four?'

Sheila had not said a word. She seemed mesmerised in the company of two such incredible women.

'Your garden looks lovely,' she said at length, 'but then it always does.' And the merest frown appeared between

Angélique's lovely brows.

'I can't think why you had that terrace there—it would have been better had you extended it to either side, three sides of a square.' And you suddenly realised that it would have been.

'Well, it's been relaid now so...'

'What has that to do with it?' Angélique asked. 'And those—what are they?' She frowned. 'Oh, I see, beds of dark-leaved begonias—so old hat, Bernadette, you must get rid of those.'

She gave them one of her beautiful smiles.

'My little sister is no gardener,' she said, excusing her, 'but I hand it to her, she tries—one has to have an innate sense of colour before tackling bedding out plants.'

Bernadette looked definitely uncomfortable.

'Did Annelise come back with you?' Beth asked politely of Angélique.

'Yes, poor little soul. She didn't want to come, but after all she must see her mama sometimes.' And she showed her lovely teeth in a sweet smile.

Glancing at Kate, Beth could see the amusement in the girl's eyes. We have a right one here, she could almost hear her say.

Bernadette glanced over at a table laid

with all sorts of delicacies, one any woman would be proud to display, and she was no mean cook, as they all knew.

'How's the cooking going?' Angélique asked her sister. 'Are you coping? I see you have attempted some ambitious dishes.' And she went over to the table and prodded here and there with a fork—but her lovely arched brows were drawn together when she turned round.

'Bernadette is a wonderful cook!' Beth found herself saying, while Bernadette threw her a grateful glance.

'Well, she's a tryer, I'll give her that,' Angélique said grudgingly, wiping her elegant fingers on one of the pretty napkins.

'And you, my dear, what do you do?' she asked Kate.

'I'm in public relations.'

'That, I believe, is in its early stages over here?'

'I didn't know that,' Kate said smoothly. 'Well, at any rate, let's say it has improved greatly since I became an assistant director.'

'In one of the best-known PR companies in this country,' Sheila said, rising to the defence of her chick, but stopped when she saw Kate's frown.

'Do you have children?' Kate asked politely.

'Sadly, no—but then, I have my delightful niece. Ah, here she comes.'

Beth could hardly believe the tall young woman who came into the room was Annelise. Like her aunt, she was taller than Bernadette, and had the same well-groomed look about her. More like her aunt than her mother, though—no wonder she got on with her so well. Poor Bernadette!

'Annelise,' Beth said, going to her and giving her a kiss, 'it's lovely to see you home again. We've missed you.'

Annelise had acquired a slight Canadian accent. 'I've missed you too, and Belinda. How is she?'

'Working in France at the moment.'

'Good for her,' said Annelise. 'Perhaps I shall have the chance to go to see her? Auntie Angélique wants to fit in a visit to France.'

'That will be nice,' Beth said, 'and how you've grown!' It sounded trite, but she was so surprised at the poise of the girl, her sophistication—quite unlike the one who had been sent home from finishing school.

And then two more guests arrived and took up Bernadette's time. She ushered them in and soon everyone was talking at once. Beth sauntered over to the window with her sherry in her hand. How on earth could Bernadette have told her her sister was quite different from her?

Annelise came up behind her. 'It's really nice to see you again, Auntie Beth. How's the rest of the family?' And Beth remembered that she had been quite sweet on Ian once.

'Jon is engaged to a girl called Laura—I think they plan to marry next year.'

'Oh, how exciting!'

'Ian is working in France, too, in an engineering firm. He joined them after he got his degree.'

'Oh, so he and Belinda are both in France?'

'Yes, although Belinda comes home in a few weeks. And what have you been doing with yourself?'

'All sorts of things, lots of sport and parties—there's a lot of socialising in Montreal, you know. And as you may imagine, Auntie Angélique is at the forefront of it all.'

'Your mother misses you,' Beth said. 'She must be so glad you are home.'

'I'm not sure I'm staying, though, I really prefer Canada. Still, I don't suppose Daddy would agree to my going over there permanently.'

'I daresay not,' Beth said.

'Now, what are you two talking about?' Angélique asked sweetly She put an arm through Annelise's. 'Isn't she lovely? So changed, I expect you hardly know her.' And she looked at Annelise proudly.

'Yes, she has grown up,' Beth said.

'Well, I expect she got bored over here,' Angélique said. 'Naturally enough.'

'And what do you hope to see while you are here?' Beth asked politely, trying to keep the coldness out of her voice.

'Oh, the London sights, Scotland, I daresay, perhaps Devon. It depends what we can fit in.'

But then it was time to eat, and the guests fell on the food, taking their plates as Bernadette stood by giving a hand.

The food as always was delicious, although by the way Angélique picked at it you would have thought there was something wrong with it. Even Annelise said, 'Super, Mummy,' and Bernadette seemed pathetically pleased.

Chilled white wine was served and coffee afterwards with Bernadette's famous profiteroles and delicious meringues that melted in the mouth, but Beth noticed that Angélique shook her head at most of the food.

How lovely she was, though, in her navy and white silk skirt and white top, exposing silky skin which radiated health, her navy high-heeled shoes showing off lovely legs.

'And where do you live, Beth?' she turned to ask.

'In Chantry Green—not far away. We have an old Victorian house.'

'Sweet,' murmured Angélique.

'It is—smashing,' Annelise said.

Angélique frowned. 'Smashing, darling? What does that mean?'

'Super,' Annelise said. 'You know, super—really great.'

For all the success of the luncheon, Beth was glad to take her leave. Driving home with Sheila and Kate, she found herself feeling quite rattled.

'What a cow!' Kate said.

'Katherine!' her mother reproved.

'Well, she is. Bloody rude and most unlikable,' Kate said. 'You know, I have a soft spot for old Bernadette.'

Beth smiled. Old Bernadette! But she thought she had too, despite the odds.

More so when the next morning she found Bernadette on the doorstep at nine-thirty, carrying an umbrella and wearing a raincoat.

'Beth, could I come in for a moment? Are you doing anything this morning.'

'Only going to the baby clinic at half-past ten. Come in, Bernadette.'

She stood the umbrella in the stand, and took off her coat. 'I won't stay a minute but I had to come—I couldn't sleep.'

'Whyever not?'

'Well...'

'Where's Angélique?' Beth asked.

'Gone to Harrods with Annelise, thank God,' she said, sitting herself on a kitchen chair. 'Look, Beth, I think I owe you an apology.'

'Whatever for?' asked Beth, putting the coffee on.

'Well, I've a confession to make. I remember telling you that Angélique was nothing like...'

'You did. 'And Beth smiled wryly. 'I must say, she was quite a surprise.'

Bernadette took off her raincoat and sat down again. 'I feel so awful. You see, I never thought she would come over here. She never wanted to before.'

'But why?'

'She hates England—always has.'

'Really?'

'Well, we're French-Canadians, and strongly French-oriented—I was too, until I met Laurie, and then I knew I would have to come to England and make the best of it. You can't imagine what I put up with from Angélique when she knew I was marrying him and coming over here to live.'

'Oh, yes I can!'

'Well, you may imagine how surprised I was when she said she was coming over for a visit—this is the first she's made after all this time. I suppose Annelise told her about the house and the lifestyle we have—anyway, for whatever reason, she decided to come and I had to keep to the rules and make her welcome and give her a little party and so on. And I thought: What will Beth think? I told her...'

Beth smiled. 'Well, to say I was surprised is putting it mildly, but I can understand your reluctance to have her visit you. She must be absolutely draining.'

She poured out the coffee and handed a cup to Bernadette who took it gratefully.

'You know, she's perfect in whatever she does—always has been. My parents think she is the cat's whiskers, and I have to hand it to her, she *is* quite something. I've always tried to copy her in every way, because she was—is such an example, and as you may imagine she always stood over me and nagged until I got it right. At school it was the same. I was never able to be my own person, if you know what I mean? "Try and be more like your sister," the nuns used to say. Of course, I like everything nice—I admire and respect what she does—but it is so instilled in me that she is the number one that—'

Imagine trying to live up to such perfection. Beth was quite horrified. Left to herself, Bernadette might have been quite different. 'It's a bit of a joke, isn't it? You must have been glad to get away from her?'

'Oh, I was, although I dreaded coming to England—but now, well, I'm so much at home here I don't want to go back to Canada. The only thing that worries me is that she has had such an influence on Annelise that I feel I'm losing her.'

'You won't,' Beth assured her, 'if you play your cards right. You've let her influence you to such an extent you've lost touch with the real you, trying to be like your sister. What does Laurie have to say about it?'

'Just wants me to be more like her. "Ask Angélique," he used to say, "and watch what she does." '

'And yet he married you,' Beth suggested.

'Oh, yes, he was never that keen on her, just held her up as an example—which you have to admit she is.'

'Well, it's difficult for you to do anything while she's here, but I think I would try to unbend a little—be a little more relaxed with Annelise. So far you seem to have spent your life obeying your parents and your sister then Laurie—and you've reacted by taking it out on Annelise.'

'You think I am too strict with her?'

'You're behaving the same way as they did to you.'

'But she's been a very naughty girl, Beth. If I'd been easier, think what she might have got up to!'

'But then she might not have felt the need to rebel.'

'I don't know—my mind is in such a turmoil. I'd better fly.' And she drank the rest of her coffee. 'You'll be late for your clinic, and I have to get back.'

She put on her raincoat. 'But you do understand, Beth? I'd hate to lose our friendship.'

'Take more than that,' she laughed, going with her to the front door. 'I'll see you soon.'

'Thanks, Beth.'

Chapter Seventeen

Looking down at the photograph in her hand, Beth smiled. It was Geoff holding Jon's baby, Toby, their first grandchild. What wonderful days they had been, when Laura had presented Beth with the baby and she had held him for the first time. He looked so much like Jon had as a baby, holding him brought it all back again. Laura, who was an only child, was in a seventh heaven of delight. They had wanted a family early, they said, so that Laura could go back to work while she was still young, for she intended to look after her children herself. No nannies for her. By the time they went to school, she would be ready to take up her career again. Young people had it all worked out, Beth thought.

She could remember how she had been at the change of life, menopausal as they would term it today. How she had become quite paranoid about babies, looking into prams, wishing with all her heart she could have another baby, the jealousy she felt of the young mothers at the clinic, so much so that she had given up working there for a time. It was not so much that she wanted another baby, it was the knowledge that she couldn't have one if she wanted to. She had no one to discuss it with, although Geoff said it was perfectly normal, for Sheila and Minna were delighted to have arrived at that stage of their lives. Thank God, they'd said, that's over!

And then Toby came along, followed by others, small children who had played on the lawn, had their pictures taken by delighted parents and grandparents. Wonderful days. What age would she have been then?

She would certainly remember her fiftieth birthday which was engraved in her memory forever. Geoff said it was a special occasion and they were going to treat it as such and really push the boat out. She had no idea what he had in mind until the evening before, when he announced that he was taking her to lunch at the Ritz.

Beth could hardly believe it—the extravagance!

'Why not?' he had asked. 'What's money?'

They had left home, Beth in a new suit she had bought for a wedding earlier in the year, and set out on a nice July day. It was wonderful just to be driving up to town with Geoff, for he normally had very little time to himself, but this he had insisted upon. They left early, in order, he explained, that they could take their time and not have to rush.

He had already told her he would like to buy her a ring or a bracelet, a piece of jewellery to celebrate this very important occasion, but Beth was not keen on conventional jewellery, she much preferred old settings or unusual pieces, so he was handicapped in that he could never surprise her, knowing she would like to choose something herself. Browsing around an antiques market or second-hand shop was more to her liking, and not something that Geoff enjoyed. Already she had a few unusual pieces of jewellery: a heavy silver bracelet from Mexico, a silver torque bracelet unearthed in Dorset, a gold Victorian signet ring—not valuable but things that she cherished.

They managed to park the car and strolled along Piccadilly and into Simpson's and then Fortnum & Mason's where they had coffee and Beth drooled over the exotic foods.

When they arrived at the Ritz she made her way downstairs to freshen up and on her return found Geoff waiting for her in one of the wing chairs. Then up into the lounge bar where a waiter came forward to take their order of dry martinis.

This is the life, thought Beth, looking around. I could come here every day and never get tired. She saw a couple of politicians, for she could always recognise faces where she couldn't remember names, and then to make her day complete, saw Iris Murdoch.

'Who's she?' Geoff asked.

'Oh, never mind,' Beth sighed. She was probably with her publisher, it looked like a business meeting, she thought, they were talking rather earnestly. How she would love to know what they were saying!

No doubt about it, she was enjoying herself, Geoff thought. He was pleased. He just wished he could afford for them to do it more often.

Drinks over, they were called to their table, and found the beautiful restaurant half full. They were seated towards the centre of the room, since most of the tables overlooking the windows were occupied, but they had a good view of the park, which looked lovely on this perfect day.

Eyes shining, Beth studied the menu then glanced across at Geoff. She looked so pretty and nothing like her age, he thought. You'd never think she was fifty...

'What shall I have?' she asked.

'You have whatever you like,' he replied. 'Whatever you want.' He enjoyed indulging her. 'It's your day.'

She took a deep breath.

'I'd like a Dover sole—but first, I think, cream of spinach soup with sage croutons.'

'Sounds good.'

They spent some time going over the menu and when the waiter came to take their order, followed by the wine waiter, Beth sat back and relaxed, admiring the beautiful dining room and the view outside. How elegant it was, and what a setting! Geoff took delight in watching her. He knew she never missed a trick, she saw everything; it would all be imprinted on her mind like a photograph.

By the time the waiter came with the soup, Beth had observed most of the diners, and it was not until someone got up to go and made their way towards the exit, that her heart leapt. Blocking her view as they had, she was only now able to see who sat at the far table by the wall in the corner. She was not mistaken. It was Minna—and Laurie Featherstone. For some reason her heart began to race, and she blushed to the roots of her hair. Geoff leaned forward.

'Everything all right? Is the soup too hot?'

'Yes—er—no, it's fine.' And as she simmered back to normality, casting the odd glance across at them, she knew that Minna couldn't see her, placed as she was, but if Laurie looked over—which seemed unlikely, he was so absorbed in what Minna was saying—then he would see her.

The last thing she wanted was for Geoff to know. He would be furious that her day was being spoiled by Minna, the fact that they were there, furious that it had caused Beth to feel uncomfortable. Best to say nothing...

It did, however, spoil her meal. She was outraged, furious with Minna. She had no real feelings towards Laurie, but Minna! How could she? How dare she? Did it mean nothing to her that they were all friends? It was obvious as the minutes ticked by that she and Laurie were very close, intimate almost. Not that they indulged in holding hands or that sort of thing, but the rapport was there to see, the smiles and the laughter. It was as if they were old acquaintances—which perhaps they were?

Beth was furious and upset, and it was difficult to hide it. Already, by the time the main course came, Geoff could see there was something wrong.

'Beth—aren't you enjoying it?'

'Yes, I am—it's lovely, delicious.' But she picked at the fish. It was hard to swallow, so upset was she for Bernadette. Well, perhaps, she told herself, Laurie did this sort of thing all the time? All well and good, but with a local woman, a neighbour? Did they meet up all the time? And what about Jimmy? At this she felt close to tears and Geoff was looking at her anxiously. 'Beth, is something wrong?'

'I think I'm a bit overwhelmed by it all. I mean...'

'Come on, that's not like you. Is your fish nice? If not, we'll send it back.'

'No, it is—' Oh, blast Minna! How dare she spoil Beth's birthday? It might be usual for Minna to dine at the Ritz but it wasn't for Beth. It was a treat. She could have wept, for Geoff as much as herself But if she told him now, she knew he would be furious.

Presently, she calmed down. What business was it of hers after all? It was nothing to do with her. The fact that she knew Laurie, and that Minna was a friend...what did it matter? Oh, but it did! And she put down her knife and fork. Thank goodness she had worked her way through the fish, although it had almost choked her.

'Now, you're sure you feel all right?'

She forced a brilliant smile. 'Yes, I'm fine. Now, what shall we have for dessert?'

Beth concentrated on the menu. Perhaps after all they were just friends? Platonic friends. Not likely! Not Minna. Best

266

pretend nothing was wrong, forget it—but how could she? Minna not a few yards away from her, with Laurie Featherstone. She bit her lip.

'I'm not sure I want a sweet,' she said.

'Oh, Beth, surely—you know how you love puddies.'

'I know, but there was a lot of that fish.'

'Well, I'm going to have one,' Geoff said, and she thought: how can I sit here while he works his way through his sweet?

'I'll have creme brulee,' she said suddenly.

'That's the spirit.'

Miserably, she sipped her wine and Geoff poured her a glass of ice-cold water which was delicious. That was better. She took a deep breath. She would tell him once they were outside. But what if the others got up to go before them? Minna could turn then and see her—and if Beth and Geoff left first, Laurie might see them. Oh, what a misery. She decided she was making a mountain out of molehill and smiled at Geoff.

'That's better—the colour has come back into your cheeks. You went so pale I got quite worried.'

Whenever she told him now, he would be furious that she hadn't said anything

267

before—well, she couldn't win. In for a penny, she thought. So I was thrown, didn't quite know what to do. Geoff furious before or after—what does it matter? But Minna—she's my best friend and I hate her! And then she almost managed a smile.

'Like to go to Harrods?' Geoff asked. 'Do a bit of shopping?'

'Let's see how we feel after coffee,' she said, glancing across and seeing that the others had finished their coffee. At that point Minna got up. She was wearing a cream silk shift which set off her tan, and carried a splendid handbag, her fair hair enhanced with high-lights, dark glasses pushed back on her head. Escorted by Laurie Featherstone, she left the restaurant.

The swine! thought Beth. I never trusted him anyway. And now at least she and Geoff were free to enjoy their coffee.

'Shall we have it outside?' he asked.

'Good idea,' said Beth, and waited patiently while he settled the bill and they made their way out of the restaurant.

Once seated, the order given, Geoff looked at her.

'So what was that all about?' he asked coolly. 'I know you, Beth. Something upset you.'

She really was contrite. 'I'm sorry, darling, honestly—I wouldn't have spoiled it for the world. In fact it wasn't spoiled, not really.'

'Yes?' And he waited.

'Minna was across the room, with Laurie Featherstone.' And she waited for it to sink in.

'I'm glad that's all it was! I thought something awful had happened—you'd come over ill or felt faint or something.'

'I'm sorry—but—well, I didn't want to tell you then.'

'Why not?'

'I didn't want to upset you. I knew you'd be cross that Minna had spoiled our lunch.'

'Well, she certainly spoiled yours,' he said drily.

'You don't seem surprised?'

'I'm not,' he said coolly.

Her mouth opened. 'What do you mean?'

'Well, are you?'

'Yes,' she said, sticking her chin out. 'I didn't think Minna would—'

'Oh, come on, Beth, Minna's for Minna—you know that—she does exactly what she wants to do—always has, and if she fancies Laurie Featherstone—well, that's that—poor Bernadette—although I'm sure she must be used to it by now—'

'You sound so cynical,' Beth said miserably.

269

'Well, let's say I wouldn't think it's the first time,' he said quietly.

'What?'

'I saw Minna's car parked in a layby when I was visiting a patient just this side of Windsor and it crossed my mind then that the man with her was Laurie Featherstone—'

'Geoff!'

'I'm afraid so.'

'Why didn't you tell me?'

'I wasn't going to start something of which I wasn't quite sure, but after this, I daresay it was—who knows how long it has been going on—they're a well matched pair—'

'Oh, I know you're not all that keen on Minna—'

'I don't dislike her—I just think you need to be put straight about what she's up to half the time—'

'I never dreamed—'

'Oh, Beth, you live in cloud cuckoo land—you think everyone is nice and kind—just because you are—'

She flushed. 'I'm not—you make me sound super-human or whatever it is—'

He put his hand over hers. 'Beth, don't change. I like you just as you are—but you mustn't fret about this. As far as they are concerned you saw nothing. Least said, soonest mended—'

Beth sat there—knowing that the first thing she wanted to do was to go round to Minna and confront her—but what business was it of hers? Geoff was right—it had nothing to do with her.

'Come on, let's go to Harrods, shall we?'

The shock gradually wore off as they wandered round Harrods, where Beth bought a pair of shoes which cheered her.

'Too tired to walk down Bond Street?' Geoff asked. 'Might as well make a day of it—'

'Lovely,' she smiled back at him. Oh, what a day—if only she hadn't seen them—but she had. Today of all days. It was fate, something like that...

Once home, it was to live with the knowledge that Minna was probably having an affair with Laurie Featherstone, and she wished she hadn't known. No use pretending it was a business relationship— or they were friends, it was obvious they were lovers. They looked like lovers, she told herself. And where would they go for their secret assignations? To the company flat?

She must put it to the back of her mind. No good would come of dwelling on it, imagining... She must act normally when she saw either Minna or Bernadette.

Bernadette was not too difficult but how to face Minna?

Oh, forget it, forget it. As Geoff said, it was nothing to do with her. Nothing at all. Still...

Fix her mind on something else: Ian's wedding to Sophie in September. Of course, she had nothing to do with the arrangements for that, for it would be in France as Sophie was French, but they would be going over to Paris for the weekend and Beth was really looking forward to it.

She smiled when she remembered Ian— so sure had he been that he would remain a bachelor. It hadn't taken long. Six months he had known Sophie, and that was that. So another wedding in the family. Which just left Belinda.

She was far too immersed in her cooking and future projects—she had been so successful in her career, her heart and soul was in it.

'You said you would marry a farmer and have lots of children and make scones,' Beth reminded her.

'Did I say that? Well, chance would be a fine thing—I never seem to meet farmers, although I got round to the scones.' And she winked at her mother. 'Don't worry, I don't suppose I'll die an old maid.'

'Don't you dare!' Beth had said.

Still, she could kill Minna...

She couldn't remember where she was when the thought suddenly struck her: Minna should be in France in the month of July. She usually went at the end of June and stayed throughout the summer, and Beth had been surprised when she hadn't called in to say goodbye.

Chapter Eighteen

Two days later, plucking up courage, Beth telephoned Minna. There was no reply. The next day she rang again. Still no reply.

She knew that it would be against Geoff's wishes, but felt she had to. She and Minna had been friends since secretarial school—Beth simply had to talk to her.

But all thoughts of seeing her were shattered when she received a telephone call from Bernadette.

'Beth—will you be in today—any time? I have to see you. Could I come round?'

'Yes, of course, late-morning. Is anything wrong?'

'Oh, Beth, I should think there is! I'll be round just after eleven.' And she hung up.

Oh, please God, don't let Bernadette find out about Minna...

When she opened the door it was to find Bernadette in dark glasses, her raincoat pulled round her, a headscarf over her shining hair.

She almost fell against Beth when she came in, and she realised there was something seriously wrong.

'Bernadette, come in, my dear. What is it?'

She put an arm round her shoulders and half-led her into the kitchen, pulling out a chair for her.

Bernadette wasted no time. 'Laurie—he wants a divorce.' And she burst into uncontrollable sobbing.

A stab of sheer hatred for Minna went through Beth, until she realised that it need not be her friend's fault. Geoff was right—she must not jump to conclusions.

'Let me put the kettle on.' The usual panacea, she thought. A good hot cup of tea. But it did work—usually—and she was playing for time.

She got out the cups and saucers, allowing Bernadette to settle down and her own heart beat to subside before sitting down opposite her. Why did she feel so guilty? Bernadette was as white as a sheet, and quivering like an aspen leaf, shaking almost.

'What happened?' Beth asked quietly.

Bernadette swallowed a sob. 'He came back from the States last night—I'd expected him the night before, and phoned New York but he'd left some days before. Apparently he came back by ship, something he hasn't done for years. Jack took the car early—he must have driven down to Southampton. I'll kill him, that Jack—he must have known.'

'He'd have been under Laurie's orders,' Beth reminded her.

'Yes, but he rushed off, not telling me he wasn't going to the airport but to Southampton.'

'Anyway, what happened then?'

'The usual thing. Laurie had a drink and went upstairs to shower and change. Came down and had a whisky. I could see he wasn't in a good mood but that often happens if he's had a hard time over there.'

She took off her dark glasses to polish them, and Beth saw that her blue eyes looked red-rimmed, the freckles standing out on her nose. Even without makeup, her skin was smooth as a baby's.

She put them back on while Beth made the tea and covered the teapot and got out some biscuits.

'Have you had any breakfast?'

'Oh, I couldn't eat a thing,' Bernadette answered. 'I feel sick—sick to my stomach.'

Beth was sure she did. She waited, standing with her back to the sink, hands gripping her arms and thinking hard. My God, if Minna was at the back of all this...

'I said: "I thought you'd be back last night, but when I rang New York—" '

' "You rang New York?" he said, his face like a thundercloud. I know he doesn't like his movements being checked. "Who did you speak to?" '

' "Johnny Danesman—he said you'd left five days ago, that you'd had a reservation on the *Queen Elizabeth*. I got quite worried, it's so unlike you to come by the slow route." '

She didn't tell Beth she had had her first misgivings then—the fact that Laurie wasn't hurrying home—but had told herself she was worrying unnecessarily.

'I'd set dinner for eight-thirty so I served it up: melon, lamb chops—he likes English lamb, and doesn't like to talk while he's eating. But before I had a chance to serve the cheese, he pushed his plate aside, looked at me, and said: "Bernadette, I've something to tell you." Just like that—as cool as a cucumber.'

She took a deep breath. 'I don't know why, but my heart sank into my boots. It was so unlike him to talk like that, then out it came.'

' "I want a divorce," he said. As simple as that.'

'Oh!' And Beth's heart turned over.

'I think I gave a little scream, I was so shocked. It came out of the blue, you can't imagine...'

Beth found her fury rising as she thought

of the implications of this. Minna.

She poured out tea and pushed it towards Bernadette.

'Drink that while it's hot.'

Bernadette took the cup with shaking fingers and sipped the tea, then put it back in the saucer.

'I think I said: "What do you mean?" I know I got up and ran over to him but he pushed me away—not roughly but by this time I felt quite faint. I couldn't believe it.

' "Go and sit down," he said. "We have to talk about this. It's no sort of life—not for you or for me."

' "But I'm not complaining," I said. "Am I doing something wrong?"

'And then he told me—he'd met someone else. My God, I couldn't believe it! I was stunned. Another woman! Well, that got through, I can tell you!

'I yelled at him, shouted...I don't know what I said, Beth, but the upshot of it was, when I realised he wasn't answering back or arguing, I stopped and looked at him. He was toying with the bread on his side plate, not looking at me, not listening, and he was deadly serious.

'Then I said: "Who is she?" '

'But he wouldn't say—just that he wanted a divorce so he could marry her.

'Beth, I thought I'd go mad. Another

woman. I don't know, I'd never thought—oh, I expect he's been attracted to other women. After all, he is a very good-looking man, and quite a catch, but I never imagined that it would be so serious. Apart from anything else, he knows I am a Catholic and can't divorce.'

Beth hadn't thought about that side of it. This really was going to be a disaster.

'I went over to him, I put my arm on his shoulders and kissed his cheek—tried to kiss his mouth. I told him he couldn't mean it—after all we've been through together, building up a lovely home, a place in society.

'But he got up and went over to the cabinet, and poured himself another drink. He asked me to join him, quite politely, and at that I went over and struck the glass out of his hand, and he grabbed my wrist and said: "Now be careful, Bernadette—this isn't going to help." And I cried, and snuggled up to him—but he took no notice—didn't even comfort me—oh, it was cruel, cruel, Beth.' And she sobbed even more.

'Where is Annelise?' Beth interrupted quietly.

'She's in London. You know she's doing that secretarial course, and sometimes she stays overnight with Lucy—to save coming home on the train, oh, I'm glad she wasn't

279

at home, but then, he may not have said anything if she had been.'

'Well, he would have chosen another time if he really means what he says,' Beth said.

Somehow she wasn't surprised. She only knew that racing through her brain was the thought of Laurie Featherstone and Minna dining together—surely, surely not Minna? He couldn't divorce Bernadette to marry Minna? It was impossible—and what about Jimmy? Her heart began to race, as her anger against Minna grew.

'So he told you no more about the—other woman?'

'No—and neither will he. I know as much as I'm going to know.'

'How does he think he will get a divorce then if you won't divorce him?'

'He says I'm to divorce him, citing an unknown woman—imagine—and he will provide the correspondent.'

' "Over my dead body," I said. "I'll never divorce you—never—'

'He looked at me as though he hated me. I believe he does, Beth.'

Beth felt so sorry for her, sitting there with her world that she had so carefully built crumbling about her.

'Bernadette, I'm so sorry—you must have felt simply awful—but you must be strong. Where is he now?'

'Gone to the office—I must talk to him, I keep ringing the flat—but there is no reply—I expect he's at the office, but I daren't ring there—he'd kill me—and his secretary—Suzanne—I bet she's in it too, she adores him—oh, Beth, what am I going to do? I can't give him up to another woman, I can't...' She blew her nose.

'I used all the arguments,' she went on. 'I'm your wife, we have a daughter—what about Annelise—but it made no difference—he didn't say much more, I was the one who did all the talking, then he said, "I'm going up now—I shall sleep in the dressing room—will you lock up?" '

Her shoulders sagged.

'I paced up and down for hours, and when I got upstairs, I went straight to the dressing room and the door was locked. Against me. Can you imagine anyone doing that? Locking the door against me...' and she sobbed afresh.

'I didn't sleep all night,' she said. 'I heard him go to the bathroom and when he came down, I gave him his breakfast, I'd put my best housecoat on and made up my face, but you'd have thought I wasn't there. He ignored me, completely—picked up his briefcase when Jack rang the bell, and he'd gone—oh, Beth what am I going to do?'

Beth really didn't know the answer.

'Well, if I were you, I'd go home and carry on as usual—do you think he'll be home this evening?'

'I don't know—oh, Beth how could he do that—I can't bear it—suppose he never comes home again?' And then she looked grim. 'But he will, he won't leave the house and everything in my hands for long, that's for sure—but he'll have a fight on his hands, I can tell you. I haven't built him up and the house and garden for someone else to enjoy—'

Beth shuddered inwardly. This could be a very messy divorce if it ever came about, she thought. She couldn't quite imagine what would be the next move.

'Look, I should go home now, just in case he telephones or has some plans—and give me a ring after lunch—'

'Oh, could I? I have the hairdresser at three—and I expect Annelise will telephone—yes, I'd better get back now—'

'Take care, Bernadette—ring me if you need me and look on the bright side—if you can—'

Poor Bernadette, she thought, watching her get into her beautiful shiny pristine car. What a price she paid for all the work and effort she put into being Mrs Featherstone, only to have him turn round and want someone else—you read about these things, but until it happened to someone you knew...

I've never liked him, she told herself grimly, but then what did that matter? She wasn't married to him, thank God.

But Minna...on impulse she went to the telephone and picked up the receiver, but put it down again. Best not ring while she was in this frame of mind. Goodness knew what she'd say that she might regret.

By the time Geoff came in, there had been no word from Bernadette. When she told him, he whistled and seemed quite shocked.

'But she can't divorce, can she? She's a Catholic.'

'She won't agree to a divorce, but anything is possible. After all, Laurie isn't one. I've thought since this morning that this was almost inevitable when you think about it.'

'Oh, yes, no doubt about it, only a question of time. There's not a lot she can do if he's determined. Poor Bernadette,' he said. 'And the girl—what's her name?'

'Annelise. I can't imagine what she will feel about it, she's never appeared to have any time for her mother. For Laurie, well, I don't know—it would be awful if Bernadette lost her as well.'

'Oh, he'll leave her with her mother if he has a new lady, I'm sure, but a broken marriage is always sad, for whatever reason.'

'Geoff, you don't think,' she said tentatively, 'that Minna—'

He turned on her quite sharply. 'Beth, don't start imagining things or putting two and two together. There is no reason to suppose—'

She turned troubled eyes to his. 'But there is, he was dining with her.'

'Yes, but it doesn't follow that Minna is the reason for the break up.'

By the time they went to bed, there was no call from Bernadette, and in the morning, when Gina arrived, Beth decided that the best thing was to wait a little longer. Who knew what was going on at SAN REMO?

While Gina got on upstairs, clad in a very expensive dress which was miles too short for her and exposed her Italian knees to some disadvantage, Beth went off to her baby clinic. She loved this time, when the young mothers, so many of them unmarried these days, brought in their tiny bundles, dressed in every colour from navy blue to scarlet. They seated themselves round the room, nowadays held in the barn of the old farm which had been taken over by the council, and undressed their babies, wrapping them in a blanket while waiting for them to be weighed.

They were always delighted when they found the baby had gained weight, sometimes as much as ten ounces, especially those who were not breast fed. They always gained the most. It was written on their card, with the date and the amount of the increase. They were so proud of their babies, who cried at the tops of their voices, especially when they went on the scales.

Beth would take them from the mother, and lay them gently in the hollow, and often she would wonder what life could be like for a lot of these young mothers, some of them as young as sixteen, still at home with parents or alone in a council flat. Some of their own mothers were younger than Beth herself. She often wondered what the future would be because some of them had never had a chance. But mothers are the same the world over, and the proud look on their faces as they showed each other their offspring, changed their nappies, and burped them if they had been fed, was universal. It was a real young mothers' get together. They loved the clinic morning, and were very appreciative of the helpers there, even though, Beth thought, they probably feel we're as old as Methuselah.

It was always a satisfying morning, a few hours well-spent, but as she drove home she couldn't help wondering if there had been any message from Bernadette yet. She had scarcely been out of Beth's thoughts, but she could hardly go round to SAN REMO—her presence there might be superfluous.

Gus got up to greet her slowly, his clouded eyes staring up at her. 'Good boy,' she said, bending down and stroking him under the chin. He loved that. Through the front door came the strains of an Italian aria—thank God for Gina, she thought. She is such a treasure.

Closing the door behind her she hung up her jacket and went into the kitchen, where Gina was mopping the floor.

'Any messages, Gina?' she asked but Gina shook her head.

'Nothing, Madam-a,' the short dress clinging to her bottom as she bent over the pail of water and disclosing her generous thighs.

She had to wait until after lunch before her curiosity was satisfied, when Bernadette rang to ask her round. It was strange driving into a house of sadness after the successful times Beth had spent there.

Bernadette came to the door, she looked awful. Red rimmed eyes, and no make up, already she looked thinner than usual.

Beth kissed her. 'How are you?'

'Awful—I haven't slept a wink,'

'You must try to get some sleep, Bernadette—you're going to need your strength—you can't go on like this.'

'Annelise is coming home this evening—I rang the college and asked them to give her a message. Then she rang me back—and you know, Beth, she sounded quite kind, as if she knew all about it—'

'Did Laurie tell her, do you think?'

'I can't imagine it—still, I shall be glad to have her home.'

It would be strange, Beth thought, if this broken marriage was to be the cause of Bernadette and Annelise becoming closer.

Bernadette led the way into the kitchen. 'He came home last night—but he didn't stay. Collected some things from his office—not clothes, I noticed, but papers, that sort of thing. He stopped long enough for a drink—didn't want any dinner—said he hoped I wasn't going to be difficult—because he intended to get a divorce come what may—'

She made a pot of coffee, and they sat and drank it, without really noticing as they talked.

'But Bernadette—what will you do? If he is adamant about this—'

'He can be as adamant as he likes. I am not giving him up to another woman, and that's that. Sorry, Beth, wild horses wouldn't make me divorce him. He wants me to see a solicitor—and of course, I refused. I said to him "Laurie, until this affair has blown over—and I don't care how long it takes—I can wait—when you come to your senses—" '

Well, that didn't help, thought Beth.

'Even if it lasts longer than the others—I can wait—'

'Did you know he had other affairs?'

'No, but I suspected. An attractive man like Laurie is bound to be pursued by women, and he is very sexy, as you know.'

No, Beth thought, I don't know, but I suspect he is—he's just not my type.

She sighed now. 'Well, I hope you succeed, for all your sakes.'

'Oh, I can be patient,' Bernadette said. She seemed to have adjusted, Beth thought. Although she looked strained, she seemed to have reached a conclusion. Almost had the light of battle in her tear-drenched blue eyes.

'This is the first time he has ever mentioned divorce, though?'

'Well, this bitch has obviously caught him good and proper, but she'll find she's met her match in me, I can tell you. There won't be much left of her when I've finished. She'll find she has a battle on her hands.' And Bernadette's face was grim.

Beth's heart sank. Minna—please don't let it be Minna!

'Oh, yes!' Bernadette cried triumphantly. 'I am more than a match for any little floozie he likes to bring home. Here—in my home? My garden? He must be joking!' And she looked quite wild-eyed.

'Well,' Beth said hesitantly, 'I'd better be going—when will Annelise get home?'

'Some time this evening—early, I expect, after she finishes at the college. Oh, I'm really looking forward to seeing her, Beth.'

'Well, give me a ring. You know where I am if you need anything or someone to talk to.'

'Beth, you're a brick. Such a friend.' And suddenly she looked near to tears again.

'Don't forget,' Beth said, making her way back to the courtyard.

It was two days before she heard from her, and then it was a telephone call to say that Laurie had been home the night before, and they had talked about it. Annelise had, surprisingly, taken her mother's side, much to Laurie's disgust.

'You make a right pair,' he'd sneered.

'It's not that model girl, is it, Sandie Bliss?' Annelise had asked, and Bernadette had turned on her, horrified.

'You mean, you knew—you met her?'

'Yes, Daddy took me to lunch with her.

289

But she wasn't the only one, was she?' she asked.

'How dare you?' Bernadette had cried. 'Taking our daughter to meet your disgusting women!' Then was lost for words.

'Don't pull your histrionics on me, Bernadette,' he'd said. 'Nothing will make any difference anyway. I want a divorce, and what's more I'm going to have it!'

'Never!' Bernadette had screamed after him. 'I'll die before I agree.'

Beth put down the phone eventually. At least Bernadette had Annelise home to keep her company. She was pleased about that.

It was Sunday morning two weeks later when Bernadette called round after Mass while Beth was preparing Sunday lunch and Geoff was having a well-earned round of golf.

'Sure I'm not in the way?' She looked deflated, lost, a shadow of her former self.

'Where's Annelise?'

'I sent her off with some friends from church—she's gone home with them.'

She took off her gloves. 'Oh, Beth... That's it—it's all over!'

Beth stood open-mouthed. 'What do you mean—all over?'

Then Bernadette's fine nostrils flared, and she took a deep breath.

'He can have his divorce. She's welcome to him, whoever she is.'

'But why?' Beth asked. 'What changed your mind?'

'He called me a Goddamned Papist!' Bernadette said, outraged. 'Enough's enough, Beth.'

Chapter Nineteen

What an awful time that had been, when the Featherstones' divorce was underway and the house contents were being divided, for it was turning out to be a most acrimonious affair. Beth tried as far as possible to keep out of the way of arguments. It was not until the beginning of September that she telephoned Minna again, having tried several times throughout August, even calling round to the house. Mrs Bonnington answered when she rang.

Beth asked if Minna was there—and the housekeeper said she was sure she was, and went to fetch her.

She returned a few moments later.

'I can't seem to find her, Mrs Meldrum —possibly she's just popped out somewhere.' But she sounded embarrassed.

'Don't worry—I'll ring again later,' Beth said.

She was sure Minna had been there.

Twice more that week she tried, but there was no reply. It was strange that Minna had not been to see her before she left for France, which must have been a day or two after she had been lunching at the Ritz.

But now to concentrate on Ian and Sophie's wedding. Before they left for France Beth tried once more and Mrs Bonnington picked up the phone. 'She's gone up to town, with Mr Alders, I'll tell her you called, Mrs Meldrum.'

'I shall be away for a few days from tomorrow, Mrs Bonnington—we are going to Paris for Ian's wedding. Will you tell her?'

'Yes, of course. Have a good trip, and best wishes to the bride and groom.'

'Thank you.'

How odd not to have seen anything of Minna for so long. Yet was it? Was Minna avoiding her, and if so, why?

Well, she'd think no more about it until they got back from Paris. Jon and Laura were flying out, leaving the baby with friends who had a nanny, and Belinda was travelling down by car with her parents.

They set off at the crack of dawn and drove straight down to Folkestone, waiting at the terminal for the ferry. Already they'd noticed the increase in the number of people going abroad—gone were the old passenger ships, now they were all car ferries.

The channel looked smooth on this September day as the cars slowly took their turn to embark. Once on board they made for the restaurant where they had breakfast and sat back to enjoy the trip and the smooth crossing, for the sea was like a mill pond.

The French coast soon came into sight: Boulogne, a bustling port with a great cathedral in the background. Once upon a time blue-coated French porters would have swarmed over the boat and there would be the unmistakable smell of French cigarettes. That had changed now, but you always knew you had arrived in France.

One after another the cars left the ship and made for the road taking them out of the docks en route to their destinations.

They drove on the fast autoroute to Paris, Belinda at Geoff's side since she was a good map reader and knew the area outside Paris better than Beth, having worked in France for some months.

Ian had booked them into a small hotel quite near to where Sophie's parents lived, just six miles outside Paris. They had no need to go into the centre of the city, for the area was to the west. The fast route soon gave way to trees and farms, and then they were in a small town with its cobbled streets and square, the usual church and market place. Just outside the town was the development where Sophie and her parents lived, a very attractive area with blocks of apartments set in well-kept lawns with trees. Each apartment had huge picture windows opening on to a balcony. Opposite was the hotel, the Lion d'Or, and once parked in the garage at the back, Geoff telephoned Ian who drove across to welcome them and to see them safely booked in.

'Oh, this is great!' Belinda said, eyes shining. Her room overlooked the car park, which was laid out like a garden, looking beyond trees to a river where ducks swam quietly by and huge willows hung their heads, reflected in the clear water.

Geoff and Beth's room overlooked the front of the hotel and up the hill they could see Sophie's home. A wide stone bridge crossed the river gliding by. It was an idyllic spot.

'I've sent a car to the airport for Jon and Laura—I'd like to have gone, but there's been quite a bit to do here. I've booked a table tonight for dinner at eight-thirty—is that all right, Dad?'

'Splendid,' Geoff said.

Beth unpacked and put their things away, and presently she and Geoff took a walk outside along the river bank. They held hands. It was so quite and peaceful, with the clear water beneath them and the overhanging trees.

'It's an idyllic spot,' Geoff said. 'We

should come to France more often.'

Returning to the hotel, they found that Belinda had been checking out the dining room.

'Beautiful,' she said. 'Overlooking the river, with round tables all dressed in pink linen. It all looks lovely.'

'Let's hope the food is as good,' said Geoff.

They pulled the curtains and rested on the cool sheets, and Geoff fell asleep for an hour before they got up and bathed and got ready to greet their guests. Downstairs Jon and Laura would be waiting for them, Sophie and her brother Etienne, and her parents. Beth hoped they would be nice—warm and likeable.

Marie and Yves Durand turned out to be just what they had hoped. Madame was a little shy, her English was not very good, she explained, but her husband was very much in command of himself and eased her gently into the conversation. Sophie looked as adorable as ever, petite like her mother, with long black hair and large brown eyes, so dark they were almost black. She had a fine pale skin, slightly freckled, which only added to her attraction. Her brother Etienne, who was fourteen, observed the proceedings with polite curiosity.

The Durands were obviously fond of

Ian and happy to have him as a son-in-law. Marie Durand soon attached herself to Laura, asking about the baby which seemed to be the one topic on which she was voluble. After drinks in the bar, which broke the ice, it seemed not to matter who spoke English and who spoke French. They were led to their table, a large round one in the corner. As Belinda had told them, the decor was very pretty, with the dark green walls showing off the pink cloths and napkins, pink roses and sparkling glasses and cutlery. There were special flowers for their table, like wedding flowers.

'I say,' Belinda said, eyes wide. 'We could learn a thing or two here.'

The meal which followed was superb. It was difficult to choose, there was such a wide selection: oysters and mussels, and to follow lobsters or meat, game or fowl. Madame Tessier, the manageress, advised them and explained the wine, deferring to Sophie's father whom she obviously regarded as an expert.

Beth admired Madame Tessier, and was intrigued by her. Efficient and brisk, she seemed to miss nothing yet was kindness itself, smiling and pleasant, ordering her waiters to see that her guests lacked for nothing.

'Shouldn't mind employing her when I

get my own hotel,' Belinda said.

'Oh, is that what you want?' Ian asked her.

'Perhaps—I'm not sure yet,' Belinda answered. She was really enjoying herself. They were the last to leave the restaurant at midnight, and said their farewells before tottering up to bed to sleep soundlessly, mellowed by the wine.

As Geoff said, it was nice not to have to drive home, and all agreed it was the best meal they had ever had.

The wedding was to take place in the Mairie, and in the morning they walked across the road, for it was not far. Inside, on wooden benches, sat the Durand family, while they were shown to the other side.

There seemed to be a host of French relatives, and the Meldrum family group looked small by comparison.

Then Sophie appeared, looking so lovely in a short dress of white wild silk and a small matching pillbox hat. She carried a posy of white carnations tied with long blue ribbons. Beside her Ian looked very English, and so tall. Beth caught her breath. She felt very emotional watching the young couple, Ian and his little French bride, and prayed that they would be happy.

The mayor conducted the ceremony in French, although afterwards he made some jokes in English at which they all laughed. It was all over so quickly then Ian bent down to kiss Sophie. They signed the register, and Beth felt a small pang that it wasn't in an English church with all the usual traditions, but told herself it was all experience. She was delighted with her new daughter-in-law, and only wished they could have made their home in England. Perhaps they would one day? In the meantime, it was nice to have a link with France.

They all made their way back to Sophie's parents' apartment which was on the first floor. Inside it was spacious, and tables were laid out with a wonderful buffet. Waiters and waitresses were on hand with champagne and Beth took hers out on to the balcony where she could look down at the wide lawns and wonderful trees. Jon stood beside her. 'Happy?' he asked.

She turned to smile at him. 'Wonderfully, Jon,' she answered. 'It's all like a dream.'

It seemed strange to have no wedding cake but that was the way in France, as Sophie's father explained. A frequent visitor to England on business, he was well aware of the differences between the two countries. There were speeches from everyone, including French cousins, of whom there seemed to be a number, and well-dressed aunts. Beth was interested in the apartment which was tastefully furnished but not overdone. A collection of silver and glass was arranged in a unit with concealed lighting, and the drawing room, which was large, had a dining area in which the food was displayed. It must be nice, she thought, to overlook the gardens from that huge window, and one could sit out on the balcony there on summer evenings. She supposed a flat like this had its advantages, especially with that balcony.

Jon and Laura took their leave early to fly back home, but Geoff and Beth stayed on until the newly weds left for their honeymoon, which was being spent in the South.

Afterwards they sat and chatted to the French family, laughing together. Soon they were like old friends. They finally took their leave in the evening, going back to the Lion d'Or where they were to stay overnight before leaving in the morning for Paris. They intended to spend the day sightseeing and revisiting old haunts, as much as they could crowd into the time before leaving for home early on Monday morning.

Paris, Beth decided was as magical as ever. Of course it had changed, there were many new high-rise buildings since she had seen it last, but somehow, Paris was always Paris. Then a quick visit to the Louvre, and a walk up the Champs Elysees where they had coffee and a snack, knowing they were going to eat in the hotel in the evening. A swift visit, at Belinda's request to the Ile de la Cîte and Montmartre—so much to see and so little time to do it in.

'It would have been nice to spend another day,' Beth said.

'We'll come back,' Geoff promised. 'Of course, you and Belinda could stay on for a few days.'

'Bless you, absolutely not. Belinda?'

'No, thanks. We'll come back,' She said. 'After all, we have a reason to now, haven't we?'

It struck Beth forcibly and for the first time when she returned home that the boys had finally gone. Their rooms would no longer be used except for visits, and even Belinda seemed to be going through some sort of crisis when she announced her intention of moving herself to the top floor, where she could have a bedroom to sleep in and a sitting room of her own.

'But why?' asked Beth. 'You've got such a lovely room.' But she could see the set of Belinda's lips, and knew that that was what she wanted.

'Well, why not?' she said with forced

301

brightness. Better not to argue—Belinda had her reasons. She missed her brothers, both married now with wives of their own. They had been special to her for so long, and although Beth had no brothers or sisters, she could understand how Belinda felt.

That next week, she was determined to see Minna if she was home, and without telephoning first, walked Gus round to Green Lawns. She hoped Jimmy would not be there, for it would be difficult to have a long chat—and anyway, if Minna was out, she would have to try again.

But she was in, Beth could see her in a far corner of the garden, while Jimmy's car was not in the garage.

She called out and waved. Minna turned, standing up straight from a kneeling position, squinting to see who it was before slipping her hand into the pocket of her shorts and taking out her dark glasses.

Beth walked towards her.

'Gosh, it's been ages. Sorry, am I interrupting? I can see you're busy.'

'No, glad of a break.' And Minna took off her gardening gloves. 'How are you? Long time no see.'

Beth felt that the atmosphere was tense or was it her imagination? The conversation was stilted, to say the least.

'Hi, Gus.' Minna stooped down to pet him, and Gus put out a paw—he adored Minna. 'Come into the house. I'm glad you called—I've got a little something for Ian and Sophie. Why didn't you tell me they were getting married?'

'I haven't seen you,' Beth said. 'I phoned a couple of times.'

'Did you?'

'But you were out.'

'Well, you know how it is. I've been busy.'

Not at all the conversation they usually had, Beth thought. It was unusually polite.

Beth waited while Minna disappeared upstairs and came down again with a wrapped present.

'Here, for the newly weds.'

'Oh, Minna how nice of you.' Beth took the prettily wrapped parcel.

'Glass of wine?' Minna asked.

'Why not? Let's drink to Ian and Sophie.'

Minna disappeared into the house and Beth sat down by the French windows, watching Gus ambling about the garden, nosing here and there among the shrubs. But Minna wouldn't mind, she would forgive an old dog where she wouldn't a human.

'Here we are, then,' she said. How agreeable she was being, Beth thought grimly. As well she might...

'So—here's to the happy couple,' Minna said, pouring out a glass and handing it to Beth. 'And how've you been?'

It was strange really, Beth thought. She had imagined going in and facing Minna, telling her what she thought of her in no uncertain terms, but here she was drinking a glass of wine, all thoughts of the Ritz luncheon forgotten—or at least temporarily.

'You went to the wedding, Jimmy said.'

'Yes, it was lovely, and we stayed at a dear little hotel where the food was super.'

She described it all to Minna, who lit one cigarette after another without any of her usual caustic comments.

'So what other news?' she asked, drawing on her cigarette as if it were her last.

'Belinda's moved herself upstairs to the top floor. I think she's missing the boys.'

'When will you stop thinking of them as the boys? They're married men now,' Minna said shortly.

'Don't you think of Hamish as a boy? I think I always will. How is he by the way?'

'Got a girlfriend, met her at university. She's from Yorkshire—very down-to-earth. He brought her to France. I like her, though.'

'Oh, I can't imagine it—bless him,' Beth said warmly, and then before her heart could beat any faster, added abruptly: 'You heard that Bernadette is divorcing Laurie Featherstone?'

Minna inhaled deeply before throwing the cigarette on to the lawn.

'Mmm,' she said. 'Not before time, I imagine. Gus! what are you doing?'

She's playing for time, Beth thought. 'What do you mean?'

'Oh, come on, Beth. He's been playing around ever since they were married.'

Beth thought she would burst before she said: 'I saw you lunching at the Ritz with Laurie in July. It was my birthday.'

'Did you get my card?' Minna asked.

'Yes, of course I did—thank you. I just wanted you to know I saw you.'

'So?' Minna asked.

'Well,' Beth began. 'I was shocked.'

'Well, you would be, wouldn't you?' Minna asked, coolly lighting yet another cigarette.

'Minna, how could you!'

'How could I what? Have lunch with Laurie Featherstone?'

'You know what I mean.'

'Sleep with him, you mean? Quite easily. He's a nice guy—and available.'

'Didn't you think of Bernadette?'

'Good Lord, no, why should I? If it

wasn't me it would be some other lady—and he is very good company and knows how to treat a woman.'

'Not his wife, though,' Beth said tersely.

'Well, she's a fool,' said Minna.

'How could you? I mean, you know them—socially. You've been to their house.'

'What's that got to do with anything?' Minna asked, taking off her glasses to polish them.

'Oh, Minna!' Beth hesitated only briefly before going on: 'Don't you feel in the least bit sorry for her?' She wondered how to put her next question. 'You're not the woman—I mean he's not divorcing Bernadette because of you, is he?'

And Minna laughed out loud before putting her glasses back on.

'You must be joking! I wouldn't have him as a gift.'

Beth found herself heaving a sigh of relief.

'I still think it's jolly rotten of you.' It was what she would have said when they were at secretarial school together.

'Look, Beth, he's a nothing. Not worth a thought.'

'He is to Bernadette. Think what this means to her.'

'That's her fault. How could she hope to keep a man like that?'

'He married her.'

'More fool him. She was necessary to his plan. After that—kaput!'

'Well, Minna, how about Jimmy? Don't you mind hurting him?'

And that did strike home. She got up and turned her back on Beth.

'What about Jimmy?'

'It's not fair on him.'

Minna swung round. 'And what would you know about it?'

She looked furious.

'Why do you think I sleep around? Why do you think I encourage other men? Why do I have to turn to other men? Eh?'

Beth was shocked, too shocked to answer.

'Because Jimmy doesn't want me.' And Beth's face drained of colour.

'Shocked, are you? Surprised? You may well be. You think he indulges me, gives in to me, I can have everything I want... Well, I can, but not Jimmy. He does all that because of guilt—guilt, I tell you.' And she hovered on the brink of outrage and tears. Beth was too stunned to say or do anything.

'I thought you'd be surprised,' Minna sneered. 'Wonderful Jimmy, kind Jimmy.'

Beth found her voice. 'Has—' She swallowed. 'Has he got someone else?'

'Not to my knowledge, he's just not interested in me. But—well, I love him.

307

Poor sod, I always have. But it's hard, Beth. I'm normal, I have the usual desires of a woman—but what would you know about it, anyway? You're so protected in your dream world, everything's all right for you, isn't it? Loving husband, three lovely children—you live in cloud cuckooland. There's a whole world going on out there, Beth, where people aren't happy, are desperate, long for love and affection. But what would you know about that, eh?'

Beth sat still, shocked to the core. She couldn't take it in.

Minna began to simmer down. 'Anyway, I saw you when you came into the restaurant. I've been wondering when you'd say something.'

'Oh, Minna!' Beth found her voice. 'No wonder you kept out of my way.'

'I thought I'd wait for you to cool down.'

'It doesn't make any difference now,' Beth said, 'for whatever reason.'

'Christ!' Minna bent down to pick up her cigarettes which she had dropped. 'When will you grow up? You're still eighteen in your mind. You think everything is lovely.' Her voice was scathing. 'No one is above reproach, but I can tell you, Beth, one of these days you'll get such a shock. Nobody's perfect—even your own husband.'

There was a silence you could cut with a knife.

Beth found her voice. Her face was deathly pale.

'What do you mean by that?'

'Nothing, nothing—I'm just trying to tell you that no one is perfect, that's all.'

But Beth had heard enough. She couldn't take any more.

'Gus! Here, boy. We're going home.'

'Look, Beth, I didn't mean that...'

But Beth was going home, to where she felt safe. Home to Chantry Gate.

Chapter Twenty

What had Minna meant? Beth worried over it, and when Geoff came in from surgery, tired as usual, for it had been another long day, she looked hard at him, trying to see in his face evidence that he wasn't as perfect as she had always thought.

He was a doctor, she told herself, subject to more rules than most men, but would he...had he...?

He was dear to her, a fine husband and father, a gentle man, a kind man. Was Minna just casting random aspersions, hitting back because she'd been hurt?

She decided the best thing she could do would be to forget the whole thing, her interview with Minna, the things they had said, put it at the back of her mind. She would never feel the same towards Minna—hadn't since she saw her with Laurie Featherstone. Neither would she entirely forget what Minna had said about Geoff...but it was all water under the bridge. She couldn't change anything now.

Adapting to a life without the boys and Belinda who was away from home so much, led her to find different things to do. A literary circle, her baby clinic, the hospital services and visiting, the occasional antiques fair...but she needed no further furnishings for the house, and had lost a lot of her old interest in sales except for finding the odd teapot or two. The garden seemed to take up most of her time, and she found this therapeutic. She could lose herself once she was out there.

Occasionally she took a day off and went up to town, or she and Geoff would drive out into the country, to Henley or Oxford for lunch, when he had his day off. They seemed to live at a slower pace now, even talked of moving to a smaller house, but each of them knew it would be the most difficult thing to do—they both loved Chantry Gate so. And it had been a good house to them, a kind house, and they looked forward to having grandchildren to stay and to play in the garden.

One day in January, Kate Rowlands telephoned.

'Beth, would you like to have lunch with me today?'

'What are you doing at home?' she asked.

'Mummy is coming back today—you know she's been staying down in Sussex with Fran while David is away? She's due back this afternoon sometime after lunch and I don't like her to come into an empty house after being away, so I've taken the day off.'

What a good daughter she was, Beth thought.

'Yes, I'd love to,' she said now.

'I thought we might try that new place in the village, the menu looks interesting.'

'Lovely idea, I haven't been there yet. What time?'

'I'll pick you up around twelve-thirty—is that all right?'

'Yes, that's fine. I'll be ready.'

She found herself looking forward to it, it would make a change from social work and gardening.

Beth heard Kate's car come down the drive, and was ready with her keys. She locked the front door, waving to Gus who sat in the hall and had hoped he was going too, and got into the passenger seat. Kate looked elegant in fawn slacks and a leather jacket, while Beth had wrapped herself up in her navy blue cashmere coat—a present from Geoff at Christmas.

It was cold but a nice day, and there was a pink sky with ice-cold translucent patches of blue and a few small black clouds that now and again allowed the sun to appear.

'I'm glad Mummy has a nice day for driving back. She'll leave early so as to arrive before it gets dark. Are you warm enough?' asked Kate. 'I can turn the heater up.'

'No, I'm fine,' Beth said, and stole a sidelong glance at Kate, for whom she had a soft spot. She knew only too well that underneath the hard shell, Kate had a warm heart—for her mother, at any rate. Knew, also, that if only Sheila would give in and move away to something smaller, like a town house or a flat, it would be the signal for Kate to do her own thing, get her own flat, for she was not going to desert Sheila all the time she stayed in that house, although Beth knew she wouldn't have admitted it.

'Has your mother really been away a week? It seems only yesterday that she went.'

'Yes. David comes back tomorrow.' They were stuck at traffic lights just outside the village. 'You know where he's been, do you?'

'No.'

'Skiing, he's been to Les Arcs—apparently he loves to ski and Fran encourages him.'

'Why didn't she go with him?'

'Hates the thought of winter sports. "I'd rather stay at home and watch Coronation Street," she said. Can you wonder that I get impatient with her?'

Beth smiled. They were as different as

chalk from cheese, those two girls.

'You'd think she'd want to go to keep an eye on him, even if she didn't join in—after all, après ski is good fun. And I wouldn't leave him out there unaccompanied with all those designing young girls if he were my husband.'

'Have you been? Do you ski, Kate?'

'Yes, I love it, but I don't get much time, and between you and me, I don't like to leave Mummy—oh, Beth, I wish she'd get a flat, either in town or near Fran.' And she sighed. 'I know she's put down some roots here, in which case perhaps she could get a garden flat locally. Then again, she could come nearer to town to be with me. It seems so pointless to run that big house with just the two of us in it, and I get fed up with the journey to and from town.'

'Perhaps she will,' Beth said. Kate had her sympathy.

'She won't. It's the home that she and Daddy loved, you know the sort of thing—and it's been a long while now. It really is time she adjusted better. Well, here we are.'

She pulled up outside the new little trattoria, pleased that there was a parking space. 'That's a bit of luck, isn't it?' she asked, dark eyes sparkling. 'Now, let's see what it's like inside.'

Beth followed her into the small but inviting restaurant which was immaculately kept, with little tables and snowy white cloths and a narrow vase on each table containing a single spring flower.

They were shown to a table in the window, which suited them, and their coats were taken and hung in a corner.

'Would you like a drink first?' the waiter asked them in a strong Italian accent.

Kate raised her eyebrows to Beth.

'Not for me, but you go ahead, Kate—I'd like some wine with lunch.'

'Me, too,' Kate said. 'Perhaps you'd bring your wine list—or shall we have a glass of house red? I'm driving, so I don't want too much.'

'Super,' Beth said. 'Now.' And she picked up the menu.

'I say, nice starters—and pasta of all kinds. This might be good, Beth, and quite cheap.'

They studied the menu and Beth chose thinly sliced mozzarella cheese and tomatoes while Kate had mussels.

'I love them,' she explained, 'but we never have them at home—Mummy won't touch them.'

'And to follow?'

They both chose cannelloni with green salad, and sat back to await the wine.

'Did Mummy tell you about David's

315

father dying?' Kate asked.

'Yes, she told me. You went to the funeral, didn't you?'

'Yes, but did she tell you all about it? Beth, you wouldn't believe it!'

'Why, what happened?'

'If my sister hasn't become the definitive Yiddisher momma, then I don't know who has!'

Beth laughed.

'The mourners wail, Beth, and if you had seen Fran, wailing away—especially when they carried in her father-in-law's hat on a cushion.

'It's a tradition, apparently. You should have heard her, holding on to David, weeping and wailing. Honestly, I was so embarrassed.'

Beth bit her lip. 'But, Fran, it's all part of being David's wife, a good wife, going along with his traditions.'

'Come on, Beth! She's not yet taken on the Jewish faith—although,' Kate said grimly, 'I bet she will one day.'

'I wouldn't be a bit surprised.'

They sipped the red wine, which was rich and fruity and tackled their starters which arrived promptly.

'Do you hear from the newly weds in France?'

'Yes, they write quite often, which is nice, or we telephone—we keep in touch, that's the main thing. Jon tells us baby Toby has six teeth.'

'I never felt I wanted to have children,' Kate said slowly, competent fingers tackling her mussels then dipping into the bowl of water provided. 'Funny, isn't it? Mind you, chance would be a fine thing. No one has asked me to marry them, although that doesn't seem to matter today. Strangely enough, I wouldn't want a child out of wedlock. I expect that sounds old-fashioned to you, but it's true. Yes, it's always been all or nothing with me. I love Fran's children, though, love to see them—but that's as far as it goes.'

When they had finished the first course, Beth sat back.

'So who is the latest boyfriend?' she asked.

'I can't give you his name. Suffice to say that he has a show running in the West End, and I adore him.' Singer, actor, producer, impressario? Beth wondered.

Kate sighed. 'I expect it will end up like all the others and he'll go back to his wife—although in this case they haven't lived together for three years. But they've never divorced.'

'Oh, Kate, couldn't you find a nice, unattached man?' Beth cried.

'You're like all married women, they always want a girl to get married, tie up the ends, make a neat job of it—but, seriously, chance would be a fine thing. They're always married, the nicest ones anyway, stands to reason.' Kate stopped speaking, as their main course arrived, piping hot and delicious, and the salad was fresh.

'Dressing, *Signora?*' one waiter asked, while the other hovered over Beth with the pepper mill.

'By the way, I was sorry about Bernadette, I like her—jolly rotten. But he was a swine, wasn't he? To tell you the truth, I thought at one time your friend might be the one involved. You know, what's her name—Hamish's mother, the artist?'

Beth swallowed. 'Minna?'

'Yes, Minna Alders. I saw her with him once but she didn't see me—coming out of the lift at Claridges.'

'Really?' Beth's voice was faint.

'Well, it's not really my business. Still, this new lady friend, the cause of all the trouble, is American, so I'm told.'

Beth was avid for news.

'Really?'

'A model—years younger than him. There was a photograph of them in one of our files. Gorgeous girl. She's over here apparently, just waiting for the divorce to come through so they can marry. At least, that's the gossip.'

Beth really didn't care who the new woman was so long as it wasn't Minna.

When they were served with coffee, Kate became thoughtful.

'What is Bernadette going to do after the divorce? Move out, I suppose?'

'Oh, yes, the house will be sold. It's on the market now so I'm told.'

'Not going back to Canada?'

'No, oddly enough, that doesn't seem to be the plan. Imagine having to face that awful sister!'

'God, yes! You know what I've been thinking, Beth? She's such an expert on entertaining and etiquette, that sort of thing, I think she should write a book on it: hostessing, cooking, presenting, how to do this and that. You know what I mean. It's terrible to waste all that expertise.'

'Oh, Kate, what a good idea! Do you think she could?'

'Well, I wouldn't mind giving her a hand—I've lots of publishing contacts skill, and after all, she does know her onions as it were. Or something else—she could open a restaurant.'

'That's a bit ambitious, isn't it? But what an idea!'

'Well, she knows all about it, presentation and cooking, doesn't she? I've always been impressed with the way she goes about things. She's such a perfectionist.'

'Do you know, I think you're right,' Beth said. 'Shall I broach it to her, do you think?'

'We could mention it to Mummy first,' Kate said. 'See what she thinks. Beth, will you have a sweet?'

The waiter had appeared with the sweet trolley. 'No, thanks, I'm afraid I've done rather well.'

'No, thank you,' Kate told him, 'but we would like coffee.'

They left half an hour later, well satisfied with the meal.

Kate dropped her outside the front door. 'Thanks for the lunch,' Beth said. 'It made such a break.'

'Thanks for coming. I'll give you a ring about you know who,' she called out, and drove away up the drive next door.

A month later, Sheila, Beth and Bernadette met for lunch in Beth's kitchen. It was a freezing cold day in February, and they were grateful for the warmth of the Aga and the huge tureen of soup Beth was keeping hot.

Bernadette was a shadow of her former self, painfully thin, her eyes enormous, huge in her small face which had lost its soft rounded beauty, and now showed sharp cheekbones and angular lines. Once it was over, Beth consoled herself, and the divorce through, Bernadette would regain her strength and gradually pick herself up again. She hated to see her looking like this.

'It is good of you girls to take such an interest in me,' she said. 'I didn't know I had so many good friends. I must say, I think Kate was a brick, going to all that trouble. I have to tell you, I am definitely interested. I like the idea of writing a book. Does she really think I could get it published?'

'When Kate decides on something, she usually does it,' Sheila said. 'She has lots of strings to pull, knows the right people, publishers, that sort of thing, and quite frankly, I don't see why it wouldn't work.'

'Well, I did have lots of training in Canada and over there much more care is taken over the presentation of meals, the dressing of the table, the approach to the whole thing. I went through the very best courses in Canada, the USA and France—my parents saw to that.' And she smiled ruefully. 'A fat lot of good it did me.'

'But it will stand you in good stead for the future,' Beth said. 'We need that sort of thing over here—it's time we had a cookery revolution.'

'I must say I agree, I think British

cooking could be great, but the thing that worries me is how I go about writing a book? I haven't the faintest idea how to get it together.'

Beth ladled out the soup, and they unfolded their large napkins.

'Oh, this smells good,' Sheila said. 'I would leave it to Kate—she has someone in mind, I think, who would help you tackle it and put it together.'

Bernadette laid down her spoon. 'You know, you have all been so kind.'

'Nonsense,' Beth said stoutly, 'it's the least we can do. You've been through a rough time and we have had pleasure enough from you in the past.'

'Tell me about Annelise,' Sheila said. 'I was surprised—I mean—'

'You were surprised that she's staying with me instead of going with Laurie? Well, I'm delighted naturally. He is being very generous over it, I must say. I expect the new girl in his life is not so keen on having a grown-up stepdaughter,' she said wryly. 'Anyway, for whatever reason, she's staying with me.'

'Good,' Sheila said. 'I'm glad.'

'And if I am honest, I'll admit it's not only because of me. You see—' she hesitated. 'She has met a young man from our church.'

'Ohhhh,' they both said in unison.

'And you know what love is—they're dotty about each other. He's very nice, Irish, as handsome as all get out, comes from a large family and I don't know what kind of future he has in front of him. But as long as he takes care of her, and is honest and trustworthy, I don't mind. Of course, they won't get married for a long time—she's still young—and she might change her mind, but I'm looking forward to meeting his family.'

'What is she doing at the moment?' Sheila asked.

'Well, you know she did every kind of course at Laurie's instigation? He insisted she did something with her life. She went through a secretarial course, cookery course, flower arranging, you name it. At the end of the day, she says that a florist's shop has the most appeal. She's working in town at that place in Piccadilly—a very junior junior, but she seems to like it. She comes home every evening, and from what she says, loves every aspect of of it and hopes one day to have a florist's shop of her own. You could have knocked me down with a feather because I just didn't see her doing that—it's quite hard work and cold—ugh!' Bernadette shivered. 'Especially in this weather. And after a time she will have to learn to go to market—very early, so I imagine at that point she may leave home and get something of her own in London. I'm not looking forward to that. Still, we'll wait and see what happens.'

'You have a great touch with flowers,' Beth said, 'she probably takes after you.'

'If I'd been told about this at one time, I would never have believed it.'

It's surprising, Beth thought, how one changes. If she had been told all that time ago that she would become fond of Bernadette, she would have pooh-poohed the very idea. People took some knowing. Her father used to say: Never judge a sausage by its overcoat, and it was true. Sometimes people had unexpected depths.

And other people, she thought grimly, are like chameleons—like Minna. They do unexpected things, things that you wouldn't imagine. But then, that was life. One long lesson and you never gave up learning.

'More soup?' she asked brightly.

'Yes, please,' they said.

Chapter Twenty-One

Beth put down the blue album and picked up the red one. Really, she should be going to bed with so much to do tomorrow, but somehow, although she had been on the go all day, she wasn't in the least bit tired. If she went to bed, she probably wouldn't sleep.

Opening the album at the first page, she gave an involuntary smile. Ah, Belinda's wedding—how lovely she looked, and so young, in cream wild silk. 'Can't wear white, Mummy,' she'd said, 'no good for my colouring.' And she had looked so pretty with her dark hair and that beautiful Carrickmacross lace veil which had come to her through Geoff's family. Harry, her barrister husband, so tall beside her, and the small pageboys, Toby and Ben, Beth's grandchildren, and one grown-up bridesmaid, Annelise Featherstone. Her own wedding had taken place a few weeks later.

And here were the boys, Jon and Ian, and their wives, Sophie elegantly pregnant. And there was Gina—bless her heart, how wonderful she looked. She had bought what must have been one of the very few absolutely new outfits she had ever worn, a suit in navy and white silk. 'Italians always wear silk on special occasions, *madam-a*,' she had said, and that lovely hat—why, she looked like a film star. Many guests had asked: 'Who is she? That attractive woman over there in the hat.'

'A dear friend of the family,' Beth had said, which indeed she was. And now Gina lived in a council flat of which she was so proud, it did you good to see the pleasure on her face, black eyes shining like jet as she showed you round.

'I entitled, madam-a,' she had said when she told Beth of her plans. 'I work in this country twenty-five years—I entitled.' So she had gone to the council offices to be put on the list, and sure enough, two years later the flat had come up.

Once Beth had asked her, 'What did you do before you came to England, Gina?'

'I look after two little girls, four and six. They daughters of diplomat, you know? Ambassador in Rome, you know? I go everywhere with them—all over Europe. I stay in lovely 'otels, very rich, very nice...beautiful 'otels. You go, eh? Taormina—ahh, you go, eh?'

Imagine, thought Beth, Gina with those two little girls, staying in luxury hotels.

'Why did you come to England, Gina?'

'I like,' came the terse reply.

'I mean, weren't you sorry to leave the family?'

'They grow up,' Gina said. 'I like family—I like this-a family, the boys, Belinda. I like.'

And Beth knew you wouldn't get any more out of her than that.

And here was Bernadette, restored to her former beauty but with a new assurance that was no longer a pretence, rising to a challenge. She really had matured, was in charge of her own life now as the owner of an agency for maids and domestic help. It was known that if Mrs Featherstone sent you someone, you could bet she would be good, her standards were so high. She was thinking of opening another in Windsor, and her two books were even now available in shops and libraries: *The Etiquette of Entertaining* and *Cooking the French Way*. Now she was working on one on how to plan the perfect kitchen.

Well, if anyone knew, Bernadette did.

And here was Kate, looking so elegant, still single. Possibly she would never marry now. Even though she had her own flat, she still spent most weekends at home with Sheila—she liked to keep an eye on her. And here was Fran with her son and two daughters, plump, pretty Fran, as happy a wife as you would find anywhere.

Beside her, tall, dark-haired, good-looking, was her wealthy financier husband. Beth sighed.

She glanced in the corner, where wrapped and ready to be taken away was the large azalea plant, bereft now of flowers, which Ian and Sophie had given them when she and Geoff left them after that wonderful holiday in Normandy—the holiday which had ended in tragedy.

Whether she wanted to or not, she knew she was going to re-live that journey back from France, the day she and Geoff had crossed from Dieppe to Newhaven on the car ferry after a wonderful holiday with the children.

She had had no sign, no way of knowing. One of her first resentful reactions had been that she'd had no warning. The sunset over the channel had been spectacular, and when the sun set, the sky had turned to a brilliant red streaked with purple then black. But darkness quickly fell when they were on the other side of the channel and drove up from Newhaven, skirting Brighton on their way. At one point, thinking the azalea had fallen over, Geoff suggested they stop and make sure it was safe. He pulled up while she checked it was still upright, giving him a glass of water from the bottle of still water they kept in the car. It had been a hot summer and the evening was still very warm.

It was dark now, lights flashing round them on the motorway, when Geoff suddenly said, 'I think it's time you took over,' in such a way that she glanced at him swiftly and saw that he was trying to ease himself out of his seat belt. Her first reaction was one of horror—what was he doing? And for her to take over at that point was odd. 'Pull over!' she had cried. 'Pull over!' And he did so. His foot was still on the brake as it came to a stop. 'I ache all over...' And he had fallen back as she breathed into his open mouth, pummelling his chest, breathing again, knowing deep down that it was too late. Incredibly he had gone. It was all over in a matter of seconds.

Getting out of the car, she was surprised that she could still stand, that she didn't collapse. Strength came from somewhere— waving to passing motorists who couldn't see her in the dark and were not supposed to stop anyway, the flash of red lights, oncoming traffic, walking to the nearest telephone, turning back in case someone ran into the back of the car, going on again. If only they had a car phone. Going back once more, listening above the roar of the traffic for a heartbeat. She felt so alone—more alone than she had ever been in her life.

At some point, she had no idea how long, before she reached a phone, a man stopped.

'What's the problem?'

'The car back there—my husband, I think he's dead.' Was she really saying those words? Her lips were ice-cold and stiff with terror.

'Get in!' was all he said, and backed up on the hard shoulder.

And then it all happened: the ambulance came, she was taken to the hospital in a police car—did they always go as fast as this? The little room where they told her, the telephone calls to Jon and Ian and Belinda. They put her up in an hotel, to await the arrival of the children in the morning, and she paced the floor all night while a storm raged, thunder and lightning flashing. The room was lit up like daylight, and she, who normally couldn't bear storms, was hardly aware of it.

Then the children's arrival, their faces, the tragedy of children losing a father, the shock, the terrifying aloneness of it all.

The coroner came to the hotel the next morning. 'The cause of death was an aneurysm.' He explained it to her, as Jon did. It could have happened at any time, anywhere.

Her breath caught in her throat as she relived that terrible time, as she had done a thousand times since. Eventually she came to think it was wonderful for Geoff who would have hated to be ill, but so awful for those left.

Everyone had rallied round, the children so supportive at a time like this, despite their own grief. Jon and Ian giving practical help, Belinda urging her to give vent to grief—'It's all part of the therapy of coping with loss'—and then to emerge on the other side, chastened in the face of death. You were not the same person again. How could you be?

'I can't stay here in Chantry Gate,' had been her cry.

Bernadette had been a tower of strength. Supportive, generous with her time, nothing was too much trouble for her. And Sheila had been through it herself, of course, the shock of sudden death.

From Minna there was nothing. Of course, she might not have known, but it had been in the English newspapers—Beth had thought she would have heard.

For Minna had moved away. Some months after the Featherstone's divorce, she had gone to France, and never returned. Had obviously made her home there, and when one day Beth saw the pictures of Green Lawns in the agent's window, she felt at once a sense of shock followed by sadness. What an end to a friendship that had lasted so long! But neither of them had made a move.

And Jimmy—where was he? Disappeared into the unknown?

But that was something else.

One day, one bitterly cold day in the New Year, the telephone rang and she went to answer it.

'Beth?'

She knew in an instant who it was.

'Jimmy!' And her heart seemed to melt as though there had been ice around it for too long. 'Where are you?'

'In London, I've just got back from New York.'

'How are you?'

It seemed such a trite conversation.

'What's more to the point—how are you?'

'I'm fine, Jimmy.'

'Are you? Are you really, Beth?'

'Yes, really.'

'Someone told me months afterwards and I didn't want to contact you and bring it all back to you. You must have been devastated.'

'How's Minna?'

'I've no idea. We divorced last year.'

'Oh, Jimmy!'

'Well, it was always on the cards. She

332

has a new man in her life now.'

There was silence for a moment.

'Hamish is married—he was in New York with me. Beth, may I come to see you?'

Her heart fluttered in her throat.

'Oh, Jimmy, I—'

'Please, Beth. I have to talk to you.'

She hesitated, playing for time—time to get her thoughts adjusted. 'You've taken me by surprise, let me think about it. Can you leave me your telephone number? I shall probably be moving soon.'

'Where—where will you go?'

'Locally, if the sale of Chantry Gate comes off. I have a buyer—but who knows these days?'

'But to leave Chantry Gate—is that what you want?'

'Oh, yes,' she said firmly. How to explain that Chantry Gate was her home with Geoff, the family home. She still expected him to be there at every turn, as he had always been there. Now, with Geoff gone, the children married, her life had changed. Nothing would ever be the same again. It was time to leave.

Jimmy was silent for a moment.

'Yes, all right, I'll give you my office number. You can get me there most days. But Beth?'

'Yes?'

'Don't leave it too long.'

She smiled. 'I won't. Goodbye, Jimmy.'

And now, she thought, the time had come. Jon had been right when he'd said: There is a time—you'll know when it is—when you can sit down and feel free to do your own thing.'

Well, she was free now—free to write, for that was what she was going to do. And now she had all the time in the world.

Leaving the Victorian bathroom, she made her way to the bedroom and tucked herself up in the large bed, realising how exhausted she was.

Thirteen months, she thought. Sometimes it seems like years, sometimes a few days. And finally she slept.

Chapter Twenty-Two

Number eight Flag Walk was the last small town house in a row of four—the end one, with a little bit more garden, the corner of which Beth had filled with bulbs and the little strawberry tree cutting, a mahonia 'Charity' which was so wonderful in early spring, the old Chantry Gate hydrangea, which had come via SAN REMO—already pale green buds were bursting on the stems. And, of course, the squirrel-proof bird feeder.

Inside the little house she had used all her inventiveness and experience to make it look larger: mirrors to reflect space, pale curtains, pale carpet, and the few pieces of furniture she had saved from Chantry Gate before she left. The children had been so glad of the larger pieces.

The house had a nice entrance hall, and a very large sitting room, L-shaped, which served as a dining area too. The kitchen was a dream, with every known new appliance, which wasn't to say that she didn't yearn sometimes for the Aga. Upstairs were two good-sized bedrooms; she had chosen for herself the smaller of the two. There were fitted cupboards and an en-suite bathroom, while the second bedroom she turned into a study so that books lined the walls. She could never give up her collection of books, garnered over the years from auctions and secondhand book shops, much loved and cherished. She had bought a double sofa bed, which could be used for sitting or sleeping once let down. A large armchair, which also served as a bedchair, and grandchildren would have to manage with sleeping bags, she thought.

It was as well not to compare it with Chantry Gate, but to adapt and accept the fact that her life had totally changed. That way it became tolerable.

She looked forward each day to her spell of writing. She used a typewriter, but Jon had been showing her how to use a word processor whenever she went down to stay with them in Wiltshire, and she felt almost ready to embark.

She found the writing came easily, and once finished, if no one wanted it, well, at least she would know she had tried. There was a time, a right time. She had been far too busy in her old life to do justice to both writing and bringing up a family. To say nothing of being a busy doctor's wife.

Well, the time for writing was now—and she wondered furthermore what her family and closest friends would think if they knew she had been in love with another man all her married life.

Of course, she had loved Geoff—no woman could help loving him in that sense of the word. He was a charming man, a good doctor, a good husband and father. But she had never been *in* love with him.

The love of her life was Jimmy Alders, always had been, but never in all those years with Geoff had she been unfaithful to her husband in word or deed. Well, one kiss, but that really didn't count.

She thought back to her single days, when she and Minna had been together all the time, sharing the flat, doing everything together. She had needed a leader, and Minna an acolyte—for whatever reason they were drawn together, the attraction of opposites.

They enjoyed life, going to shows, concerts and museums, and never seeming to lack boyfriends. They joined the tennis club in the local park, and in the summer months spent most of their time there.

They had been working for two years when an old school friend of Minna's, a French girl called Celeste Tessier, wrote to ask her over to France. This was followed by a letter from Madame Tessier who said she would be delighted if Minna would come to stay at their lovely house near Montpelier where they always went for six weeks in the summer to get away from the heat in Paris. Perhaps she could stay for a month?

Minna looked up from the letter, so excited, until she saw Beth's face.

'Won't do us any harm,' she said. 'We live in each other's pockets.'

'Thanks, Minna!' Beth said, and then laughed. 'You go—I would if I had the chance.' Knowing she would miss Minna more than somewhat. But Minna was right—they did spend too much time together...

It was a glorious summer that year, and Beth spent most of her evenings in the park, playing tennis or having tea in the clubhouse. She had a holiday booked for September when she was going up to Scotland to see a distant aunt. Until then she'd be perfectly happy—and then Jimmy Alders turned up.

She couldn't have said what it was about him that made him stand out from all the other male members of the club. True, he was reasonably good-looking, and had the most wonderful eyes. He had only had to look at Beth from those golden eyes for her to feel she was going to swoon. Was this what falling in love felt like?

He was a good tennis player, as she was

herself, and they played singles, enjoying each other's company, went for walks whenever he wasn't wanted at the film studios where he worked, and by the third week they were like old friends.

His home was down in Hampshire, near Bournemouth, and he had a small flat in London near the studios. He had started out as a photographer, but turned to films when it was discovered he had a gift for taking moving pictures. Now he was a cameraman and a good one, he assured her.

They went for long walks, talking to each other like old friends. He told her about his work and his aspirations to write and become a director—Beth was so happy in his company that she scarcely noticed Minna wasn't there.

Minna was due home one Sunday and expected late in the evening. It was late afternoon when Beth and Jimmy finished their game and were having tea on the terrace. The sun was going down towards the west when suddenly Minna appeared. Beth ran over to her. 'Minna! I thought you'd be back tonight!'

'I caught an earlier train,' she said. 'Who's this?'

Afterwards, Beth remembered that Jimmy and Minna had stared at each other for what seemed like an eternity. Minna looked stunning. Her skin was golden, she was slim as a reed and her hair sunbleached and piled on top of her head where it caught the light of the setting sun. She wore dark glasses, but took them off and squinted until her eyes had adjusted. Jimmy didn't take his eyes off her.

I could have walked away at that point, Beth told herself later, and he would never have noticed.

Once the ice was broken, they all laughed and Minna told them about her holiday. Jimmy was riveted, eyes fixed on her, listening hard for she could be very amusing. But gradually the smile left Beth's face as she realised that he was really smitten.

'Come on,' Minna said, taking over, 'let's go home, I've brought back a bottle of champagne from France—let's celebrate.'

What, Beth asked herself, were they celebrating?

She wouldn't want to live through that period again, she thought now. The misery of watching the two of them together. They seemed so right somehow. It was the most miserable time of her life. She knew in her heart she had lost him, and couldn't even blame him, for there was a magnetism about Minna—always had been.

He was captivated by Minna, she was almost like a drug to him, and gradually as Beth took more and more of a back seat, they became inseparable.

At that time, Beth, as miserable as she had ever been in her life, could hardly bear to watch them together, and decided to get accommodation nearer to her job. She found a bed-sit in Regents Park and settled in to face a new life, without Jimmy, without Minna. It was the hardest thing she had ever had to do.

Then Jimmy was sent on location to Canada and Minna went with him, and a few weeks after that Beth met Geoff at a Christmas party.

She liked him enormously, they got on well, had a lot in common, and if their relationship was without the depths of emotion she'd felt when she had been with Jimmy, she told herself that that was something she might well never experience again. The excitement of being with Jimmy, the way her heart fluttered when he was anywhere near, the way he looked at her—what good did it do to think about that?

She and Geoff drifted into an easy friendship, they liked the same things, enjoyed each other's company, so that when he asked her to marry him, Beth did so gladly.

She did love him, she told herself and it wasn't as if she hankered after Jimmy whom she knew now was lost to her for all time.

She heard from Minna from time to time, heard that she and Jimmy had married and had settled temporarily in the United States.

The birth of Beth's son less than a year after the wedding cemented their marriage, and when eighteen months later Ian was born, their happiness was complete.

She had only seen Minna once in that time when she made a brief visit to see her and her two young sons.

Much later, Belinda was born, and Geoff had the daughter he always wanted.

She was pleased for Minna when she heard she had a baby son, Hamish, but it was when she came back finally to England and announced her intention of coming to live near them, Beth was secretly horrified.

On their doorstep! Could she bear it—was it too far back in the past to matter? Beth told herself firmly not to be weak. To count her blessings, Geoff, the children, their lovely home—and try to recapture the old unclouded friendship with Minna, the way they were before Jimmy appeared.

Only once when she and Geoff visited Minna and Jimmy and he had kissed her—even now her face flamed as she remembered—she had looked straight at him, into his eyes, before fleeing. By then she knew he wasn't happy. That his marriage to Minna had been a mistake. His touch was electric and she had hurried outside the house, her mind in a turmoil.

A lost love, she thought now, but with the passing of the years, could she have been happier? She doubted it, she had much to be thankful for, but it still hadn't stopped her heart yearning occasionally for what could never be.

When Minna had gone to France, presumably to stay there, for she had never returned from that last visit and the house was up for sale, Jimmy had come to see them. He had joined them for dinner and told them Minna intended to stay in France.

'What will you do?' Geoff asked. He was fond of Jimmy.

'Well, I'm away a lot, working on location—we'll have to see.'

When he left them, he had shaken Geoff's hand and wished him well then approached Beth, whose heart seemed to have turned to stone.

Suddenly he threw his arms round her, and she felt his heart beating hard against hers. When he let her go, she swayed.

'Goodbye, Beth,' he'd said. 'All the best.' And then he had gone.

'Poor old Jimmy,' Geoff said, coming back from locking the front door. 'I think he finds leaving that house quite a wrench. Sad when you think of it, pity they couldn't have made a go of it.'

Made a go of it? Beth thought. Was that what she'd done—made a go of it?

Now she'd made up her mind. The move was over and done with and she knew it was time to call Jimmy. She'd carefully kept his number.

'Come to lunch,' she invited. 'Around twelve?' He was not to know that her heart was beating fast as she said it, despite promising herself to keep calm.

Now she checked again the dining table laid for two, with the crystal wine glasses and the narrow flute of freesias, her linen table mats and silver cutlery.

Glancing at herself in the mirror, Beth wondered if he would find her very changed. Of course, she was plumper, more rounded. Her hair was still fair, if greyish, and there were lines where there hadn't been before. But this wasn't about looks, she thought. It was something more than that.

It had just gone twelve when Jimmy's car drove up the short driveway and parked, and he rang the bell. When she opened the door, they stood staring at each other for what seemed like an eternity. She had only time to notice that his hair was quite grey before he took her in his arms and held her tightly. He didn't kiss her, just held her.

'Beth,' he said finally, letting her go.

She led the way into the sitting room and he looked around before sinking into a chair.

'You can't imagine how often I have dreamed of this happening,' he said.

'Don't talk. Not yet. Shall we have a glass of wine or dry sherry? Perhaps a whisky?'

'Wine would be good,' he said, and she went to pour it. 'Dry white, if you have it.'

She smiled and brought him a glass, placing it down on the side table, where there were some cheese biscuits and nuts.

She brought her own glass and sat opposite him, smiling gently, not saying anything.

He looked around. 'This is nice,' he said. 'Cosy—comfortable.'

She nodded. 'Yes, it is. I was very lucky to find it.'

She had imagined this moment many times, but now that it was here, found it difficult—so much had happened since they last met. He had divorced Minna, and Geoff was gone—so much water under the bridge.

'Tell me about Hamish,' she said. 'I was so pleased to hear that he was married.'

Jimmy seemed relieved to have been given a lead.

'Yes, she's a lovely girl, an American, they're very happy. Hamish is working in New York—they got married there—and I rather think he will make his home there permanently. He's producing television films.'

'A chip off the old block.' She smiled.

'And what about the family—fill me in. It's ages since I had news of them.'

And that broke the ice. Together they talked of her children and grandchildren, and finally Geoff's death, which she just told him was sudden without going into the awful drama of it all.

They sat down to a lunch of salad and fresh salmon followed by fruit salad and coffee, and by now they were both relaxed, aided by the rest of the bottle of wine. He talked about his film work—but still he hadn't mentioned Minna.

They were sitting having coffee when she took the plunge. Minna had to be mentioned at some time or another.

'So you divorced?' she said.

'It was inevitable. I'm not sad about it although divorce is always sad in one way.'

'Jimmy, when did you—' she hesitated.

'Find out I'd made a mistake? Married the wrong girl?' He gave a quirky smile, but she met his eyes without flinching.

'Very soon after we were married.'

She frowned. 'But, Jimmy, why did you stay? You could both have had your freedom—found other people.'

'Beth, I don't expect you to understand but I felt guilty. Knowing I'd made a mistake and it wasn't Minna's fault. I was determined to make a go of it. We went to the States and Canada but it made no difference, it wasn't going to work. But when I broached divorce a couple of times, she wouldn't agree.'

'She loved you, Jimmy.'

'I know,' he said. 'Do you think I didn't know that? And then there was Hamish, and I thought we should at least stay together until he'd grown up so I gave in to her all along the way—gave her everything she wanted, even to coming to Chantry Park to live. She wanted to be near you, that was the irony of it. She really needed you more than you needed her.'

'What she really wanted was for you to love her,' Beth said gently.

He shrugged. 'I know she found lots of consolation.' There was no answer to that.

'Jimmy, you don't think she ever suspected that...'

'You and I had been—close?'

She nodded.

'No, I don't think so. I'm pretty sure not.' He reached over and put a hand over hers.

'Have you been happy?' he said, amber eyes searching hers.

'Very happy, Jimmy. I've been so lucky.'

'And what are you doing with yourself these days?'

'You're not to laugh! I've made an effort at writing, and I must say, I'm enjoying it.'

'That's great!' He looked genuinely pleased.

'And you?' she asked.

They were more at ease now. The years seem to have slipped away.

'I'm going on location for a new film,' he said. 'To India,' he said, and saw her face light up.

'Oh, Jimmy, how wonderful!'

'Come with me, Beth.'

She stared at him, open mouthed. 'What?'

'Come with me. Have you ever been to India?'

'N-no—'

'Then come with me—why not? Just as friends, Beth. I've never been, either, and we could see it together. I wouldn't ask any more of you, Beth, no more than you wanted, anyway. We could stay just friends, as they say.'

What on earth would she say to the family?

'Oh, Jimmy, I don't think so, I really don't—'

'Not just as travelling companions?' There was a twinkle in his eye. 'Not much fun travelling as a single these days.'

She smiled back at him.

'Let me think about it.'

She knew she would go. After all, wasn't this the beginning of the rest of her life? What was she waiting for? The family had their own lives. She had the rest of hers to look forward to.

She looked across at him and smiled, meeting his eyes.

'And could we see the Taj Mahal?'

'Oh, Beth!'

He reached across and took her hand and held it tight between his own.

This Large Print Book for the Partially sighted, who cannot read normal print, is published under the auspices of

THE ULVERSCROFT FOUNDATION